THE
NOVEMBER
GIRL

THE
NOVEMBER
GIRL

LYDIA KANG

Entangled Publishing, LLC
2614 South Timberline Road
Suite 109
Fort Collins, CO 80525

Entangled Teen is an imprint of Entangled Publishing, LLC.
Visit our website at www.entangledpublishing.com.

Edited by Kate Brauning
Cover design by Miguel Parisi & Erin Dameron-Hill
Interior design by Toni Kerr

ISBN 978-1-63375-826-1
Ebook ISBN 978-1-63375-827-8

Manufactured in the United States of America

First Edition November 2017

10 9 8 7 6 5 4 3 2 1

To Sarah
Who encourages my strangest ideas and
fuels the bravery to make them real.

The wind in the wires made a tattletale sound
When the wave broke over the railing
And every man knew, as the captain did too
'Twas the Witch of November come stealin'

"The Wreck of the Edmund Fitzgerald"
Gordon Lightfoot

Chapter One

HECTOR

There's a foolproof method to running away.

I know the wrong ones all too well. This time, there'll be no mistakes.

I'd left my cell phone, fully charged, duct-taped beneath a seat on a Duluth city bus. If they track it, they'll think I've never left town. Acting scared and paranoid is a giveaway. Wearing a hoodie is no good, either; they'll think I'm a criminal. With my height and my brown skin, I get enough sideways glances as it is without more advertising. Nah. I make sure the clothes I've stolen from my uncle are clean and defy gravity, instead of sagging on my hips and shoulders. I carry a hiking backpack, not a high schooler's version.

This khaki down jacket I got from the Salvation Army. It's the nasty kind only worn by grown-ups with flat, worn-out souls. And I carry my armor of pleasantness like a plastic shield, pretending it's the most normal thing in the world to board the ferry to Isle Royale on October 4, the last day it runs to the island.

I make them all believe I belong on this damned boat.

A line of people waits to board the *Quest II* at the dock. They're all middle-aged, with that middle-aged sag that weighs them down. The air around Lake Superior is cold, but humid and acrid from the rotting wood of the pier. The sky hangs with clouds of pale gray. It doesn't look like rain's coming, but the color paints a thin gloom, and fog skims the lake. I zip my jacket up higher.

A bald white guy calls out names for passengers, his pudgy, callused hands gripping a clipboard. His belly's softly round above his jeans. My name is fake, of course, and my fare paid in cash, to leave no trail.

"Goin' alone?" he asks, friendly-like. The gap where he's missing a canine tooth only shows when he smiles.

"No. Meeting my wife there. She works at the lodge," I say, performing lines I've carefully rehearsed. Luckily, I've got a face that could be twenty-five or fifteen, depending on my clothes. So, I'll let them think I have a real life. I've even got my dad's old wedding ring on my fourth finger, but I hate how it feels on my hand. Confining. My palms get sweaty and I shove my ringless hand into my pocket.

"Don't forget the last ferry leaves at one o'clock, tomorrow afternoon. It'll be crowded."

I nod, but my stomach dives into the center of the earth. I pray he won't notice that I'm not on it. I try to walk by, when he points to my backpack.

"Hey. Next time you come, bring a different bag, will ya?"

I shift uncomfortably, conscious of the line of people growing on the dock. "Uh, why?"

"Black bags are bad luck. They sink ships."

A passenger behind me yells through his beard, "Ignore him! Norm's superstitious. He made my wife throw away a rose I gave her. Right into the trash, because they're bad luck on boats. He won't run the ferry on Fridays. Lucky they shut down in November, too."

"Why November?" Ah, God, Hector. Shut up, *shut up*.

"The worst storms come in November," Norm says quietly. "There's a name for them storms, the ones that sink ships. The Witch o' November."

There's something about how he says "witch" that bothers me. Some people love to say stuff for the drama of it. But this guy glances nervously at the lake, as if it were listening.

I nod at him. "Got it. No Fridays, no flowers, no Novembers. And I'll bring my blue backpack next time," I say with a smile, though the conversation is killing me. My hands are swampy with perspiration. The boat sways beneath my feet as I walk past the other passengers. This late in the season, they're probably Isle workers helping to close up for the season. Because from tomorrow until late spring, the Isle Royale will be empty.

Except for me.

It's the perfect hideout. No one will look for a runaway on an island that's purposely deserted every winter. I've covered my tracks too well. I'll hide out here until mid-May, when I turn eighteen. And then I'll be free, and there will be no more leashes. No more living under that roof that punishes me with thoughts I can't stand.

I'm doing my uncle a favor, really. He complains about the bills, how much it costs to raise me, how the money my dad sends is never quite enough.

But it's not about the money. It's what we never talk about that chases me from that house.

I've lived with him since I was six. I know he'll report me missing when he finds out. I know that deep in his heart, he might hope I'm never found. By then, the island will be uninhabited. On Isle Royale, I'll be where I don't belong.

I'll fit right in.

The two engines of the *Quest II* are already rumbling, water boiling to a hissing fury by the propellers. The mooring lines are cast off and the fenders secured. I sit in my corner seat inside the boat, itching to read the maps, notes, and pamphlets I stuffed into my coat pocket. I'm not supposed to look like a tourist. My phantom wife supposedly works on the island, after all. When the force of the engine pushes me against my seat, I glance up.

Lake Superior stretches out in liquid stillness, a yawning expanse of dark water that unsettles me and makes me sweat even more. Behind us, the sparse buildings of Grand Portage shrink farther away. The black forest swallows everything as the boat pushes us forward, until there's no trace of humanity on the horizon.

For almost two hours, I fake like I'm asleep in my corner seat. It works; no one talks to me. The boat pitches up and down on the growing swells, the lake water occasionally spraying my face from one of the open windows, but I pretend I'm dead to the world. I'm hungry for sleep, but my mind is wrung too tight to relax.

I think of which part of the island I'm going to live on, how to stay warm, how to eat enough. Looking on the internet hasn't been helpful. All I know is that pit toilets and leave-no-trace camping rules abound. Isle Royale isn't exactly a popular or luxurious tourist destination. Then again, that's why I chose it as my refuge.

Finally, a cramp in my thigh forces me to sit up and change positions. The second my eyes pop open, a voice chirps nearby.

"Takin' a late vacation?"

I jump inside my skin. An older woman in head-to-toe khaki is sitting a little too close to me. There's an Isle Royale National Park logo on her coat. Shit.

"Nah. Too late. Just meeting my wife. Maybe I'll be able to spend more time next July." I swallow dryly and my heart trills. What if she looks for me on tomorrow's ferry, or asks who my wife is? What if she knows everyone on the island and catches my lie?

"That short a trip, eh? Well, not much to do now, anyway. Weather's turning." She shifts her large, square ass and motions out the window. In the distance, the dense clouds kiss the lake's surface. "You make sure you get off this island before the witch gets ya."

There we go with the witch again. What's with these people? I give her a blank look, not wanting to engage, but she takes it for a question. Great.

"You know. The November storms. Where you from?"

She stares at me in that impolite way that makes my skin crawl. I know what she sees. She's trying to guess what I am. Not who, but what. I'm some crooked puzzle piece that bothers them. *Indian! No, Native? Oh, wait— Hapa, right?* I have "double eyelids" that my Korean mom called *sankapul*. She was so proud of that little crinkle of skin. I made sure to cut my hair so the thick waves were under control. The lady studies the angles and colors of my face—pieces of my parents. I hardly recognize which parts belong to whom anymore. As if ownership ever mattered to either of them.

The lady narrows her eyes—she still can't figure me out but doesn't want to ask *that* question. What a relief. She tries again. "Are you from Grand Portage?"

"Oh. No, we're from…" I can't say Duluth, which is where I'm really from. But despite practicing the lie in my head on the bus ride, my brain is all *DuluthDuluthDuluth*. I stutter, remembering the small town on the shore I'd picked out on the map last week. "Uh. Um. Grand Marais."

She keeps babbling on about places to visit next time I come, flashing an artificial smile of false teeth. Her upper plate keeps coming loose as she talks to me, so her *S* sounds are more like *sh*. She says things like, "Now that's a nice place to shit for a view of Duncan Bay." Normally I'd laugh, but nothing is funny now. I don't want to be chatty. I need to be ignored.

After a few minutes, I can't be polite anymore. I've taken three buses from Duluth to get to this damn boat, and I'm so close. Last thing I need is some square-assed lady committing verbal diarrhea all over me.

"Sorry. Where's the men's room?" I fake my best nauseated look and hold my stomach.

"Oh! Bathrooms are aft," she says, thrusting her thumb behind her. "We have Dramamine on board. Scope patches. Sea bands?"

I nod politely and bolt past the other passengers, who give me plenty of room to pass.

I push through the door to stand on deck. Isle Royale is in view now, with Washington Harbor yawning open a passageway for the boat. Evergreens cling to the rocky shore on either side. There are scant houses and docks as the boat turns gently to enter the bay's inlet. The water sparkles from the sun cracking through a slice in the clouds. We'll be docking at Windigo soon. I'm almost there. As I inhale to empty the stale cabin air from my lungs, something on the shore catches my eye.

It's a flash of amber, and at first I think it's just sun reflecting off the water. But it doesn't flicker like reflected light. It almost seems to glow, like the harvest moon beaming against the backdrop of dark evergreens—but it's daytime.

It's a girl, standing on the shore. She's dressed in dark colors, which is why I could only see her face at first, and now, a dab of pale hands clasped together in front of her. She stares back at me, and her face changes—subtly, like when a blink changes sunset to evening. Though she's far away, I swear she went from smiling to frowning. Or maybe it was frowning to smiling?

Something in her expression tugs at the center of me. It's a terrible feeling, and wonderful at the same time—like waking up on Christmas, and realizing that, damn, the waking up part is already over. As I squint to get a better look, the door to the inner cabin swings open and that same chatty lady steps outside. Ugh. I can't handle any more conversation. I shuffle toward the bathroom. But when I check over my shoulder for one last glimpse of the girl on the shore, the rocky beach is empty.

I try to push aside the vision of her face as I search for the bathroom. Inside, I lock the door with nervous fingers. There's a stainless steel toilet that's stained anyway, and the tiny compartment reeks of fake evergreen deodorizer and piss. The mirror is broken and divides my face on a diagonal.

The wind must be picking up, because the floor pitches me left, right, left, and waves slap the boat. I close the toilet seat and sit down, placing my bag on my lap. I unzip it. Half the space is taken by an old sleeping bag. The rest is crammed with beef jerky packets, baggies of bulk dried fruit, nuts, oatmeal, and a collapsible fishing rod I stole from Walmart when I worked there this past summer. Since my uncle took every paycheck, I couldn't spend a penny without him knowing why. I push aside the food, touching the changes of clothes, thick winter gloves (also nicked from Walmart—it was a good summer), a sewing kit, all-weather matches, a tiny enamel cooking pot and water bottle, and some bathroom stuff. Folded within a flannel shirt is a good camping knife. And inside my jeans pocket is enough money to buy me a ferry ticket in May and a bus ride to someplace that isn't Duluth. I've got the clothes on my back and the skin over my bones.

That's all I have.

I'll have to break into a few houses, maybe the park ranger's quarters. On the bus up here, I realized I'd need an ax to chop wood, but it was too late. I couldn't afford to buy one or risk stealing something that big, so I'll have to find one on the island and a place with a wood-burning stove. There will be no electricity. No phones, either. Hopefully I'll survive the five months and get out on the first ferry before anyone can find me. I zip my bag up and exit the bathroom. I can see the dock at Windigo now.

I might die before May comes. But if it happens, at least it will be on my terms. I watch, almost without blinking, as the shoreline grows closer and closer.

I'm almost there.

I'm almost free.

Chapter Two

ANDA

I saw him on the ferry.

Every day, I've stood at the shore to watch the disinterested ferry pass by. The passengers are always the same, their faces set with familiar expressions of anticipation, or the green bitterness of seasickness, or the blankness of one who knows the lake and the Isle so well that nothing is new. But this boy was different.

We shared the same expression. And what's worse, he could see me.

No one ever sees me at first glance. They don't care to, they don't want to, they want to but they can't. If they're searching hard enough for something, then sometimes it can happen. Father tries to explain why, but none of it matters. This boy—this boy—he saw me. Immediately. And it felt terrible, when his eyes touched my skin. I search inwardly for a similar feeling, flipping through file cards of memory. And then I find it.

Magnifying glass. Sun. Dead aspen leaf. Boring a pinhole of smoke and fire with that focused sun.

Yes. Yes, that. That is what it felt like when he saw me.

I was standing on the shore, waiting for one more day to arrive, the day that everyone would leave and the island would be mine. The bamboo-like rushes were rotting underfoot, and the juniper behind me scented the wind with its spicy notes. Grebes flew overhead, too smart to stay near me. I could feel the eagerness of the boats, wanting to get away and dock for the winter, to be safe. I knew my father paced inside our home. Anxious to leave me alone. Frightened to leave me alone.

Standing on the shore, I let the icy lake water seep into my shoes, weighing me down. I watched the passenger boat pass by, the last one that would bring anyone onto the island. And I thought, *Soon. Soon, you'll all go far away. You don't want to be here when November comes.*

But this boy saw me.

No one ever sees me.

Run, Anda.

I listened to her voice and ran away, terrified.

The next day, I sit on the floor of our small cottage, cradling the cracked weather radio in my lap. I'm impatient, fumbling with the tuning knob. Words stutter and struggle for clarity between bouts of static. Finally, I hear the automated woman's voice from the NOAA station consistently, a beacon from the battered machine.

Southwest winds ten to fifteen knots

Cloudy with a 90 percent chance of rain after midnight

I close my eyes and listen to the drumming of the truth. The rain is coming. I feel it beneath my skin and on the tip of my tongue, like a word ready to be spoken. No matter what time of the day, the words from NOAA are a comfort. They may be robotic recordings, but they're slaves to the wind and temperature, just as I am. With the radio on, I am not alone.

Areas of fog in the morning
Waves two to three feet

"Anda. You know where the spare batteries are, don't you?" My father's heavy steps creak the oak floorboards. He's pushing aside a pile of driftwood I've left in the middle of the kitchen floor, trying to open the cabinet by the stove. He shakes the box of batteries at me, and when I don't respond, he puts them back with a sigh.

I say nothing, because the weather service is buzzing in my head, and there's a warning laced in there.

Pressure is dropping rapidly

"Anda. My boat leaves soon." He strides over to where I'm sitting by the fireplace. He wishes he could come closer, but he won't. It's October. He's sensed the seasonal change that already sank its claws into me when the fall temperature fell. I push a lock of hair out of my face, and static crackles the ends of my strands. I'll have to cut it again soon.

My legs are crossed, and I'm still in my nightgown. His boots stand a precise three feet away. If I looked closer, I'd see the worn leather become jean-covered legs, then a thin and carved-out torso, as if a stiff wind had permanently bent his back years ago. He'd be unshaven and his white hair mixed with brown and occasional copper, like the agate I found broken on the lakeshore only days ago.

"Anda." There's a slight strain in his voice. Perhaps he's getting pharyngitis. "It's time for me to go." He seems to be waiting for something.

The voice on the radio fades into static again. I fiddle with the antennae, but the radio is telling me it's tired of talking, that I need to go. My father takes his coat down from the wall peg. A suitcase and backpack sit by the door, ready to flee the cottage. If the door were open, I imagine they'd tumble down the gravel road just to get away from me.

The air inside the cabin has grown stifling. The cabin's telling me to get out, too. I get up and put on my rain parka, then shove my bare feet into a pair of duck boots. Father stares at my eyelet nightgown, coat, and boots with bare ankles above, hair still messy from a restless night. Asleep, I'd seen brown skin and knowing brown eyes from a face on the ferry staring me down all night. I only escaped when I woke up.

Father picks up the suitcase and opens the door. I grab his backpack. There is a tag printed with a name, SELKIRK, in permanent ink that's smudged nevertheless. I study it for a moment, and then my eyebrows rise. Oh. Selkirk. That is our name, isn't it? I slip my arms through the straps and wear it backward so my arms can support the bulk of it. He watches me waddle down the stone steps and shakes his head but says nothing.

He doesn't need to tell me that there are civilized ways to dress, or to say good-bye to your father. Before he leaves you, secretly, on an island so inhospitable that everyone abandons it when autumn hits, an uppercut that won't be dodged. We have been through this before. Arguments don't work when one side is a tidal force that has no basis in rational thought.

I can't remember the last time I lost an argument. He knows what happens when I don't get my way.

My nature upsets him. No, "upset" is the wrong word.

Fracture, rend. That is what happens to Father. So when November arrives, when the strength of the weather resonates with my need more than any other time, that is when he leaves. I am more dulcet the rest of the year, but it is not easy. Birth and growth are sweet to him and everyone else, but not for me. I do what I can to draw from what death occurs in the broad summer, but it's scant. I've given up on explaining it all to Father, and instead, I wait for November for my time to renew myself.

Not everyone is happy with this arrangement.

It's a mile-long walk to the dock. Since there are no roads on the island, we take a wooded hiking trail through ghostly paper birch trees and balsam fir that lend their spice to the air. Any tourists have long since left, and we pass a campground that's quiet but for a few seagulls pecking about the footprints of the departed.

As we crunch along the path, my father polishes his glasses and rattles off a list of things he must tell me. "There's enough fuel for the kerosene heater if you keep it on low. I've left food in the pantry to last until I come back in early December. There's a pot of that homemade strawberry jam that you like so much."

"I like strawberry jam?" I ask him.

Father stops walking. His sorrowful eyebrows sag above his eyes. And then I realize, I've already forgotten, haven't I? Parts of me—the human slices of what I am— are already fading. They have been fading more than ever these last few years. This saddens him.

"Yes. You like—you used to like it." He clears his throat. "Anyway, Jimmy will drive me over in his boat in December. The first aid kit is fully stocked. Try to be frugal about the batteries, if you can…"

None of it is terribly important, but it relieves him to

unload his thoughts. I'll carry them for a while, but these are the things I would prefer to keep close: the scent of his beard after he's been on the dock all day, like lake water mixed with ashes. The lines on his knuckles, permanently stained from his carpentry work around the island. And his irises. Tiny circlets of white and gray that resemble the eyes of an Isle wolf.

Voices seep through the tangle of spruce trees. The dock is just beyond, and the low purr of the ferry's motor grows louder. Among the fallen leaves, a dead deer mouse lies on the trail, thin and stiff. I crush it underfoot and smile. From the trail behind, a couple catches up to us. They live in one of the rare houses beyond ours, and their backs are burdened with heavy packs.

"Hey, Jakob. See you on the boat?" the woman asks. She walks past, her elbow swishing against mine. She doesn't catch my eye. She doesn't say a word about my nightgown, and neither does the man. They are worried about making the ferry and do not make an effort to see me. Like the broken branches off the trail and the dead mouse, I am invisible to them in these moments. This brings me comfort, but nevertheless, their brush by me feels icy.

"Yep. See you soon," Father responds. Beyond the web of trees ahead, the couple joins the group at the pier. My father stops and lingers in the shade to face me. His eyes crinkle with concern. "Anda. I could stay."

"You can't be here with me," I say. "No one can."

"Then come with me," he asks, helplessly.

I sigh. I lift my chin and let him see me. Really see me. Just as he is more to me than a list of supplies gathered to provide for his child, I am more than a girl who wears a nightgown to hike in the woods, whose hair crackles with static when it gets too long and flyaway.

I am November on the island. I am part of the lake, and the earth, and the rusted steel of the shipwrecks. He cannot stay to see what will happen. He's witnessed too many Novembers with me here, seen that destructive synergy when he can't tell the difference between me and the storms. My body rebels when he tries to take me away. But staying with me will kill him, piece by piece. It's already started to kill him, fissuring his face into a million wrinkles, years deep.

His death cannot help me.

And so I choose to stay on the island, because the other option is a reality I can't even comprehend. I cannot fight my nature. I cannot be what he wishes me to be, all year long. That part of me that is Jakob, my father—that part has been fading more every year. Soon I might be the waves on the water, just as my sisters have become. It is the natural history of us. He knows this. He can't stop it.

"No. I must stay," I remind him.

He nods. His eyes sparkle with redness and moisture, and I let the backpack slip off my arms to the ground. He picks it up and hoists it over his broad back.

"December first. I'll be back." He takes a step closer. "Don't let them see you," he warns, tossing his head toward the dock.

As if that matters. As if they ever try to see me.

He waits for my embrace, his arms arcing towards me, a bear trap ready to be triggered. A brisk wind blows at us from off the water, and my white hair twists around my face in a riot. My father loses his balance and is forced to take a step back. I can't touch him. I cannot.

Once, I could do these things. But I'm forgetting. Once, he taught me to read and cipher and do arithmetic, and all of it is more dream than memory now. I've forgotten what one should do and feel when a father leaves his daughter.

I wring my hands together and blurt out, "Don't forget to sleep." My fingernails dig into my knuckles. "And eat," I add. "You should eat food. You should…wear sweaters."

Father smiles gently at my efforts. "Good-bye, Anda. Be careful."

"Careful" is such a strange word. To be full of care, overflowing with sentiment. The nature of care is solely for those with whole hearts to give. The word is an antonym to everything I am now, and my father's words are a strangled wish, rather than a warm farewell. He crunches away down the path, and I stay in the shadows of the forest as he approaches the boat.

I watch from behind a particularly fat spruce trunk. A tiny iridescent dragonfly is entombed under a blob of sap, and my heart lightens a single gram. I lean close to the tree, letting the sap stick to my own fingertips, watching my father shake hands with the last residents of Isle Royale. As he boards the full ferry, he turns and looks over his shoulder. His eyes scan the grove of spruces, searching for a last glance good-bye, but his eyes never find me.

The mooring lines are untied from dock cleats, and the engine roars as the vessel pulls away. Usually, I feel a frantic sensation when watching the last ferry leave. Panic mixes with sheer loneliness, but it's fainter than in previous Octobers. I breathe easier once the boat motors its slow exodus into Washington Harbor.

I push back from the tree. A sudden, sharp crack of a stick sounds from nearby. Likely it's a moose. I turn around to walk the mile hike back home when I freeze.

It's the boy.

Through the columns of bushy evergreens, he stands there with hands against rough bark, just as mine were a few seconds ago. He's so tall. Six feet, maybe an inch over. His skin is darker than the usual shade worn by the tourists who blanket their skin with titanium cream. His face stakes no claim with anyone and refuses to give its secrets. He's surprisingly graceful as he steps back. Well, not so graceful. He doesn't know how to walk in this pine forest without making noise. He doesn't see me yet. He's still watching the boat in the distance, his face a mixture of relief and worry.

What is he doing here?

Almost as soon as the thought enters my head, his head swivels toward me, as if someone slapped his face in my direction. Our eyes lock on each other, and his face fills with wonder. For a full minute, we just regard each other. Astonishment forces its way into my chest. A very human sensation, one I haven't felt in years. The slight wind disappears, pushed away by our mutual atmosphere of surprise.

Finally, he seems to rouse himself with a deep breath. He looks like he's going to say something.

I spin around and run.

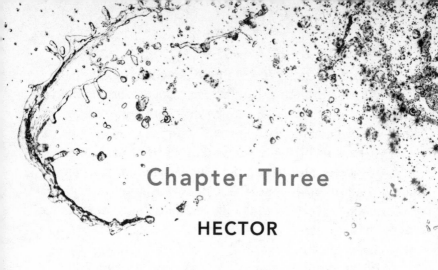

Chapter Three

HECTOR

Holy shit.

It's her. The girl I saw yesterday, before I landed. My heart punches my chest a million times a minute. She stands there staring at me, her pink lower lip dropped in surprise. She's wearing a lumpy parka on top of—wait, is that a nightgown? Her bare ankles are twigs sprouting out of muddy boots. A tangle of white-blond hair, all different lengths, adorns her head. Looks like she attacked her own head with scissors and no mirror. And she has that amber skin that reminds me of autumn.

We freeze, staring at each other for almost a minute. Why is she here? Who is she? Why the hell is she dressed like a homeless woman from downtown Duluth? Is she going to scream at me?

I take a deep breath, trying to figure out what to say or do. As soon as I open my mouth, she spins around and tears through the trees, back onto the narrow hiking path.

I don't follow her. I'm still too shocked. Did I really see what I saw? Is she hiding here, too? I mean, at least

I'm prepared. Sort of. I've got a backpack full of food and a plan for shelter all winter. That girl probably has no clothes, no food—I mean, she looks like she doesn't even know how to make a sandwich.

Great.

What if she calls the police? There's supposedly a pay phone somewhere on the other end of the island that takes credit cards. Only, she looks like she wouldn't have a credit card.

I start heading back to my camp, not knowing what else to do. My brain feels all unsettled. The island is like two hundred square miles. I'll probably never see her again. I inhale cool air and pause. Right now, anyone on this island doesn't want to be found, or else has a death wish. If it's the first, then we have no problem. If it's the second, I might be in trouble. I rub my forehead as a headache sprouts in my temples.

There's no room in my brain to worry about one more thing.

Chapter Four

ANDA

I run all the way home, clunking down the narrow trail in my ill-fitting boots. In my head, I can still see the boy staring at me, his mouth readying to form a word. I imagine what it would have been.

Hello.

Why.

Who.

Go.

But the answer never materialized, because I couldn't stand inside my skin and wait for it.

This cannot be happening.

I'm not alone on the island, and the ground below my feet is off-kilter. There was a constant in the equation before. And now the equation has changed, not to my liking.

Normally, in autumn, a seed of wind will come toward the lake. The lake water, warmed from a summer full of solar energy, nourishes it from below. And I can coax it into something absolutely savage, far bigger than it intended to be. It is chaos that is orchestrated, nurtured, groomed. It is what I do.

But he's brought an altogether different element of chaos, and it confuses me utterly.

Then send him away.

Her order is sound advice, but it's a distasteful command. And I wish to stay here, to hide, to become a crack in the weathered bones of the cottage itself. I want to run away from him, into forgetfulness.

Anda. Send the boy away.

I nod meekly.

The warm air of the cottage is thick syrup in my lungs and is anything but soothing. *Get out, get out,* it seems to hiss. I'm not welcome home. It knows there is still something I must do. I leave and pause outside the cottage, sniffing the air. Yew and bearberry are waxy and green nearby, parading their health. The loamy humus brings a symphony of scents demanding attention, but I ignore it all. Now is not the time for me to tune the balances of the island. Instead, I let the pressure in the air infect my lungs. My eyes close and I speak out loud.

"Southwest winds ten to fifteen knots. Cloudy with a ninety percent chance of rain after midnight."

Call it a prayer or a weather forecast, but it works to keep me calm. I force myself to think, to use sensibility, not sense. An uncomfortable shift for me. It's this boy's entire fault, making me think outside of myself.

The Washington Creek campgrounds, near Windigo. That is where he must be. I turn around to see the cottage door flapping a complaint in the light wind. It urges me on, knowing I would rather sink into the depths of the lake and forget everything. I'm terrified of letting that boy see me again. No one ever sees me.

November is coming. Get rid of him.

Or I will.

The cottage door slams shut like a thunderclap, and I run.

Chapter Five

HECTOR

Forget the headache. Forget the girl.

I need to focus on living and surviving. I can handle this.

It's about a two-mile hike back to where I hid my stuff. Yesterday after I'd disembarked, I'd listened to the required boring lecture on camping before quietly disappearing down the nearest trail. The campgrounds were already deserted, but I couldn't take the chance of being found inside one of the camping shelters. I'd found a dry, hidden ring of evergreen trees and sat there hugging my bag, twitching every time I heard a twig snap. It was only a few hours before I was starving. There was no way a fire would be a good idea, so I rummaged through my supplies before taking out one precious bag of trail mix.

God, it had been cold. When you're hiding and not moving, your heat gets sucked away so easily. After the sunset, I'd curled up in my sleeping bag. Having been on constant alert since I ran away, my brain was fogged, begging for rest. I didn't want to waste flashlight batteries, and it's not like I had anything else to do. I hadn't brought any books, and island pamphlets were shit for company. Which left me thinking. And I didn't like what I was thinking about. So I slept.

Or at least I'd tried. I shivered all night long, because the wind forced its way into my sleeping bag. Rocks and sticks dug into my side, and my folded hands made for a crappy pillow. Now here I am. I'm dirty. I probably smell like a locker room drain. And my left shoulder aches from sleeping on the ground, but I'm alive, I think, as I walk back to camp. It's a damn long walk, but I have all winter. I'm in no rush.

But I'm not alone.

The memory of that girl in her parka and nightgown won't leave me. Worry seeps into my bones, but I can't let it stop me. In the meantime, I'm starving. *Again.* Maybe today I should start fishing, since the food I packed is only for emergencies. I'll also have to start exploring the rest of the island, maybe the ranger's quarters and the camp store. There might be an ax and leftover food supplies. I'll need to build a fire, since I have no intention of becoming a sushi lover anytime soon.

Cracks and snapping twigs echo in the forest, but they're mostly from me. And yet I stop in my tracks constantly to do a three-sixty. I don't see the girl, or any other animals, but I can't shake the feeling that there are eyes on me. Through the far trees, the lake ripples with a twinkle, as if winking at me. A few gulls cry out far above, circling. Somewhere on this hunk of island, there are wolves.

I spend the rest of the time hiking back to camp gripping the hilt of my knife.

The temperatures slowly rise to the point where I'm a sweaty mess after half an hour. Soon, I recognize the clustered trees where I hid my stuff. An empty plastic bag lies on the path only a few feet away. I pick it up, shoving it into a pocket. It could come in handy. I can't waste stuff that other campers left behind. A few steps farther, and I see more plastic on the ground. This time, it's a Ziploc bag. It's riddled with puncture holes, and a scattering of peanuts roll around inside.

Wait.

Oh, no.

I tear through the brush to my hidden camp and glimpse a flash of orange and black fur. A fox scurries away into the brush with a tiny yip of glee.

"No, no, no, *no*."

It looks like a cherry bomb exploded in my bag. The zipper has been tugged open only a few inches, but it's enough. My stuff is everywhere. The jerky bags have been ripped through, and some are empty. My bathroom stuff has been left alone, but the food baggies have been tossed everywhere. Oats and curly dried apples mingle in the dirt.

I howl a string of curses at myself and the fox, but mostly myself. How, *how* could I be so goddamned stupid? Who knew foxes could get into a bag like that?

Well, I should have known. I'd punch myself in the face if I could right now. I deserve it. Stupid fuckup.

I collapse onto the pine needles and drop my head in my hands. Panic rises in my chest, hot and acidic, and my head feels like it's going to explode. A voice chants inside my head, but it's not my own.

How could you be so careless, Hector?

My shoulders hunch over the pine needles. I can only make myself so small, but I try, even if there is no uncle pacing back and forth before me. I hunch over further, cringing, shaking my head, but I hear it anyway.

"How could you have lost your job? This house costs money. The food you eat costs money."

All I want to do is go to my room, lock the door, and pretend I'm dead. That would be a relief compared to this.

My mouth is so dry, but I force the words out anyway. "Maybe we can ask Dad for more money."

"No. No. He does enough for us already."

I say nothing. When he gets like this, there is nothing I can say that won't make him more furious. Even my silence fuels his anger. Though I'm almost the same height as him, he's twice my weight. He has the same intense eyes as my dad, the same strong nose, but being half brothers, my uncle always passes for white. People who don't know us always ask if I'm adopted. They look at my uncle like he's a saint.

When my uncle sees the clothes hanging off my lean frame, he tells me I'd be more of a man if I didn't have my mother's piss-yellow blood in me. And then inevitably after his tirade, he'll apologize. He'll beg for me to forget all about it. I'll find him staring at me in that greedy way that makes me want to crawl out of my skin. But he's not at that point yet. He has more anger to spend before he gets there.

He yells and yells, and eventually, all his complaints empty out. His feet stop pacing and land in the square of rug where I'm staring. His hand rests on my shoulder.

I like it there. I hate it there.

"Look. I'm sorry." He sighs, but I refuse to look up to see his face. "I lose it sometimes, since money's a little tight. I don't want to stress out your dad more than he already is. Take this." He hands me a few bills. "Go pick us some TV dinners and two beers. Fill out a few job applications while you're at it."

I nod and walk quietly to the truck, while my uncle paces the living room behind me. I take the truck and drive down the street, parking in the lot by the FoodMart. In the cupholder, there's a crumpled pack of cigarettes with two left. A book of matches has been shoved into the cellophane wrapper.

I love the smell of a freshly lit match like I love the smell of gasoline. I could incinerate the truck, but that wouldn't get him out of my life. I could have made him angrier and tempted him into pounding me with a golf club. But no, he'd never do that. He's too clever for such obvious violence. He gets money from the foster agency for keeping me, even though we're family. He'll lose that if he hits me.

On the record, everything is my fault. I'm the one who skips school. I'm the one failing English and history. I'm the one who won't listen to teachers, always on the cusp of throwing a punch. I'm the one who got dragged to the doctor every month for a year, because I was throwing up daily for no reason.

He never takes me to the doctor after the blackouts, though.

Every time I've run away, the police have just brought me back. I could go out and pick a fight, but there are quieter ways to contain my fury. So he leaves the cigarettes for me.

It's the kindest thing he does for me, and he has no idea.

I light a cigarette and take a few deep puffs, letting the smoke curl deep inside my lungs. Maybe it'll kill me from the inside out. I push up my left sleeve and read the scars there. Ten round burns, each one more healed than the last. Within me, the fury boils and scalds, waiting for release.

I take the cigarette from my lips, aim, and close my eyes.

My eyes snap open.

My whole body is shaking, and it's not cold out. Inside, a craving turns itself over and over in my stomach, different from the hunger I'd felt before. There are no smoldering cigarette butts out here. It's just me, but the compulsion to quiet my anger claws incessantly.

My hand falls automatically to the knife at my waist. I unsheathe it and watch the flickering light through the treetops reflect on the blade's edge. My thumb tests the sharpness, gently touching it all the way to the tip without pushing hard enough to draw blood.

I roll up my left sleeve and rest the blade against the skin just above my last scar when a cry pierces the quiet.

Chapter Six

ANDA

I understand, in a split second, what he's going to do. I've done it a hundred times in my own lifetime, but never with a knife. I don't need a blade. But it's like watching the act in a mirror: witnessing the breaking of another human is somehow altogether obscene.

Every day, the push and pull of life around me is a harmony I struggle to curate. Everything—the microbes, the fungi, the bats—everything trying to consume and destroy each other. Relentless. Human death is an inevitable fragment in this cacophony. My sisters surrendered, well before I ever set foot on the Isle, to the simplest part of the cycle, the most giving part—the ending of things. They beckon for me to join them, and in November, they sing most sweetly when I've taken a ship.

Father is glad that I wait until November, but it's November that waits for me. The winds and temperatures and decay, they restore me like no other month of the year. But now, here—I couldn't have ignored the rift in the lake-tinged scents in the air. I'd followed the coppery tang that came from this warm body, this boy.

I came here to tell him to leave. To say that he didn't belong. But the sight of the knife on perfect skin—it incites me to emotions I can't process. I understand what I must do, and not do, and the clash of the two is a massive wall of hot air hitting a cold one, swirling together to make something bigger, more frightening.

No, Anda.

The boy presses the knife harder against his skin, and finally I unstop the word that has lodged in my throat.

"No!" I scream.

My body shrieks at me for speaking. It's angry, and a punishing, twisting sensation in my back makes me gasp in pain. The wind rises and whips against my cheek. He jerks his hand away, but the sudden movement causes him to nick his skin with the blade. A welt of red blooms upon his arm, followed by a tiny trickle that winds down his wrist and drips onto a plastic bag at his feet.

The boy stares at me, and I stare at the ruby drops on his skin. This blood does me no good. What I need now can only be found at the bottom of a lake. Blood on land only satiates normal human needs, like lust, or hate. And I am not normal.

"Jesus! What are you doing here?" he asks. The words sound like an accusation. I'm too shocked by the blood to flee or answer. He's still standing there, unmoving. Fatigue wears on him like a hundred years of rain on sandstone. The backpack gapes dumbly, its half-vomited contents of torn plastic bags strewn about.

"Why did you do that?" I know part of the answer already, but I'm desperate to own the rest.

The words shock him into movement. He hastily sheathes the knife. His body is so tall that even the trees seem respectful of him. His hair is thick and curly, though disappointingly, it is trimmed short. For a moment, I wish I could tangle my nails in it. I shake the thought away.

He pulls his sleeve down, and the droplets of blood seep through the dark green fabric. "It was an accident."

"But you're lying!"

He pauses and his head ticks back. "What are you doing here?" he asks again. He's dodging my answer, as I am his. We're both stones skipping on the lake, trying to avoid sinking into the depths. It's inevitable, though. Maybe he knows it, too.

He takes a step closer with a crunching boot, and I take a step back, almost simultaneously. As dance partners do. We're still the same distance apart, and neither of us has gotten anywhere with this conversation. My heel hits something hollow, and I look down to see a water bottle that must belong to him.

The shard of sunlight that had been brave enough to show itself suddenly disappears, and the grove of spruce becomes shaded within seconds. The NOAA forecast woman's voice echoes in my mind.

Pressure is dropping rapidly

The air around me begins to change, imperceptibly at first, but then prods me with a knowing gust of cool air. It's coming. Not a big storm, but big enough I can already feel its strength gathering about me, pressing me to seek the shore. I turn away but hear footsteps in my wake and realize he's following. The air swirls and hits him straight in the chest. I watch him stagger back and blink dazedly, holding his arms to shield himself from the dirt and dead leaves pelting his face. The water bottle skips and dances over the rough ground, rolling away to *clonk* quietly against his shoe.

Tell him to leave. Make him go, Anda.

I open my mouth and take a deep breath. Instinct tells me to listen, to do what is right. The pain of resistance twists again in my back, making me wince.

Do it, Anda.

When silence continues to scream inside my brain, she pushes a little harder. The wind whips the dying leaves around us in a slow whirlwind. He doesn't see her, but I do. The brown leaves rise and take shape behind him. There is a head, a matronly dress. She takes this form because it's what Father tells me she looked like. She is as motherly as the dead tresses of trees could be.

Anda. Tell him to leave.

"The wa...water." It hurts to speak. I swallow and clench my fists. "Boil it, or the parasites will eat you alive."

The leaves fall unceremoniously to the ground in a faint *whoosh*, the spell broken. I spin around and head to the shore. This time, he doesn't follow me.

All the way to the lake, I hear nothing but the lamentation of the rising wind and her voice, scolding me.

Chapter Seven

HECTOR

Parasites.

Man, I always worried about the hell that surrounded me every day in Duluth. The school administration, my uncle, my bosses, the punishing winters, the infrequent letters from my dad—they were always trying to kill me, bite by bite. Now I have to worry about being a different kind of victim.

The girl's footsteps recede into the woods as the wind rudely smacks my face. Well, I guess she's not trying to kill me. I blow out a breath and pause to touch my sheathed knife when a sliver of pain on my arm reminds me—I'm cut.

I was this close to slicing my arm open on purpose. And then she showed up, and I ended up cutting myself *by accident*. I actually forgot what had upset me so much, which never happens. The only times I forget are when I black out, but the thoughts that fill the void after that are far worse than what went missing. But this girl—she made me forget myself, in a good way. There's nothing in my life that's ever worth distracting me away from…me.

Under my sleeve, the wound is shallow and already wears the darker red stain of dried blood. It stings, though. I'll have to keep it clean so it won't get infected. I laugh, and the sound startles me. I can't believe I care. And yet here I am, trying to survive. The contradictions have always confused me. It's easier when I have a clear thing to run away from.

Things like my uncle. Him, and everything that house knows—I will always run away from them.

I've got to survive until May. I must.

I spend the rest of the afternoon picking through and retrieving the cleanest bits of food left over from the fox attack. I find one of the nearby camping shelters. There's no bunk bed, just a wooden floor and no mattresses. The front of the shelter is just a screen nailed to a wooden framework. The wind still slices into me just as easily as before.

It's a roof, at least. Not bad.

It's not good, either.

One thing is for sure. I need to get more food, or else I won't have much of a body left to protect this winter. I put all my stuff in the shelter, then leave with my fishing rod and a few obnoxiously colored lures. The gray clouds above are close and heavy, as if they're too wiped out from the effort of staying aloft. If they slammed to earth and swallowed everything up in fog, I wouldn't be surprised. I wipe a sheen of sweat from my face. I thought that being outdoors wasn't supposed to make you claustrophobic.

After a half-hour walk, I'm back at the dock in Windigo. It's so strange to stand on the wide planks without a single person in sight—a contrast to the busyness only hours earlier. Somewhere out there, the Duluth police are searching for me. For a moment, my uncle's distressed face fills my head. He's worried. Genuinely worried. He's holding his phone, ready to call my dad in Germany to tell him what's going on. The phone shakes in his hands. But what I hear isn't him talking to the police. It's his voice from only a few months ago, after one too many shots of Jack.

You're my best friend, Hector.

Your father leaving you with me — it's the best thing that ever happened.

Sometimes I get mad, but I'm not really mad. You know I love you, right? Right, buddy?

I squeeze my nails into my palms, forcing the thoughts away.

Stop it, Hector. No pity.

I jog over to the visitor center, which is shut up and closed, but I peek through one of the doors to see if there's anything worth stealing.

A taxidermied wolf sits in a Plexiglas box in the corner. It rests on its haunches, stuffed and sewn into a stiff, howling position, facing a seven-foot-tall skeleton of a moose. The tip of the skull is pointy as a spear, and the dead teeth grin permanently at a joke that's probably not funny.

It's all for the sake of education, but the whole thing creeps me out. The enclosed wolf howls silently for what it can't really howl for anymore. Maybe it's sad the moose is dead. Maybe it's sad that the moose can't be eaten. Who the fuck knows, but it's depressing as hell.

I walk away to the end of the dock as fast as I can.

I put the fishing rod together at the joints and study the lures. I've got three that came from a kit, along with a bobber and some weights. I choose between a dopey minnow, a baby frog with a hook sprouting out of its ass, and a Day-Glo orange worm with green sparkles on the smashed end. Hooray for variety.

I tie the worm to the end of the fishing line, along with

the weights and bobber. I watched a few videos about fishing, but I don't actually know what I'm doing. The one and only time I went fishing was seven years ago. I got invited to a fishing birthday party. My uncle was in a rare mood and actually let me go. I was the only kid who didn't know how to fish, and the birthday boy's dad had to show me everything.

"You hold it in your right hand, like this. Put this finger down on the release button." He stood behind me the whole time, showing me how to cast, congratulating me when the worm I'd crucified on the hook actually plopped into the water, a reasonable ten feet away.

I didn't smile at my success.

"So…I guess your dad's not much into fishing, huh?" he'd asked kindly.

"My dad loves fishing."

"Oh." The dad had shifted in his sneakers. I could practically hear the wheels of confusion grinding inside his blond head. "So…why didn't he teach you?"

I couldn't say a word. Imaginary cracks fissured in my chest. Dad had sent me letters every six months, ones that I couldn't understand for years because I couldn't read a damn word until I was eight. By the time I could make sense of the pages, it was an explosion of information. Stuff I didn't want to know, and stuff I *really* didn't want to know.

He was at this army base, and then another. He was fishing in Florida on leave, catching tarpon for the third time. He hadn't heard anything from my mother, had I? Was I being a good boy? Was I being respectful of my uncle, who was nice enough to give me a settled, normal life?

He'd asked questions, wondering what I was becoming, never coming close enough to the Duluth city limits to retrieve the answers himself. I wrote back, but the responses that arrived afterward gave no indication that he read them at all, or cared about their contents. He was a one-way street of words on paper.

"Hector? Are you okay?" The birthday boy's father had put his hand on my shoulder. It was heavy with pity and radiated this nauseating warmth. I'd turned around and knocked it away violently. My fishing pole had fallen with a messy splash into the pond. I don't remember the rest of the day. Didn't matter anyway. For me, the party was over.

The wind picks up on the dock, and I stand to cast into the water. My hands are cold and shake with nervousness, which is stupid. There is no one here watching me make a fool of myself fishing. Well, except for the girl. I scan the shoreline carefully, searching for any glimpse of human anywhere. In the distance, I spy a thin curl of white smoke coming from the shoreline trees about a mile away, but then it disappears.

My first attempts at casting my rod are ridiculous. I forget to let go of the release button too late, and the lure winds jerkily around the tip of my rod four times. Another time, the bait plops straight down into the water and snags on a mossy stick. After a few more casts, I manage to get it out and away from the dock. As the little white and red ball bobs on the surface of the water, I smile grimly. I don't need anyone to teach me how to do this.

I end up sitting on the end of the pier when nothing happens after the first twenty minutes. My nose runs from the cold and I wipe it on my jacket arm. Occasionally, something twitches and tugs the end of the line, but I reel in nothing. It's like the fish know that there's nothing but death waiting, so why bother? A rubber worm isn't worth it.

When there's nothing but you and a lot of silence, your head ends up filling with crap you didn't want to be reminded of. Instead, I try to think about the girl. I wonder where she is. Who she is. Why she's here. What she eats.

But mostly, I wonder who she's running away from. Why else would she be on Isle Royale?

My mind fills with the stuff you see on the evening news, and it makes my stomach burn. I can't think of an answer that isn't horrible, so I make up all sorts of fantastical stories about her, like she'd run away from a Florida circus where she was forced to do backflips off elephants all day. Or that she's a biology illustrator who's drawing different kinds of fungus for a living.

I have no one else to keep me company. Soon, the curve of her cheek and the glint of her gray eyes become so familiar. Her eyelashes are wispy. Her eyebrows curve slightly upward in the middle, making her seem like she's always about to ask a question, or doesn't understand the one you just asked. She's a little scrawny, like she could seriously use a steak dinner. I could describe her to a police sketch artist, if I had to. And then I wonder, what crime is she capable of committing?

Huh.

Killing mosquitoes is the only thing I can imagine.

Hours go by. The sun is getting low, and I'm a little panicked at having caught nothing. Just as I stand to pull in the line, a mighty tug yanks on my fishing pole. I almost drop it in the water, then pull it back with my sweaty hands and reel as fast as I can. I yank the tip of the rod up every few seconds, zipping my catch in, and then a flash of silver breaks the water and a tail flips spray into the air. I whoop out loud, then reel even faster.

"Please, please, please," I pray to nobody. Afraid I'll push the release button by accident, I grab the line when the fish is only a few feet from the tip of the rod.

God, it's beautiful. And really fucking small. It's maybe seven inches long, barely over a pound, shiny greenish-gray with cream-colored speckles all over and a slightly hooked mouth. My lure is sunk into the side of its mouth. Right where the barb juts out, there's blood. It's red like mine, which momentarily surprises me.

It thrashes around so much that I put it down on the pier and pull out my knife.

"Sorry. It's you or me, little guy." I raise the blunt end of my knife above its head. But I hesitate. Its glassy eye stares coldly back at me. After an eternity, I bring down the hilt of my knife and hit it hard on the top of the head. It flops a few more times, then goes still.

I start gutting the fish and scale it like I remember seeing on some TV show once. I don't remember it being such a disgusting mess, though. A whole lot of blood for a small fish. I seriously wish I'd caught a bag of Oreos instead, or a giant ham sandwich. I'm not a huge fish fan, and the prospect of stepping into the new role of fish serial killer isn't helping at all.

When I was a little kid, back in Korea, Mom used to make fish in the only way I liked it, with a hot bowl of steaming rice and plenty of *banchan*. I'm almost homesick for it, except that I don't really know what homesickness is. Maybe I'm just sick. I try to blur my thoughts and refocus them on my mom's face, but I can't see it. I can feel her arms around me, above the heated floor of our room. But I can't see her face.

I look down and there's a dead animal in my hands. For a moment, I wonder how it got there.

Pay attention, Hector.

My hands are bloodied and slippery, and now I reek like pond scum. The scales fly everywhere when I scrape the body with my knife. I must have at least four or five on my face. But soon, I'm done. I've got food.

I rinse my hands and the headless, gutted fish with bottled water. As I head back to my camp, the thin curl of white smoke appears above the tree line about a mile away again. It's on the way back, so I head toward it, hoping it's what I think it is.

Taking the path back to the camp, I find the source of the smoke. It's a tiny little cottage, hidden from shore by a layer of maple trees devoid of leaves. The cottage seems dilapidated until I realize it's only weathered, not abandoned. Thin pines grow close, hugging the walls. A curlicue of smoke rises from a stone chimney, and the windows are all closed up with some battered-looking metal shutters. There's no peeking inside this house. Still, it's small, and she must have broken in. No one on the island would have stayed here, and I doubt anyone would stock it with food to waste over the winter.

I take out my knife and saw the tiny fish in half, then leave part of it on the stone step of the back door. I walk away quickly. Hopefully a fox won't get it before she does.

There's always more fish to catch. Anyway, I owe her for the water-boiling comment, and for something else. It was nice to not think about myself for a while.

At the thought, I jog back and leave the other half of the fish on the step, too.

Chapter Eight

ANDA

It begins with the fish.

I find it on the back step of the cottage, a small corpse of an offering. At first, my nose flares at the scent. It's beheaded, chopped in two, and smeared with blood. Scales stick to it here and there, violently displaced from that unnaturally smooth skin. The belly has been inexpertly torn open in the tenderest of places, anus to gills, leaving a jagged maw with fascia and silken skin hanging in ribbons.

There is only one person who could have left such a thing. The boy.

Is he trying to scare me? Is it a warning, a herald of what he might do to me? The air pressure around me drops like a stone, and I draw the clouds about me. Mist dampens my forehead with comfort as I stare at the carcass. And then my father's good sense enters my brain.

Anda, it said. *It's food. He's trying to feed you. He worries for your body.*

It is kindness.

"Oh." I stand there dumbly for a full five minutes, until

I finally pick up the pieces with my hands and bring them inside. I rinse them out with cooled, boiled water and place them, small and lonely, on a plate. I stare at them for at least an hour before deciding what to do. I dig into the small trove of cookbooks that Father kept in the kitchen cupboard and study the "sea delights" section. Every word is a bit of prayer.

Sprinkle generously with salt and pepper.

Dip gently in an egg wash.

Dredge thoroughly in cornmeal, well-seasoned.

Fry in butter until golden brown.

Serve with a wedge of lemon.

I only have a few eggs. Father left me with enough food to last a month. But the eggs will go bad anyway, so I use one and follow the recipe instructions as if they were sacred law. The skillet soon hisses with browning butter, and I lay the pieces in. Droplets of hot fat skip out of the pan and hit my skin, making me dance and dodge, squealing. My face near the stove feels scorched, and I burn my left fourth finger.

I laugh the entire time.

Finally, they are done. I burned half of the fish, but the cottage smells of good, cooked food, and the walls smile at me. Father has tried to do this for me. He'd create dishes to tempt me to eat. Berries like jewels, so pretty that they made me cry. Or cubes of cheese that I wouldn't touch, because they smelled of their true origins—of rotted, curdled, glandular secretions. His care was only suitable for a normal human girl, because it's all his mind can imagine. He tries, so hard. But his attempts are slippers that don't fit, that chafe at my edges constantly.

But this one viciously murdered fish feels just right for someone like me.

Too fitting.

I find a piece of nice clean newspaper from the stack by

the fire and wrap half of the fish in the paper, watching the oil stain the newsprint with dots of dark gray. I study the gift I've made, cradling it in my hands. A strange sensation tickles my fingertips.

I believe it's called pride.

And then I leave the cottage. It is easy to find him, though it's dusk. I go to the last place we'd seen each other and follow his footprints to the camping shelter where he's made his new home. From a distance, his footsteps shuffle a quiet rhythm. His blurred form moves about inside.

I watch him enter a patch of light where the tired sun carelessly appears for a second. He runs his hand through his dark hair and touches his stubbly cheeks with wonder, as if time had sneaked up on him and surprised him with the truth that he is, in fact, a young man now. He stands inside his shelter and looks out, but I can tell that his eyes are focused inward. He is thinking, seeing something I cannot.

I feel left behind.

I don't like it.

But I am here, Anda. I will never leave you alone.

I dismiss her voice, trying to concentrate.

Usually when campers come to the island, they busy themselves with hiking. They point at the mergansers and grebes that alight on the waters. They swat at the thirsty mosquitoes and pore over trail maps. They never see me. But this boy has seen me. Something, inexplicably, has changed. I can smell it in the air.

Suddenly, as if nudged by a thought, the boy gathers his fishing gear and leaves, heading for the shore.

I'm tempted to follow him, but my hands are full and that isn't my purpose. Carefully, I push at his shelter door, which opens with a traitorous *creak*. Inside, it's starkly empty, compared to when the others come. They bring bottles of oily insecticide, complicated cooking units, and expensive water bottles. They hang clothes from the trees that are always some shade of khaki. Their shoes are sturdy, with bountiful straps and colorful laces.

This boy has one bag, and his belongings remain nestled inside, terrified of abandonment. I watch the bag, wondering if it will speak to me. But there are no murmurs of filth or desecration. There are dark things, yes, but they hide skillfully and won't reveal themselves to me. I concentrate harder, prying, as fingers would do on a closed oyster. Still, I hear nothing.

I hesitate with my newspaper packet of cooked fish. Finally, I decide to leave it on the floor by his sleeping bag, but just before I place it there, the wind enters the shelter.

Do not, Anda.

Do not.

The cool air twists about my ankles, and she tries to pull me away. But it is just wind, and the wind is part of me, too. I hear a sigh of disappointment when I place the parcel on the wooden bed. Then I run home.

All the way back, she berates me.

"I didn't start this," I explain aloud. "He started it first. I'm paying him back. Now we're even."

You're using reason. You're defensive.

"I am?" I wonder. It's a delightful sensation. Foreign. "Why, yes. Yes, I suppose I am."

When I reach the door to the house, something isn't right. Something in my center, a gnawing. When I enter the kitchen, the scent of butter and salty fish assail my nose, pulling me forward. The cast-iron frying pan is now cold and glossy with congealed brown butter and bits of crusty skin. I lift it to my face and take a cautious lick. I lick it until it's clean.

So this is what hunger feels like.

Chapter Nine

HECTOR

Shelter, shelter, shelter.

Outside of eating enough, it's my main goal right now. If I'm going to survive here until I turn eighteen, I need shelter. It's all I should be thinking about, but things keep happening. Weird things.

Today it was a hat.

It was sitting on the ground at my campsite. I knew it hadn't been tossed there by the wind. First of all, there's nothing left behind on this island. The campers practically spit-shine the pine needles, they leave it so pristine. Also, the hat brim was weighted down with about twenty pounds' worth of rocks to keep it from blowing away.

Kind of overkill, but charming anyway.

I've seen tourists wear these kinds of hats. The ones with the floppy brim and an elastic cord that cinches under your chin, because how else will muggers know you're ripe for the picking? Normally, I wouldn't be caught dead in something like this, but I know she watches me. Yesterday, I spent the whole afternoon squinting into the sun and cursing when I went fishing. It's hard to fish when one hand is being used as a visor. Hence the hat.

I don't often see her, but there are other clues.

Two days ago, I froze my ass (and arms, and legs, and junk) off after a quick dive in the lake water to bathe. The shower units at Windigo have been turned off, and I couldn't stand my own stink anymore. I had to wrestle on dry clothes over dripping wet skin. Not fun. The next morning, there was a tea towel hung on the tree outside my shack. Which means she saw me naked. Jesus, yes, she saw me naked.

Two weeks ago, it was a battered old badminton birdie. What do they call it? Oh, yeah. A shuttlecock. The kind with the plastic feathers and the little white snub tip. A few days had gone by and I hadn't seen her. I had gotten caught up with my plan to winter-proof my shelter. I'd tried but failed to break into the ranger's quarters—the doors were steel and the window too small to slip through. So it was this camping shelter or nothing. The front wall is basically one huge screen, and it's got to be covered. I'd spent days and days gathering broken tree limbs, or sawing them off myself, getting my hands all gummy with sap.

And it's hard to work on shelter when I'm so hungry. Twenty-four hours a day, my empty stomach screams at me. I'm ravenous when I sleep, if that's even possible. I've already eaten through all my food supplies. My attempts to ration spectacularly failed after four days with no fish. The dreams of Whoppers and crisp, salty fries and Wendy's Frosty shakes don't help. My pants are already hanging on my hips more, and I'm tired all the time.

But tiredness and hunger aren't the worst. I can't stop thinking.

I think about Dad, and if he's talked to my uncle about

whether they've found me. If he really, truly needs to leave Germany to come figure out where I am. Or I think about my mom. Is she happier in Seoul without me? Does she still eat Botan Rice Candy, or did she really only buy that for me?

I remember what it was like to wake up after hours of oblivion, my mouth dry and rancid. Seeing the newest Halo for Xbox on my bed where my uncle had left it. Maybe twenty bucks. Something that says *sorry*. Also, *shut up*.

And then I would start forgetting about my shelter, about surviving, about hunger, and my mind would become a cesspool of thoughts I don't want or need. And that's when I'd see it.

This broken little shuttlecock, nestled in my sleeping bag. I put it in my pocket, went back to sawing off branches, and spent those hours and hours pondering *why the fuck is a shuttlecock on a nature preserve in the middle of Lake Superior?* Actually, maybe that's why. Because she knows, somehow, that when I have nothing to think about but myself, I start longing for a cigarette butt. I start reaching for my knife.

I haven't tried to hurt myself since she stopped me, days ago.

So in between shelter-building, I've become her fishmonger. A really sucky fishmonger. I fish every day, but I'm not lucky enough to catch a fish every time. Still, I'm getting better and better at it. Feldtmann Lake has become a favorite place to go, despite the long-ass ten-mile hike. I know which shady spots are the best, and the fact that the fish bite most when it rains a little in the early mornings. The rod and reel have become an extension of my body when I cast. The fine monofilament begins to make a proud callus between my thumb and forefinger when I feel the line for bites.

For a while, we had this pattern. I'd spend all morning fishing. If I was lucky, I'd be able to leave a fish cleaned for her on her back step. I always wait by the back door and listen carefully, but I don't hear a creak or a whisper inside that house. And I don't try to say anything, or knock. Talking is so damn complicated. It involves explaining things, like who I am and why I'm here. She doesn't try to chat me up, either. I relish this wordlessness we have.

Meanwhile, there's some sort of weird wind current where she lives. The gales there always push hard at my back. Tiny pebbles have bounced along the ground and hit my shins. Twigs smack my hands like an old schoolmarm with a ruler. The air around that house hates me or something.

Then I'd go back to camp, work on weaving fir tree branches together with what rope I have. I make sure they point downward and overlap, so they'll shed rain. During my breaks, one of my precious matches goes to boiling a gallon of lake water for the next day. I'd brew some spruce tip tea, wishing it was chunky soup, and chew some of the hard resin I'd gathered. It's a nightmare version of gum—crumbly at first, before it threatens to lock your jaws together forever, but at least I get to chew on something. I'd boil the fish bones from the day before and make a broth, before I inevitably cave and inhale a remaining precious handful of nuts or dried fruit from my bag. And then I'd saw and break more branches for the next day, just so I could have my back turned for about an hour. And she'd deliver half a cooked fish to me by early evening.

Well, almost a half fish. I started noticing that my portion was getting smaller and smaller. She'd been hungrier, I guess. Or maybe her own food supplies were running out.

Today, the temperature dropped. I mean, it's always cold, but this was a new cold that completely blasted through my jacket and pants, too easily. So I shiver inside my clothes and wear both pairs of pants (and my new hat), but it worries me. It's only late October, and the weather will get worse. It's a good thing I bathed off my grime yesterday. It took five minutes to bathe, and hours to warm up again. That water today might kill me if I dunk myself again.

Every time I've tried to wash, she's been there. I know it. I don't always see her, but everything gets really quiet all of a sudden. There's no wind, no birds singing. The surface of the water becomes glass. Once I saw her face peeking behind a tree, and I caught her eyes. She made sure not to be seen the next time.

Strangely, I'm never embarrassed by her seeing me bare. I'm no nudist or anything. But her eyes on me are never an intrusion or lewd. More like fascination. Like how a person might notice a shiny rock or an interesting moth.

But then after I got used to this bizarre voyeuristic thing, something weird happened.

I'd walked knee-high into Lake Superior instead of one of the interior lakes to wash up after fishing. As I splashed the icy water over my arms, I waited for the calm. And as expected, the surface of the water quieted to stillness.

Something appeared in the water. It was only about ten feet away, and the water was pretty clear, since the wind was low. Rusted beams tangled with chains, some old rotten canvas fabric, and an algae-covered hull.

A shipwreck? This shallow, right in Washington Harbor?

I rubbed my eyes and looked again, and suddenly there were no rusty beams, no pieces of a ship. Only a skull, with a face half rotted off and a fish snaking into one open eye socket.

"Shit!" I'd screamed, backing out of the water so fast I tripped and landed on my back on the shore. Hyperventilating, I sat up and peered into the water.

It was gone. All of it, gone.

Maybe I'd been hallucinating from hunger or sleep deprivation. I didn't see it again after that. But it definitely helped me to stop caring about being clean.

I may be dirty for the rest of the season. But one thing's for sure, I'll be freezing all the goddamned time, too. After a week, I finish my wall of branches. I'm really proud of my work, though it looks like I'm living in a kid's play fort. And yet I shiver every night inside. I try banking the other walls with branches, but it does no good. The rain sheds nicely, but the wind practically scoffs at my work. Sometimes I suspect that the wind around that girl's house purposely tries to find me at night, sneaking between the down layers of my sleeping bag. Because when I sit up and try to shift, or go outside to take a leak, the punishing wind immediately backs off. Like a crook walking away from a crime scene, whistling as if nothing happened.

Whatever. Now I'm really losing it.

And then one morning after I'm done fishing, I return to camp to find it got hit by a windstorm of some kind. The wall of branches I've so carefully woven are totally wrecked, like a mini tornado untwisted all my knots and scattered the branches.

Fuck.

So, right. I need a new place to stay. Today, I gather my stuff. Minus all the food I've eaten (and the fox ate, too), it's a lot lighter. I take the foot trail back to Windigo and walk past the dock to search for houses along Washington Harbor. I see a few, but before I can get any closer, the wind picks up. The green firs along the shore shudder, and the surface of the lake is slapped into sharp, breaking peaks. There's a strange, distant keening sound. A storm is rising for sure.

I hike up to Feldtmann Ridge to see if there are cabins there I can break into. Clouds hang low in the sky, the color of smudged ash. There's a freighter near the horizon, like the ones parked in the Duluth port that dump coal and stuff. My worry over the weather turns into simmering panic when the clouds above start to churn in greenish-gray poufs. It's going to rain, and I can almost smell the lightning about to strike. I'm in the wide open. I turn around to head off the ridge, closer to the lake and lower ground.

That's when I see her.

Chapter Ten

ANDA

Not now. Please, not while he can see me.

I'd gone to the water's edge after following him. The pines grow right to the edge of the lake, where there is only a rocky ridge separating land from shore. I stand on the precipice of a large boulder, swaying.

The air pressure is low, so much that my skin might expand monstrously against my will. The clouds lust for me to change, beseeching me to enter the water. Droplets from the surface of the harbor spray my face, and I drop my bottom lip open. The mist is a drug on my tongue; sweet and delicious and bitter, all at once. Though the wind begins to push the trees this way and that, my hair hangs untouched. My nightgown doesn't swirl against my ankles, as if I'm sheltered within a bell jar.

She cries for me.

I miss you, Anda. A year is so long. I made this for you.

I'll give this gift. Be a good girl, and give me what I want in return.

"It's not yet November," I say calmly, though my heart

pummels my chest from inside. "I promised Father. I must wait until November." The color red thrums within my ears. My mouth is dry. I'm thirsty. So thirsty.

I've always been able to hold off until November, when Father can be gone, and when my need and the wind knit into something bigger, more satisfying. But now, my want seeps past the confines of what I've done in the past. I've been changing more than I realize.

She wants me to cooperate. To do what I do after holding back all year for his sake. And for the first storm of the season, I'm lost.

I don't know how to be, when this boy is so near.

He came down from the ridge to escape the lightning and found me instead, fifty feet away. Too far; too close. I couldn't hide in time. Because I had followed him again, like I have every day. Quietly, from within the shadows. It has become my normal, something I never owned before.

But I've found that I own many things now. Possessions. Things like cooking fish in spattering butter every day. Finding treasures to give to the boy. I'm not collecting diamonds or gold. I am not a greedy human who tries to surround herself with glitter and jeweled beauty, so these things don't count. When I find things with weight, like a lovely, spotted, red-capped mushroom—*Amanita muscaria*, only somewhat poisonous—I don't keep it. I blink at it fondly, and then leave it for him. Because when you own things, that's the beginning of the end.

He's beginning to own you, Anda. And you belong to me.

I pause. With every give and take with this boy, is something more accumulating? Perhaps I just don't know what to call it. But I can feel it, and it's beginning to consume me. It's different, being consumed, instead of being the one who takes and takes, every November, without mercy.

The storm is strengthening because of my presence. The invisible bell jar that keeps the wind from touching me is thinning. My toes tingle, and my hair crackles with electricity. I've felt the weakening, the draining of my self, for weeks now. I've held it at arm's length for too long. I am weak. Too weak.

"Wait, wait!" I cry out, only to find that my lips are closed. But there is no more waiting. The invisible bell jar around me turns to nothing. The boy's eyes lock onto mine, but soon I can't see him anymore, because I've already closed my eyes to him. To everything.

With a single sigh, I let the storm take me.

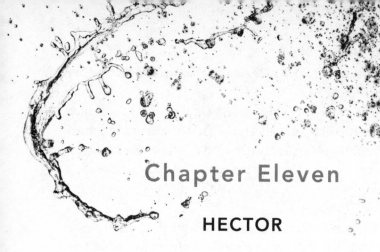

Chapter Eleven

HECTOR

She stands there on the rocky shoreline for a few minutes. When I get close enough, I see her eyes. They're black as wet lake stones. It confuses me, because I swear they were gray. She seems to focus on the trees behind me, like I'm not even there. But the oddest thing is how the wind doesn't seem to touch her. I'm squinting because of the dead leaves flying through the air, swirling around my head, threatening to scratch my eyes out.

But nothing's touching her. Not a hair on her head moves. The hem of her nightgown doesn't even flutter.

What the hell.

"Hey. Hey! Are you okay?" I yell, which is a joke, because between the two of us, I'm way, way more freaked out. And then suddenly, it's like a veil between us rises and she sees me. Her eyes latch on and it makes me shiver, because everything feels wrong. Like my eyes have just committed a crime. And I open my mouth to yell louder, when the laws of physics decide to suddenly function again.

The wind swirls her nightgown around her pale legs

and her hair goes science-experiment-static-wild. Her eyes close and she turns to step into the water.

Oh, Jesus.

The girl takes one deliberate step after another, until she's thigh-deep in the freezing water. She doesn't even flinch. Her nightgown darkens from the lake water. She's still going.

"What are you doing? Hey! Hey!" I yell at her, but she's still not listening to me. I crash through the brush, trying to reach her, but I'm not fast enough. She's already waist-deep when I jump into the lake, the icy water knifing up my legs and making me gasp. "Stop, stop!" I scream at her, but the wind has picked up and she can't hear me.

The cold water weighs down my boots as I slog closer when the wind hits me like a body slam. I stagger back, falling backward into the lake, wet to the shoulder. When I shake the water out of my eyes, I catch a glimpse of the girl's white hair disappearing beneath the surface. She's twenty feet away, too far away. It's just like a nightmare, when you can't move fast enough.

No, it's worse than a nightmare. Because this is really happening.

Chapter Twelve

ANDA

The storm is immense. I've been paying so much attention to the boy that I've become distracted, not even realizing how large it's become. The lake is releasing its captured summer warmth, mixing with cold air from the north, sodden air from the Gulf. It twists and coils about the lake. I don't need the radio to tell me what I feel.

Winds are rising to thirty miles per hour.

Waves at six feet along the south coastline.

It's a vicious song in my head, the twisting winds that gather strength when I sigh.

A heartbeat pulses near me. Vaguely, I remember the boy. His rapid pulse is too small a quarry for me right now. It isn't the salty warmth within his blood vessels that attracts me.

It's the *St. Anne*.

She's a beautiful laker, she is. A longboat, with a narrow waist and smooth lines. Small for a freighter, only six hundred feet long. With a belly full of dolomite, she's only just passed through the Soo Locks yesterday evening.

She's a mere nineteen miles from the Isle, still visible to human eyes from here. If all goes well, she'll be in Duluth's port by evening tonight.

All will not go well.

The *St. Anne* has been lucky enough to escape the fate of many of the freighters her age. Her steel is more brittle than the bones made by steel mills today. She creaks with tiredness. She aches for the scrapyard. But scrapping is the tidy way for a freighter's life to end. Beaching the ship ashore, where her captain will shake hands with the hangman and turn a blind eye to the coming feast. A crew who's never known her will gnaw her apart like ants on a carcass. There is no glory in scrapping.

I swirl the wind tighter about her, bringing them closer to sixty miles per hour. Twenty-nine hearts beat faster. Hands are on deck and below. Water is entering through a crack in her hull that they've yet to discover. I smile and force the water in. The crack widens. The ship lists to the side, ever so slightly, and more water comes on board, into one of the hatches.

Twenty thousand pounds of dolomite isn't that much, but the *St. Anne*'s middle is hogging now, sagging from the weight as it did at port. But with the winds and the water, the stress is too much. The captain issues a distress signal.

It's too late. Their fear is an electric sourness on my tongue. The crew are scrambling for lifeboats, being hurled against the metal of the ship's interior skeleton. I'll not let them go. It's a gift, really. They fight so hard, when relief is so close, so close. Their panic pains me, almost as much as the dragonfly with its leg snapped off in the tree sap, more than the dark-eyed junco that struggles out of its cracked shell.

I've waited so long. Eleven months is a long time to

go without the breaking of such creatures. I fed sparingly on the growth in spring, on summer greenery, but they are nothing to the feed of a wreck. I reach in the water to grasp the body of the *St. Anne*. The shattering of her is a symphony. Her two halves are uncleanly rendered apart, filling with water and sinking quickly. Within her fractured body, the sailors' bubbled screams are silenced. The north wind's penetrating strength has chilled the water and quickly numbs arms and legs punching through the depths, attempting to rise. Twenty of the crew have made it onto the rafts, but nine have not.

They are mine.

The sourness on my tongue changes to the iron tang of torn metal as the *St. Anne*'s bow hits the sediment of Lake Superior. The stern swirls and falls three hundred feet away, but it isn't the boat's demise that will fill me.

The nine are struggling within the crushing pressure of the lake's depths. Metal crushes thighs and cracks rib cages; some float freely, corked and trapped beneath what was once a floor, now a casket's closed top. The glacial water shocks their muscles, stiffens them prematurely. Water pours into their throats, their larynxes spasming, forbidding any last scream. I listen as the hearts thrill with a frantic rhythm before the lack of oxygen strangles each muscle into a slower pulse.

The first heart slows to a still. In that moment of savage surrender, its spent energy becomes mine. The trilling hunger in my bones is somewhat quieted, finally. I will be glutted before long.

Smiling, I barely notice the hand gripping my wrist.

Chapter Thirteen

HECTOR

Oh God. Where is she?

One second she was there, and the next, she was underwater. I surge toward the last place I saw her. The sky rumbles, and powerful wind spits lake water and stings my face. I squint, trying to protect my eyes.

My soaked clothes weigh a thousand pounds, and I hyperventilate reflexively from the gnawing cold. My sodden boots drag me down, and I can barely kick. Minutes go by, each one feeling like a century. Soon, the shoreline is frighteningly far away, and it's an effort not to think, *holy shit, I might actually drown today*. It's everything I can do to not panic. Drowning is everybody's worst fear, but stupid Hector didn't think of this before he dived in the water, of course.

The surface of the lake is prickling from raindrops. Swells that weren't there before bob me up and down, and I swallow water once, twice. I spin around, kicking hard to stay afloat.

And then I see something. The tiniest smudge of white color pushing away the darkness, maybe about ten feet away, inches below the surface. Whatever it is, it's sinking quickly. With a huge breath, I surge forward and kick, my muscles already burning. I reach forward, down, grabbing into the wet void at anything. My fingertips graze something soft. I lunge again, and burning skin meets my hand.

I grab wildly, and my hand closes around a thin limb—ankle or wrist, I've no idea. I yank and pull, trying desperately to bring her to the surface. I grab her small waist, jerking her up so her face stays above the water. Her eyes are shut. The lake splashes around us, and water pools in her open mouth. Oh no.

What's more, I can't seem to move her. Something's snagged on her legs, as if she's chained to the bottom of the lake. I kick harder, and a wave of water crashes over both our faces. I cough and sputter, fighting to drag her to shore. She's still tethered somehow. With a massive grunt, I throw us both closer to shore, and something gives way beneath us. We're loose now, our limbs flailing.

My muscles start to scream from effort as I kick my waterlogged boots and paddle with one hand. I end up flipping onto my back, arching my chest and kicking while towing her torso under one arm. It takes forever, we're out so far from the shoreline. My feet finally touch the gravel bed of the lake and I drag her onto the narrow shore. I flip her onto her stomach to let the water empty out of her mouth. My heart is pounding so hard it's going to bust out of my rib cage. I turn her onto her back, ready to do mouth-to-mouth, chest compressions, whatever it takes. Her eyes are partly open now, trancelike, but she's breathing—miraculously. My cold fingers clumsily feel for a pulse in her neck. A tiny throbbing nudges stubbornly beneath my fingertips—her heart is beating. Her nightgown is sodden and clings to skin that burns beneath my fingers, hotter than cement in the summer.

She's got a fever. She must be sick and delirious.

"Shit, shit, shit." I hoist her into my arms. Before I head back to Windigo, I turn and stare at the lake's horizon. That big freighter that was passing by is long gone, but its absence sends a chill down my spine.

I start carrying her back to Windigo. She's a dead weight, and my heavy, wet clothes and the pounding rain don't help. I've been eating barely half a fish a day for the last two weeks. I've lost a lot of muscle. So every footstep is an effort. My biceps and quads are screaming with pain when I finally make it to her little cottage.

As I reach for the back door, I'm sure it's going to be locked. But the door is wide open, welcoming us.

The door is never, ever open.

I kick it farther open with a dripping boot. The cottage is really tiny. There's a pair of old rubber boots and a collection of four skeletonized umbrellas by the door. Miniature piles of lake rocks — what are they called? cairns? — are piled here and there over the wide plank floors. A stone fireplace is dark and cold, facing a single lumpy couch and a braided rug. Just beyond, a cramped kitchen still smells of buttery fried things.

I heave her in my arms again and walk down the hallway, finding two closet-sized bedrooms. One is super tidy, with a single narrow cot topped with a neat plaid blanket. The other has no bed, just a little nest of twisted blankets, next to piles upon piles of animal bones, feathers, and more rock cairns.

I have a bad feeling that she sleeps in the nest of blankets, but decide instead to put her on the cot in the cleaner bedroom. Her body sags onto the thin mattress, soaking the bedding. Her eyes are still only at half-mast, seeing nothing. In the gloom of the cabin, I can't see the difference between her pupils and her irises. Her eyes are all one stormy dark gray. And her skin is still burning hot.

After I withdraw my arms from her body, I hesitate. I miss holding her already, though my biceps are cursing from exhaustion. But that's not why I'm hesitating.

I can't let her sleep with these clothes, wet to the skin.

There is one chest of drawers in the room. The top three drawers contain men's clothes for a guy built much heavier than me. But then in the bottom drawer, I find another nightgown, this one made of indigo cotton, with cotton lace at the neckline. There are also jeans and long-sleeve shirts that would fit a girl like her.

So she does actually live here? Why would she stay behind? Where's the dude? If it's her father (because she looks like my age, maybe younger) why the hell hasn't he come back to get her?

I shake the questions away. I want to know, and I don't. And anyway, someone needs to change her into dry clothes, and I'm the only somebody around. My heart starts tap-dancing inside my chest as I peel off my own wet jacket and kick off my boots so I don't feel so weighed down. After carrying her for so long, my hands tremble from her absence.

I pick up the dry nightgown.

"I swear to God, I have the best intentions," I tell her, nervously clearing my throat. The wind thrashes against the wall, and the metal shutters outside tap a Morse code against the window panes. "Okay." I swallow and pick up the dry nightgown. "Here goes."

It's hard to unsee what I see when I change her clothing. Unblemished skin, dabs of deep pink on bronze, and the softest curves I've ever seen in real life. She's absolutely beautiful, and it's not just because I've never seen a girl naked before.

There was Carla. We'd worked at Walmart together two summers in a row and messed around a few times in her car after work. Carla was plump and pretty, with smooth white skin, brown eyes, and harsh black bangs that knifed across her forehead. And she didn't go to my high school, which meant my low-caste reputation was unknown to her. She actually didn't care that I wore regular shorts instead of swim trunks when we went to the public pool once. She'd make me sandwiches when I'd brought nothing for lunch, or had no money to buy anything.

"Tell me about it," she'd say. She didn't elaborate on what. That was obvious. She wanted to know everything. About the scars, the rickety bicycle I rode to work, how I spoke to no one but her. In fact, we didn't talk much at all. One day, she just took my hand and pulled me into her car after closing, and I let her. That was how it started.

Her questions at first didn't seem like a demand; more like an open door. At first, I gave her what she wanted. I told her the scars were mine; that my mother was still in Korea and no, she never called or wrote. I hadn't seen or heard from her since she put me on the plane when I was six, because she actually thought I'd be more accepted here. My dad wasn't happy to have what he hadn't wanted to begin with. And my uncle, well, he needed the extra cash.

But eventually, after I'd stopped answering Carla's questions, she stopped asking. Summer ended, and she didn't ask for my phone number.

I didn't miss her. You can't miss what you never really had, can you?

And I don't blame her for walking away. It's not like she was giving and I was taking all the time. I wasn't giving and I wasn't taking anything. Ever. You can't date a brick wall. It stops being mysterious and ends up just being…a wall.

But this island girl. She's different. She gives, but there is nothing expected in return, really. She's not trying to fix me, or heal me, or new-age me to death. She asks no questions. And I've asked none, either. It's such a relief, not having to unearth things you don't want to.

And what's more—anyone who stays stranded on Isle Royale in the winter, on purpose, has problems by definition. Seriously bad side effects from living. Somehow, I know hers are a tsunami compared to mine. Maybe part of me thanks her for the perspective. To be the least fucked-up person on a whole island—well, that's a gift, too. Even if there are only the two of us.

Finally, the girl is dressed in her clean nightgown. I've sweated inside my clammy, sodden clothes. Inside the narrow hallway closet, there are fresh sheets and another blanket. I carry her to the sofa and peel off the damp sheets of the cot, then cover them with dry bedding before bringing her back.

Soon, she's tucked in, dry, and sleeping soundly.

I should go back to my cabin, but I don't want to. My evergreen wall has been destroyed, after all. And I need to make sure she wakes up okay. The wind and rain outside shake the shutters again, and the chimney moans. I've never been more glad to have a reason to stay in place.

As I sit on the sofa and stare at the ashes in the fireplace, I feel distinctly odd. Emptied out, but not in a bad way. Even though I almost saw a girl drown, even though I nearly drowned myself, I don't feel freaked out like I should. Looking around at this tiny cottage with its strange, unconscious occupant in the next room—I don't feel like tearing off my skin. I don't feel like fleeing, for the first time in years.

Huh. Imagine that.

Chapter Fourteen

ANDA

I've never had a dream like this before.

I'm in a foreign city. Everyone is Asian and speaks a language I've never heard. It's winter, and the cold air is ravenous, gnawing warmth away from people in their thick coats and scarves. Hurrying along the crowded sidewalk, there is a little boy—a toddler—and his mother. His skin is deeper, like aged oak, but hers is pale as parchment. They have the same dark eyes. Beautiful eyes.

The city street is busy and full of metal, wheels, voices, walls of steel. There are cabs and cars bumper to bumper. Steam from car exhaust and manholes rises here and there. Neon signs flash from the buildings above, and a constant din of honking horns, voices, and engines roar together in a garish cacophony.

The mother's hair is tied in a messy black ponytail. She makes no eye contact with anyone as she pulls the boy's mittened hand down the street. Her shoulders hunch over, burdened by the city air above. Two businessmen murmur to each other as they approach her. They are going to pass her and her son on the sidewalk.

One of them shouts at the mother, pushing out his chin to add punctuation.

Yanggalbo.

Somehow, I'm allowed to know what this means. *Yankee prostitute.*

He points to the boy, who cowers against his mother's legs, but she isn't enough shelter. Not from them; not from this.

The other businessman reaches out with his middle finger and presses it against the boy's forehead. He pushes it firmly away, as he might a dirty object.

Gumdungee-ba.

Look at this black animal.

The boy reels from the finger-push as if it were a slap. The mother squeezes through them, trying to get by. Passersby stare rudely. No one says anything to help. Some of them wear the same expressions of disgust as the men; others' eyes widen with pity and fear. The first businessman spits on the child, and his toddler eyes register shock as he recoils. His mother scoops him up and runs down the street.

The boy doesn't cry.

Why isn't he crying?

His eyes are wide open. They see everything, empty and accepting.

They see me. He blinks, and I open my mouth to say something. But nothing comes out, and I wake up with still no words on my tongue.

Dazedly, I take in my surroundings. I'm in my father's room, in a clean nightgown. It's night. My skin is dry and thirsty, and I'm air-hungry with panic.

How did I get here?

The last thing I remember is the lake embracing me.

The crack of the *St. Anne*'s hull, a jagged sound of purity. The deliciousness of nine hearts beating, and the first heart arresting in exquisite silence. The dreams of the dead usually infect me for hours afterward, but this time, something changed. This was not the dream of a lake sailor. I'm sure of it. And what's more, I'm not in the water, where I ought to be after such a feeding.

And then there was the boy. He was there, and saw me, and then I saw nothing.

"You're awake."

He hovers in the doorway. He's here. In my father's house. He holds a steaming cup of something, which means he's used my father's kitchen. His pants hang loosely on his hips, and he's wearing a hole-ridden T-shirt instead of the bulky jacket he usually has. His arms are lean and roped with muscle. He's thin and tall, a knife on end. I lift my eyes to study his face.

Those eyes.

They were in my dream.

I immediately look down, feeling like an intruder in his memory. The dead, they give me their dreams as payment for their relief of life. But I have given nothing to this boy. What did I take that I should see such a vision?

My hands splay across the fabric of my nightgown. This wasn't the one I was wearing when the storm found me. It's different. Which means he must have changed my clothes. Interesting. I had been curious, watching him shed his clothes to bathe in the lake. Perhaps he felt the need to reciprocate. How very interesting.

It takes a while for me to find words. Mentally, I try out a few, like "who" and "go" before flicking them away. My tongue moves, finally.

"What...what day is it?" I whisper hoarsely.

He twitches, then cocks his head. These are not the words he'd expected to hear. What did he think I would say? Get out?

"It's, uh...Friday."

"No. What is the date?"

"Oh." He shuffles his feet and searches the ceiling for an answer. I do, too. There's no calendar up above us. I don't know why he's looking there. His lips move, counting silently.

"It's October twenty-fifth, I think," he finally says.

Six more days. November is coming, and I wasn't even able to wait. I used to have more control than this. What will Father say? What if he had been here?

The boy should have been taken with the nine. He's owed to you and to me, she says. *He ought not to be here.*

"You ought not to be here," I say, obediently.

His eyes contract with hurt. "I know. I'll go soon. I just wanted to make sure you woke up okay. I think...I think you had a seizure or something."

"Seizure," I repeat. How violent. And I should know. Violence simmers in my blood, but this is a different word. Another type of taking without asking.

"You know? A spell. You were so out of it. I thought you had a fever, too. You actually walked into the lake."

"Yes."

"So you remember?"

"No."

His eyebrows furrow. "I don't understand."

No, you wouldn't, would you? I want to say. The walls of the house sigh. The house likes him, the way it likes my father. It wants him to stay, but the air around me stifles me, making it hard to breathe. It slips like molasses down my throat, coating my airways.

The house always wants to protect me, whereas the storm and the winds…they. It. She. She is far more jealous. I can feel her need clawing at me to keep me close, like she does my sisters.

The nine were not enough, because I wasn't able to take them all. She knows it, and I feel it, too.

Eleven months is a long time to wait, my dearest.

Beyond the door, I can see the window in the main room. Raindrops from the storm cling to the panes of glass. They rearrange themselves into a face that judges me.

Mother.

The burning will begin again soon. Though a tension in my body has been pacified since the sinking of the *St. Anne*, I still feel unsettled. I search for the feeling—it's urgent, in a way that won't be ignored. It gnaws at my center.

I *should* make him leave. After a storm like this one, I usually feel energized, grounded. But I don't. The boy took me away too soon.

I stare at him, inhaling courage. I prepare the words in my head:

You must leave.

You should leave.

You ought not to be here.

I open my mouth, and he inhales, too, ready for my words. The unsettled feeling in my center worsens. The boy already seems dejected, as if knowing what is to come. As if he's heard it a thousand times.

So finally, I speak.

"I am hungry."

Chapter Fifteen

HECTOR

I'm surprised. I swear she was ready to throw a knife at me. After all, I'm a strange guy in her house. She's probably freaked out that I changed her clothes.

"I'm . . . hungry," she says again, plaintively. Her eyes are large and innocent, and the gray of her irises sparkle. They don't have that dead look like they did when she walked into the water. Whatever made her zone out is gone, leaving a thin, famished girl behind.

I nod. I've never fed another person in my whole life. I only know how to make cereal or microwave chicken potpies, for God's sake. But she's been sick, after all. Later I can ask her more about why she's here.

I take a step forward and hold out the steaming mug in my hands. Her eyes grow rounder, as if I'm offering a cup of sweetened cyanide.

"It's hot honey water. My mom used to make it for me when I was sick."

I'm careful not to hand it to her. I just set it on the three-legged stool next to the cot as an offering. She watches it warily, like it's going to bite.

Weird. So weird, this girl.

But I like her. Anyway, we're not exactly strangers. We've been spying on each other for a few weeks now.

"I saw crackers in the kitchen," I say. "I can get some for you. And then…when you're feeling well enough, I'll leave."

"Well enough," she echoes. She smiles shyly, and I back out of the room.

I root around in the kitchen cupboards for the crackers. The ancient box of saltines must be an artifact from the early 1980s, but the squeaky packets inside are thankfully unopened. I investigate the tiny box fridge and am greeted by an emerald-green high-heeled shoe. Uh. Okay. Perched in the door is a pot of strawberry jelly, sitting as far away as possible from a lonesome bottle of Gulden's Mustard. A few pounds of butter occupy the lowest shelf, along with an empty egg carton.

It's been a long time since I tried to make anything in a kitchen. I remember spending hours on a kitchen floor, making rolls of *gimbap* with my mom, getting more rice stuck in my hair than on the sheets of crisp, oiled seaweed. She never complained that my messy rolls were any worse than hers. I wonder if she still makes them.

I smear the jelly on the crackers, one by one, and arrange them in a circle on a china plate. It feels like some once-in-a-century ritual that I've never been included in before. And yet the whole time, I grin like a kid at a carnival. I can't remember when I've smiled this much in my whole life.

...

It's been a day.

At first, she stayed in bed. I gave her the plate of crackers and jam, and she picked the first one up delicately, nibbling the corners off, then the middle, bit by bit. She was less polite about the rest. Actually, that's being nice; she shoved them down so voraciously, I was glad my fingers weren't near her teeth.

After the third plate of crackers and jam, I realized sooner or later, I'd have to go fishing. Her cupboards had only a couple pounds of flour and sugar, and I'm no cook. I take the empty plate, licked clean of crumbs. She watches me with that unblinking way that freaks me out ever so slightly.

I have to ask. "Why did you do it?"

She drops her bottom lip. "Do what?"

I try not to roll my eyes. Does she need me to spell it out?

Her eyelids flutter and drop. "Oh. You mean the lake. Why I went into the lake."

"Yeah, that."

She says nothing, just plays the marble statue that she's so good at. I'd fill the silence with a dozen explanations— seizures, maybe sleepwalking, I don't know. Finally, she speaks. "Why did you come to the island?"

I swallow and touch the doorframe, ready to walk out of the room without an answer, but something roots me in place.

"I…" My eyes drop to the floor. "I needed to be here."

"Me too," she says in a whisper.

I turn around to leave. I can't take this conversation, cryptic as it is. All I know is it's enough for now.

While she was asleep, the storm finally ended. Looking out the window to the lake, there was an uncomfortable number of boats on the horizon. I found a pair of binoculars in one of the drawers, and they showed me exactly what I didn't want to see. Coast Guard ships. At least half a dozen, plus a helicopter. Why were they out there? I watched for a good hour. Once, the helicopter and a large Coast Guard boat swept into the harbor here before leaving again. They're searching for something. God, I hope it's not for me. But then again, helicopters and ships don't look for runaway Black boys. Never in this lifetime.

I kept watching on and off that day as the girl slept. But the activity didn't lessen. Whatever they're looking for, they haven't found it. Maybe someone's sailboat capsized or something. Who knows.

Now, not knowing what to do with myself, I crouch by the fireplace, crumpling balls of newspaper to make a fire. Not now. I couldn't risk having that smoke attract the Coast Guard to this house. But maybe when whatever's going on blows over out there, a fire would be nice.

"We mustn't burn things."

I turn around and there she is, in her blue nightgown, standing only a foot away. I want to yelp and jump a mile, but force myself not to.

"So how do you keep warm?"

"We mustn't burn things," she says again. And then, when I wonder if we're somehow communicating in different languages, she points to the stove. Oh. It's attached to a portable fuel tank outside the walls. I'd seen it when I walked around the house the other day. I forgot that they like to use fuel for camping and cooking on this island. It's a nature preserve, after all. They can't be burning down all the trees. Or cutting branches to make shelters. Whoops.

"You must be freezing in here," I comment.

"You must be freezing out there."

"I have been."

"You shouldn't be here."

"Neither should you."

We both hesitate. Because the next question is obvious. Why? Why are we here? But to say it out loud hurts more than knowing. Maybe she's thinking the same thing, because she bites her lips together and stays quiet.

I guess we'll sit on our secrets for a little longer.

"So...uh...there are a lot of Coast Guard ships out there." I gesture to the window. "Any idea why?"

"They always come after a sinking."

Sinking? So maybe someone did lose a boat after all. "How do you know?"

She opens her mouth to speak, then bites her lip again. Then opens her mouth. Like she's fighting the urge to tell me bad news. The boats, the helicopter. I've driven past so many car crashes they seem ordinary now. A price you pay for being on the road, if you're stupid or unlucky. But a ship sinking really freaks me out. After getting my head forced underwater at the public pool by meathead kids one too many times, drowning is one of my worst nightmares. Well, aside from the one I've been living.

"Do you have a radio?" I ask.

She nods and pads over to the fireplace, where a small battery-powered radio sits on a pillow, as if it were a pet dog. She hands it to me and I turn it on, twisting the dial until a crackling news station comes on.

"—still searching for survivors, though the chances... water temperatures are low...seven bodies recovered and identified...James Johnston and Casey Merrick have not been found..." There's a lot of static, but I get the gist.

"Oh my God," I whisper. "Seven people died?"

"Nine," the girl says, matter-of-factly.

I sit on the floor, suddenly tired. "Oh my God. I can't believe this."

She responds by staring out the window. The helicopter is doing another pass of the coastline.

"Man, I feel so sorry for them."

"The twenty will get their chance, too," she says, soothingly.

I look at her cockeyed. "What twenty?"

"The survivors. They'll die, too, someday."

This girl, she makes no sense. "I meant," I say slowly, as if maybe English isn't actually her first language, "that I feel sorry for the guys who died."

"Why?"

This time, I'm the one who's silent. What is wrong with her? "Uh, because dying is bad…especially if you don't want it to happen yet. It's just…bad." I'm not able to hide the edge to my voice.

"It isn't. Death doesn't nullify life. It brings more of it." Her lips pucker the smallest bit. She's miffed at my argument. "The molecules of your body came from other things that died. You eat dead things, too."

"Well, yeah, but—" I struggle for a moment, because what she says is true. Decomposition and fertilizer and Simba and the circle of life, whatever. I get it. I'm more than the fried fish I ate yesterday, but somehow it doesn't seem worth saying. Finally, I say, "Life is still worth fighting for. That's all." I'm embarrassed at my simple words. I sound like a meme, and I'm a hypocrite. Life has beaten me down with brass knuckles, and here I am, running and hiding. I'm not the best lawyer for this argument.

The sound of the helicopter blades beating the air cuts into my thoughts. Reflexively, I hunch my shoulders and duck, though there's no way they'd be able to see inside the house, let alone through the window.

"It will be like this for a week," the girl says.

"Until they find the last two," I add.

"They won't find the last two," she says with a confidence that makes my skin crawl.

Chapter Sixteen

ANDA

I know this aversion to death. Father has it, too.

I've also seen the fear on his face before. It was only a matter of time. But Father didn't recognize this fear of me, not at first. Unlike other children, I remember all of my existence since I arrived on the shores of Isle Royale. I remember being milk-fed, only a day old, and vomiting up every white drop. Father quaked in fear that I would die, not realizing I sought a different kind of nourishment. I remember being so angry, not being able to speak when my infant mouth lacked the tone and control to do so.

And yet I forget things. Too many things. Like the fact that once, I enjoyed strawberry jam. Or that there was joy to be found within other months of the year. It wasn't always about November. And now it is nothing but.

I remember other things, too. There were days in my first years that Father would watch me tend to a patch of rock cress among a collection of stones near the house. He couldn't understand why I would weep every time they grew an inch. He couldn't see the roots forcing their way into the soil, pushing aside other lives for their own sake. He is blind to parasitism, in the guise of spring greenery and plumpness. But I know that pain has to be nurtured for the surrender later. I don't like it, but there is an order in the world that even I cannot undo.

Years ago, Father found me smiling for the first time. He panicked. My chubby hands were curled around the wrung neck of a scarlet tanager, blood and red feathers all the same color, the smear of crimson on my triumphant cheek. It would not have to go hungry any longer or be buffeted by the winds on its journey southward. Calypso orchids and thimbleberry plants would sigh with contentment, their roots threaded about the skeletonized remains someday. I didn't know why, but taking the bird was easy compared to what the struggling rock cress offered.

Here, I had found relief. And in my father's face, horror.

In that sliver of a moment, I hurt in a place I couldn't quite locate. I felt this way because I am partly my father, and my father is apt to mourn the ending of things, unable to see that twilight and dawn occur at the same time, everywhere. Is death not a gift to the living? If there were no death, would not the world corrupt itself and shatter into its own unalterable ending? This taking and giving on the island, abolishing one life to nourish another—it must be nurtured. Still, his pain was ten times mine, yet worse for me because I bore witness to it.

So I started to make allowances here and there. I made an effort to live off the flourishing springs and summers, though they made me clench my teeth. And I orchestrate deaths, too. Father is not upset by a wolf consuming an infirm, old moose, but he is upset by my splintering the bones of a living calf at a mere thought. So I save my most violent renderings for when he is gone, when November is eager to unfurl its energy my way.

These are things I learn, and do, to live. To keep him happy.

But the death of humans and ships is my domain as well, and it can't be suppressed forever.

November is coming in a few days. And I am still hungry. I, too, must live.

But this boy's eyes bore into me like Father's, that flickering of human sentiment that lights a fading piece within myself. I can't forget the way they looked at me, pained, when I asked him why death was such a terrible thing.

Perhaps I can wait a little longer before I let another storm bring me a ship.

I can be patient. Can't I?

Chapter Seventeen

HECTOR

We don't speak for the rest of the day.

After our conversation, I couldn't shake the feeling that this girl had something to do with the deaths of those sailors. It makes no sense, of course. She was less than thirty feet away from me the whole time it was happening, and then she was unconscious.

I don't understand, but my gut says I should probably leave this girl alone and flee far, far away.

But I stay. She's not quite better. She looks frail, the way she'll refuse to move for hours at a time, just lost in her thoughts. Maybe it's selfishness, but taking care of her makes me feel good. I experiment with the flour and sugar to make some really bad pancakes, and she gobbles them down. Her appetite is a great distraction from everything else. That evening, she consumes another sleeve of crackers and jam, plus a load of biscuits as dense as rocks. She watches me, but says nothing. Not like she's afraid of me—I get that plenty already, just walking down the street in Duluth—but like she's afraid of what I think of her.

Smart girl.

But after a while, even I can't bear the silence. When I pick up her dirty dishes, I say, "I wish we had more strawberry jam. We're running out." I pause, because she's staring at me from her thin bed. But her eyes brighten at my comment. "Uh. I guess you like berries." Dumb thing to say, but silence makes me talk without thinking.

"Strawberries are not berries," she says.

Since when? I want to say. "Then why are they called—"

"They aren't true botanical berries. They are an aggregate accessory fruit." When I say nothing because the definition does diddly for me, she adds, "A false fruit, or pseudo fruit. Like pineapples."

I lean against the wall by the door, dishes still in hand. "Wow. I didn't know that."

"I don't know things, too." She sits up in bed, eyes brighter. "You like to eat fish. Why?"

I laugh. "Because I have no choice? Not much else to catch on this island, and I don't plan on eating a moose." She waits and seems to know that's not the only answer I'm capable of giving. I focus on a hangnail and explain. "Well, my mom in Korea made it for me every Sunday. She'd sprinkle it with salt and cook it until the skin got crispy. I don't really like fish any other way."

"But no butter." The girl pouts.

Oh. That's right. Her version has been a bit different. "Hey, butter is good. I like the butter."

She smiles, and we just hang in that silence for a minute, not knowing what else to say. Soon, her eyes flutter. Before long, she's asleep again, and I wonder how a convo of berries, fish, and butter could be so exhausting.

The next day, I spend the afternoon with the radio, listening to more about the sinking of the *St. Anne.*

Apparently, she was an old ship and bent too much in the middle from her heavy cargo. It's weird to hear about a ship that's over fifty years old, dying in such a way. But then again, all things have to die, right? Even ships. It's sad, though. Funny how I care more about an old boat than my uncle or my dad.

There are still Coast Guard ships on the horizon. I put away the binoculars when the girl exits the bedroom. She eyes the binoculars on the kitchen counter where I put them and curls her lip a little, like she's cussing at them. Weird.

"They'll be there a week," she says again, as if I forgot our conversation yesterday. I nod, but this time, I'm not bringing up the evils of the sweet Siren song of death, so she actually smiles at me. "Are you well?" she asks me.

I want to laugh. Well? Does she mean healthy? Intact? Sane? "I have no idea," I say.

She grins at my response. What the hell? Sometimes I think if she were stuck here with the varsity football quarterback, the one who's going to Princeton on a full ride and looks like fucking Tom Brady, she'd have torn him to shreds already.

Her white hair rises a little in the front from static, and sticks to her forehead in that annoying way that only happens to people with superfine, stick-straight hair. My head is covered in thick black stuff with a stubborn wave to it. Static runs screaming away from my head, as do combs and brushes.

She battles with her own strands for a moment, trying to push them back and flatten them down. She huffs with annoyance and marches to the kitchen, where she pulls out a large kitchen knife from a drawer. She grabs a hunk of hair in one fist and holds the knife to it.

Holy shit. "Hold on! Geez, what are you doing?"

"I'm cutting it," she announces.

That would explain why it's four different lengths and so irregular. "Don't you have scissors?"

She blinks at me. Apparently, logic is some orange-winged creature she's never met before.

"Oh." She puts the knife down and rummages through a drawer full of twine, pamphlets, and keys that probably don't open anything. She pulls out an old pair of long shears with black handles, the kind that teachers always have at their desk. And then she grabs another handful of hair and starts to hew at it with the scissors.

"Wait, wait." I put my hands up to stop her. "Let me do it."

She freezes with the open blades against a hunk of hair.

"I'm no expert, but I've watched the barber do this a million times, so…I'm a visual expert. Sort of."

For a whole minute, she just stares at me. It's distinctly uncomfortable. This girl would win the world championship of staring contests. This girl would make a damn fish blink.

"All right." She takes the scissors and puts them on the counter.

I go back to the bedroom, where the three-legged stool sits beneath the now-empty mug of honey water. When I carry the stool into the kitchen, I notice that the stone cairns dotting the floor have been moved aside to make room for the stool. Oddly, the stones are still perfectly balanced on each other. If I'd moved them that fast, they'd just be a scattered mess.

I pat the stool, and she bends over and pats it, too.

I frown. "No, I mean, sit down here."

"Oh." She plops down and I stand behind her, reaching to pick up the scissors. I hope they're not too dull, or else this is going to be as effective as cutting with spoons.

"How short do you want it?" I ask.

"Short."

"Uh. Can you be more specific?"

"Like Jean Seberg."

"Who's that?"

"Jean Dorothy Seberg was an actress born on November 13, 1938. She starred in thirty-eight films in Hollywood and Europe, and died of a barbiturate overdose in Paris at the age of forty." She turns to see my expression of undiluted surprise, then points to my head. "It was short. Like yours. Shorter, even."

I nod. Okay. Short it is.

I start cutting bits off here and there, aiming to keep it about an inch long. I try not to touch her skin, but it's hard not to. Especially when I start snipping off the bits at the nape of her neck. I do what the barbers do, and capture a lock of hair between two extended fingers, then cut it off on the palm side of my fingers to protect her skin. Her neck is so soft, like velvet or silk. And it's still really warm, like she's got a furnace within her body.

Every time I pinch another bit of hair and nestle my fingers against her neck, she blinks and swallows. And I blink and swallow. I'm not used to being so close to girls. To any girl. Carla's a faint memory these days.

No one at my high school wanted to have anything to do with me. I oozed leperdom out of my pores. The truth is, most people want normal when it comes to choosing friends or hookups in school. Complicated is for the movies. Complicated gets you shunned faster than a case of publicly announced chlamydia. Complicated always ends badly. My life in the last ten years has only ever been school, my uncle, Walmart, and those letters. Those shitty letters.

There was never room for normal.

"What's the matter?" she asks.

I've stopped cutting, forgetting where I was. I'm not in Duluth anymore. I'll be eighteen in a few months. I've left it all behind. All that matters right now are these scissors, and this girl.

"Nothing," I say. "I'm almost done."

Her white hair is cropped short now. She looks like a pixie, or some sort of elf. I shuffle to the front of her and reach for some longer wisps of hair near her forehead. She leans closer to meet me in the middle. The neck of her nightgown bows open, and I see the tops of her breasts when I look down.

God, she's so beautiful.

I swallow again and will my body to not embarrass me. I go from novice haircutter to an expert in seconds, desperate to finish before my whole body fires up like an inferno. I finish off the last few pieces, put the scissors down, and step away. "It's all done."

Her long, delicate fingers touch her head all over. She smiles, delighted. She stands up and approaches me, her breasts tenting the front of her gown. I take a step back, and then another. I'm afraid to be so close. She'll know I'm attracted to her. I wish my body would calm down. Soon, my back hits the stone fireplace, and she closes the distance between us. She points at me with a tapered index finger, reaching until her finger pad touches my neck. It's not a delicate touch, but deliberate and oddly aggressive. I get the distinct feeling that she's feeling the pulse in my neck. It must be going a mile a minute. She opens her mouth.

"My name is Anda."

Chapter Eighteen

ANDA

His face flushes a faint dusky pink beneath his chestnut-colored cheeks. He smells of the boreal forests of the Isle. Of trees and cold lake water and musk. He meets my eyes, but there is a hint of panic there. He doesn't like me to be so close. Well, no one would, if they knew what I was.

But he doesn't know. So why is he afraid?

His pulse beats hard and fast under my finger. So much power and life there. So exquisite. My vision blurs a little.

Push, Anda. Push a little harder. Make it stop.

I shake my head and ignore her. My hunger is sated for now, but there is yet a need I can't identify. What I want is to feel his short, scraggly beard and compare it to the stubbly moss that grows beneath paper birch trees. My finger rises against his throat to touch his jaw, rough with stubble, and he moves away abruptly. I'm left pointing at him, a needle turned north.

I finally drop my arm to clasp my hands, wishing I could touch his pulse again. It was nice being close to that warm, living river under his skin.

"I'm Hector," he blurts out.

His name is centuries old. I like this. It makes me feel like we've met before, that maybe our histories have a more distinct beginning.

"Hector was the firstborn son of King Priam and Queen Hecuba, a descendant of Dardanus and Tros, the founder of Troy," I inform him, happy to know something.

He gives me a puzzled look again. I'm getting used to this expression of his. "You are like, the queen of Wikipedia."

I don't know what that means. So I just keep talking. "Hector was slain by Achilles and his corpse mistreated for twelve days."

"Yes," he says, a little impatiently. He won't look at me anymore. He shifts his body from foot to foot. He's antsy to leave. It's better, really, for him to go away. I can't stop imagining my fingers stretching across his neck, pushing on those tender points and damming those red rivers for eternity.

Stop it, Anda.

Oh, why is he here?

He ought not to be here.

"I...I should find some food," he stammers.

I stare at him.

"I haven't been able to get enough fish, and your kitchen is running low on stuff. I thought...well, it would be wrong..." he murmurs, scratching his sparse beard. I've a notion to cut it off, so I can unearth the planes and angles of his cheeks. Would he trust me to be close to him with a razor? Would I trust myself? He clears his throat, and I clear my head of thoughts of blades kissing skin. "But I don't think we have a choice."

What is he talking about?

"We need to break into the Windigo camp store."

"Oh!"

Hector's face is full of concern. "I'm sorry. I thought I brought enough food. I was so wrong. And then there was the fox. Even if I'm lucky enough to get a fish every day, it's not enough for two people." Hector bites his lip, and I've a notion to bite his rather than mine. "There'll probably be a lock. Maybe I'll need a piece of metal or something…"

Breaking a door or taking objects means nothing to me. They are things easily fixed and replaced. Mother and I care little for the creations of men. They'll get torn down by dust and time eventually. Sometimes we simply allow the performance to happen before time's curtain rises.

But Hector is troubled by this. For someone who's living on an island he's not allowed to be on, I find it odd that this would bother him. I hear him mutter things like, "Maybe I'll pay them back later. I could mail it anonymously…"

He heads toward the back door and shoves his feet into his boots. On goes a thick flannel shirt and his heavier coat, and he empties out his backpack. As he reaches for the door, I follow him, but he puts a hand out.

"No. You should stay here. You haven't been well. I'll bring some food back soon, okay?"

Father would say similar things, but his offerings didn't help me. With Hector (and I like to say his name in my mind—Hector. *Hector*. It's sharp and shiny, at the same time) it feels like we are on the same side of caring. Falling toward the same charred destination.

Suddenly, I don't want him to leave. It's easy enough to bring a wind against the cabin, and when he opens the door, I shut it. Hard.

"Ugh. This wind!" he says, pushing against the door.

"I should like to come with you," I say.

Hector pushes the door, and it bobs open before the wind slams it shut again. "Jesus!"

"I should like to come with you," I say again.

Hector lets go of the doorknob and stares at me, his face still and watching. He suspects something.

He knows. Anda, don't play. Just kill him.

I push away her words. A dark shape hovers outside the window, but I ignore her. Hector stares at me like I'm a wild beast.

He speaks slowly and quietly. "All right. You need to get dressed. Wear warm clothes. It's pretty cold. And we need to make sure the helicopters and boats don't see us, so don't wear anything bright."

I nod. My nightgown swooshes as I turn into the bedroom to search for clothes. The weather is the least of my worries now. I am the weather; I don't need to shield myself from myself. But I should be cautious. The boats and the helicopter are searching. I'm more visible when people are looking in earnest, especially for pretty things, like corpses.

I should wear something appropriate, only I'm not fully sure what that is. I take out everything from the drawer where my clothes are. There is underwear, and chemises, and tops. Jeans. Socks. Most of them have not been worn more than once.

I shed my nightgown and pull on a pair of underwear, then a thin white cotton camisole with a satin band at the edges. Father bought these over a year ago, and they're both a little too snug. Should I wear two pairs of pants? One? All my shirts at once? Hector said it would be cold. Cold to him and to me are disparate things. The idea of clothing layers confines me and I already miss the looseness of my gown. I gather up all the garments and bring them into the main room, where Hector is busy watching the search boats with the binoculars.

"What should I wear?" I ask.

Hector turns to look at me. I drop the armful of clothes onto the floor and his eyes go immediately to my bare legs, and then my breasts, stretching the camisole thin. Not the clothes piled on the floor. He nearly drops the binoculars, then clumsily places it on the windowsill. "Uh."

It's the only word that issues from his mouth for several seconds, while he drops his eyes to the floor. He's still not looking at my clothes. Finally, he seems to shake himself and walks over to dive his hands into the pile at my feet.

"Uh. This shirt. And uh, this one, with this sweater on top. Wear these long johns beneath the jeans." He won't meet my eyes. I've done something wrong.

The emotion is fleeting but familiar. Father is never disappointed in me; he understands what I am. But when I was smaller, when children came to the Isle with their parents, I longed for them to see me. My heart was partially a child's, once, and it had its childish needs. But when other children's eyes went through me, past me, I always knew I'd done something wrong. Just by being me, I was wrong. It was a flavor of hurt that only a child may know so keenly. It was a hurt I have been more than happy to forget. Except that I haven't, because I feel it now. The fear of inadequacy, and being passed over for my allotted portion of kindness that all humans crave.

As I start dressing, I say, "I'm sorry."

"Don't be sorry."

"I've upset you."

"Oh, you haven't upset me." He laughs, but it's a tinny, artificial laugh.

I've buttoned on two shirts and the sweater, but I pause before grabbing the pair of waffled long john pants. "What is it?"

"Uh, nothing."

"You're lying."

Hector's brown eyes go wide with wonder at my accusation. A faint ruddiness suffuses his cheeks again. Perhaps he's ill?

"Anda. Look. I'm trying to...concentrate. And you're standing there in your underwear."

"Yes."

"With me. I'm practically a stranger."

"Yes, practically. Technically, not really."

He runs his hand through his hair, exasperated. "You're beautiful, okay?"

Beautiful. I have never been labeled as such. The tourists use words like this to talk of the sunset, and the water, and the sky. I'm so used to being unseen, much less complimented. For some reason, it makes my stomach growl, in a good way.

Hector goes on. "It's just...really distracting. And I don't know what to do. You're not quite...normal."

"Is that a bad thing?"

He splays his hand in protest. "Oh, no. Take it as a compliment. Really. It's kind of a relief."

"I see." I let his words untangle themselves in my mind. So this is politeness. "Well, then. You're the most abnormal boy I've ever met."

He laughs so loudly, it's like bells chiming. The walls of the house smile. It's not used to this much mirth in a whole season. Hector's eyes go to mine, and his teeth gleam prettily in the dimmed light of the house. I've never seen him smile before. "I like you, Anda. You're so uncomplicated."

I nod, but inside, I'm frowning.

You have no idea, Hector.

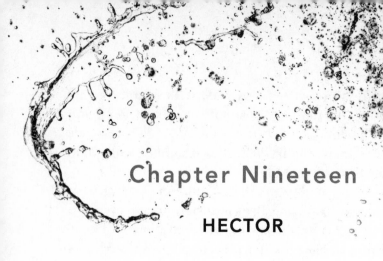

Chapter Nineteen

HECTOR

When Anda and I leave the little house, we set off on the mile toward Windigo.

A few times, we have to duck underneath the fir trees to escape the helicopter that flies a little too close. I keep stealing peeks at her, because she looks so ordinary. With her jacket, jeans, boots, and backpack, she could be just any other hiker around here. Except there are none, of course. But even with the trappings of normalcy, something will always poke its way out to remind me—she isn't. She'll stoop to pick up an interesting rock, but instead of looking at it, she'll taste it. Or she'll pick up a nugget of soil and smear it between her palms for a sniff.

The thing is, I'm so damn curious to know why she's here. Why she left herself isolated. Where her father is, and why she's so freaking odd about...about everything. She eats food like she's never eaten anything but rocks and dirt her whole life. Sometimes she seems so innocent and clueless, and other times she's almost unhinged and dangerous. I haven't even had a chance to ask her about where she's gone to school, or what grade she's in, even. Assuming she's a teenager, which I think she is.

She's a huge mess of inconsistencies and conflicting pieces. Just when I get a good view of her, like a kaleidoscope, she turns and the image transforms into something completely different.

I open my mouth to ask one question. One piece of truth, or history. She tips her head toward me, eyebrows up. There is fear behind her wintry eyes. Somehow I know, if I ask, I'm going to lose anything we've gained in the last few days. Is it worth it? Should I try?

In a low voice, she asks, "What is it, Hector?"

I want to know, but I don't, because everything is so much easier this way. Ignorance wins out, at least for now. But I know we can't pretend for much longer.

"Oh, nothing." I smile. I can wait a little longer.

And Anda smiles back—so brightly that you'd think the sun just rose on Isle Royale for the first time ever. She reaches out to my face but pulls her hand back before she touches me.

"I like your mouth," she says. It's such an odd comment that I smile wider. "That," she says, pointing for a split second. "I mean, your smile."

Then I grin even harder. Never got a compliment like that before. "Well, I like yours, too. A lot."

Anda touches her lips and looks down. I think I actually made her blush.

When we get to Windigo, we head straight to the camp store up the hill. It doesn't take long to break into the building. With a big rock, I bash the old doorknob over and over until the screws loosen, then force the door open. It's dark inside, but my eyes adjust quickly. The whole store is small. A cash register greets me, sitting on a table along with bowls of Isle Royale magnets. To the right, there's an empty refrigerator that probably held sandwiches and cold pop.

On the left of the cash register is…heaven. A whole display of Snickers bars, Crunch bars, Almond Joys. The boxes aren't full, but luckily they're not all empty. Past the rows of sweatshirts and tees are a wall with cans of soup and crackers, along with some freeze-dried meal packets and MREs. My brain gathers the inventory and I frown. There's no way these will last me until May, much less the both of us. I explore a back storeroom, but it's only got empty boxes. I don't care for the Isle Royale knickknacks, but my heart races over the few camping items still lining the walls. But before I touch the camping gear, my hand shoots out for the candy.

I immediately grab a slim, flat Hershey's bar and tear off the wrapper, cramming bite after bite into my mouth. The chocolate collapses between my teeth and melts into gooey syrup on my taste buds. I wolf it down in thirty seconds flat.

"God, this is the best chocolate bar I've ever had in my whole life," I say through the last mouthful. Anda's watching me, as if waiting for her turn, so I hand her one. She carefully peels back a corner of the bar, the plastic wrapper crinkling in her fingers. She takes a large bite.

Her eyes roam all over as she rolls the bite around in her mouth. She doesn't look like she's enjoying it at all. Her eyebrows pinch together, her jaw shifting from left to right, and finally she swallows. For almost a minute, she just stands there and stares at her bitten bar, like there's something wrong with it.

"You don't have to eat it," I say, reaching to take it away. Anda immediately pulls it close to her chest.

"Oh. It's fine," she says, her eyes wide. She turns from me and walks toward the back of the small store, but I can tell she's cramming down bites like I just did. Maybe she didn't want to look like a pig. I want to laugh but stifle it.

I'm stuffing the few granola bars and soup packets into our bags when she returns to my side. The Hershey's wrapper is empty in her hands, and telltale smears of chocolate decorate the corners of her mouth.

"I think I should try this one. Just to see if it's okay," she says, reaching for an Almond Joy.

"Suit yourself."

She does this three times, taking a bar and walking around the tiny store, returning with an empty wrapper and a nonchalance over the fact that she's inhaling candy bars faster than a kid on Halloween. At this rate, she'll outeat the entire candy supply on all of Isle Royale in no time.

"I guess your dad never let you have candy?" I ask.

"No. Well, I never wanted it."

"Oh. And now?"

She eyeballs our bags, which I've stuffed full with a small portable stove with a cooking can, several containers of white fuel, a handheld water purifier with extra cartridges, plus extra-large water bottles with an Isle Royale logo stamped on the side. Eyeing the wealth with a critical eye, she grabs a few more Hershey bars and tries to hand them to me.

"Anda, I don't have room. We can come back again."

She frowns and puts the Hershey's bars into the pockets of her jacket anyway, until there are no more left on the bottom shelf. Then she leans over and shoves several Mr. Goodbars, M&M's, and Twix bars into the large pockets of my coat, as if the real estate there belongs to her. I don't mind. It's kind of nice, having her feel like I'm some extension of her. When she's done, all the food in the camp store is gone. Plus, we look like we've sprouted candy from our hips and chests.

She smiles. "I think we're ready now."

I grin. I really, really like this girl.

"You have chocolate on your mouth," I tell her, pointing. Anda wipes her lips with her fingertip, then licks off the candy. She looks at me and points right back.

"You do, too."

I lift my hand to wipe my face, when she steps forward and grabs the shoulders of my jacket, pulling me closer. Her face inches away, she scans my face and zeroes in on my lips hungrily. She looks like she's going to bite my face off. I freeze, and she hovers, so close, with her eyes cast downward. She carefully licks the edges of my mouth.

Oh. My. God.

The silky tip of her tongue travels from the corners of my mouth to the full part of my lips, tasting me and finding the tiny islands of chocolate I'd unknowingly left behind. I can't breathe. Her lips barely touch mine as I inhale her sweet breath. I don't even know what I'm doing when my hand slips behind her neck and pulls her that half inch closer to melt her mouth fully against mine.

Anda freezes. Our lips fit together seamlessly, and hers are warm and soft beneath mine, open just a little. I realize I've stepped over a line, and that maybe, just maybe, I should backpedal. I start to pull away when Anda's fists squeeze my jacket lapels, preventing my retreat.

Her tongue tastes mine, and I go dizzy. I let mine explore a little, not knowing exactly what I'm doing. She tilts her head, and then our lips slip together, fitting as if this is where they've always belonged.

I've kissed girls before. But kissing Anda is like starting

over. I don't know what the hell I'm supposed to do all of a sudden and it's just...amazing. All I know is God, I better not screw this up. Finally, she pushes me gently away, blinking like a sleepy cat.

My heart is hammering faster than anything. Anda touches her lips and smiles down at her fingertips.

"You taste much better than rocks," she says before exiting the store and walking into the sunshine.

Thank God for that.

Chapter Twenty

ANDA

I've done something wrong.

Hector doesn't speak to me all the way back to the cottage. I catch him touching his lips, as if I'd somehow burned them with my touch. These things shouldn't bother me. I have other concerns, like the *St. Anne*'s lost crew. They aren't lost to me—in fact, I know that James Johnston's bones are already beginning to show from the ravages of hungry lake creatures, and I know that Casey Merrick is partially buried in sediment churned up by the storm. Both are confused by the disengagement of life from their selves. Usually, I let their dreams intermingle with mine as their bodies fade, but I am not there in the lake, as I should be.

I am with Hector.

A stiff wind blows hard against me, making me list off the path home.

"Oops!" Hector reaches out to steady me. "Okay?"

It's odd, how he checks in with me this way. He seems to search for an answer to satisfy him, like "Yes" or "No" or "May I hold your shoes?" I stare him down, trying to understand his intentions, and he looks away, discomfited by my eyes. He consciously steps farther away from me, and I don't like this, either.

I don't know what to do.

Because you're trying to be something you aren't. Stop trying.

But she's incorrect. Part of me has always belonged in the realm of humanity, but I keep having to remind myself of this. And now I'm remembering things like mewling hunger, and clothing, and care. They are utterly complicated, like the English language and its mockingly arbitrary rules, but I am enjoying practicing this side of myself with Hector. I want to stay here. I should like to lick more chocolate off the corners of his mouth, if given the opportunity.

Yes. I would like to stay here awhile.

You're making a mistake. You'll suffer.

I ignore her.

"Look at this fellow." Hector stops on the side of the path.

I step closer and see a tiny beautiful blue-spotted salamander among the sticks and detritus of fall. This time of year, they aren't out and about. Their blood gets more sugary to prevent them from freezing, and they stay hidden beneath rocks.

The salamander is dead.

Hector points. "Look, there are more."

And there are. Six or seven, out in the open, dried and dead from the cold and exposure. Usually the island creatures understand the timing of things. I make sure that the balance is kept, the cycles of renewal and slumber. But something is wrong. I didn't sense that their death was coming. Worse, it has come too soon.

"They shouldn't be out here where they don't belong," I say, more to myself than to Hector.

"Tell me about it," Hector says, and I look at him sharply. The wind is strikingly quiet, letting me absorb his words for a change. She wants me to admit the truth, and also show me a warning. *This is what might happen. This is what you've started.*

Hector shivers from the wind at his back. A wind that I didn't create.

"Let's go home," he says.

Home. Such an odd word, one that hasn't fit into my world. The cabin has its moods and whims, and tolerates my presence. Father is not there. I am used to fitting into a space larger than anything a human conceives of—in crevices and pockets and atmospheres of pressure that aren't comforting. But when Hector says home, for once I actually understand him.

"Yes," I say. "Let's go home."

That week, I count down the remaining days to November. After the *St. Anne*, I am tepidly appeased, but it isn't enough. The closer to November it gets, the more trouble I will have controlling myself. I had decided not to bend to my nature because of Hector, but as the hours go by, my needs will try desperately to surpass any rationality.

Hector spends hours listening to the radio. He watches the Coast Guard ships decrease in number and eventually leave the wreck site of the *St. Anne*, and he watches me, too. Furtively, out of the corner of his eye, such as when I'm eating. He doesn't comment when I leave a plate of food alone.

I am hungry, and I am not.

It's a strange thing, needing food. Listening to the complaints of your body all the time and obeying the whims and growls of flesh. But my physical hunger sometimes feels like a phantom, standing in for something far more nourishing.

Hector and I finish the last of the flour, making pancakes. Father knew how little I ate, and the food stores he'd left were more a token of care than anything substantial. There is no more jam, no sugar. The new provisions from the camp store are piled on the countertop, but it's a small pile. Hector watches that, too, like it's going to vanish if he turns his back. And yet when he spies me studying the pile from afar, he'll quietly bring me a wrapped bar before I can ask if it's okay to eat. Even though we've nearly outeaten the tiny house.

And not just that. The house has grown too small for us, though the math doesn't work. We're still just two people, yet together, we've managed to expand and become something that needs far more space than these walls. I bump into him constantly. The house seems keen on keeping me off balance. Hector doesn't seem to mind; he cannot hide his smile every time we softly collide.

I look out the window, staring at the clouds, but they're ominously silent. So I turn on the weather radio and sit with it for almost an hour. Hector thinks I'm simply concerned with the forecast.

West winds nearing forty-five knots by afternoon
Hmm. Already angry with me, it seems.
A slight chance of thunderstorms in the early evening
That's a threat. Or an invitation.
Temperatures holding at forty-five, dropping to thirty overnight

It's funny how I used to listen to the forecast to tell me what I already knew. It was a spineless friend that would parrot my own thoughts and feelings. Now I'm needing the radio to interpret for me. I'm becoming an outsider in my own life.

The day before November 1, Hector wakes up and makes a breakfast of oatmeal. He watches me carefully as I lift the spoon to my mouth. I swallow and repeat until the bowl is empty. He barely lifts his own spoon. His own gruel has gone congealed and cold as he watches me lick the bowl clean.

"That oatmeal was salted," he says.

I blink at him, not knowing if I'm supposed to answer.

"I substituted sugar for salt. A lot of salt. On purpose."

I blink again. What is he trying to say? But he only gets up to eat his oatmeal alone outside the house, staring at where the wreck of the *St. Anne* should be.

That's when I realize he's testing me.

He does it several times that week. Once, he tells me, "Anda, it's windy outside," when it isn't. The air is so still, it hangs heavy like curtains in a shut room. It's another test, only I'm not sure if I should fail or succeed. So I bring the wind. It hits Hector so hard that he trips and falls backward, agape.

"Yes," I agree with him. "It's windy outside."

Another time, he remarks on how he misses the green leaves in spring.

"Fall is always so gloomy," he says, which confuses me. A cycle is a cycle, and the cycle is magnificence itself. But it upsets him. When I don't respond, he goes outside and paces next to the house. I've already forgotten that I need to be careful about what I do. I ought to conceal myself and what I am, but it's not easy when I've never been able to hide from him. Not once.

I lift my forefinger, pushing against sleep and slumber inside the soil, and force a marsh pea vine into the cutting air, letting the pea flowers bloom with pink and purple duskiness. Hector sees it immediately. His eyes widen as he watches the display, before plucking the narrow stem bedecked with flowers. He stares and stares, turning it left and right. He stares at them so long, the sun sets hours later and he's still fixated by their ghostliness in the dark.

Chapter Twenty-One

HECTOR

None of it makes sense.

I hold the flower until it wilts in my hand, and then lay it carefully on the ground. In the gloom just past twilight, I can still see it, the pale pink against the soil's darkness. As soon as it touches the ground, it disintegrates. When my fingers touch where it was, the only thing that comes away is ash.

I don't have words for the theories forming in my mind. There are too many things that don't make sense. Part of me wants to leave and run clear over to the other side of the island. But part of me knows that somehow, I'd arrive and find her waiting for me.

There are too many reasons to stay. Like having a bona fide roof over my head. And the fact that Anda doesn't ask me questions or psychologize me to death. I haven't ever spent this much time in the presence of another human and not felt like running away. It's narcotic, the feeling I get being around her.

That night, I wash up and get ready to sleep. Anda has

been in her room, door closed, for hours. I don't bother her. Since I've camped out in her place, she hasn't asked me to leave. And she doesn't say things like "good morning" or "good night." I'm relieved not to abide by all the fake words that people use. It used to bother me when people said *hi, what's up*. Because they didn't really want to hear the answer, the truth. So I wouldn't answer. That may explain why I have no friends.

I curl up on the sofa, pulling a nubbly knit blanket over me, and shut my eyes. It's a relief knowing that my uncle isn't in this cabin, or on this island, or within a hundred miles. Even with the camping, I've never slept as peacefully as I have on this island, frozen ass and all.

Just when I'm drifting off, a shuffling noise rouses me. I don't move, just listen carefully. It's a shuffling of feet, and I crack one eye open in the darkness. The moon is full and shining through the window, casting a weirdly bluish-metallic rectangle on the floor near the sofa.

Anda walks to the window where the moonlight is streaming through, and the light illuminates her white hair like a halo. She stares out the window at the moon on the lake water. Her hands are balled in fists, like she's quietly struggling with something. There's a tiny plop. I raise my head just a bit to see a liquid splash on the floor. Is she crying?

She turns. It's too late to hide that I'm awake. Her hands are still in fists, and her eyes are red-rimmed and hostile.

Oh shit. Here it comes.

She steps closer to me, and I don't move a muscle. I'm afraid to look her in the eye, but that becomes impossible when she kneels by the sofa and we're face-to-face. There are a million emotions across her features, and none of them are peaceful. She reaches out, and her warm hand slips right under my jaw, right against my windpipe.

It's a weird gesture. If this were a Marvel movie, she'd have lifted my whole body by the neck to fling me through a wall. But she just holds her palm there. And then something changes in her face. Curiosity flits across her features, and her fingers move from my neck to the patchy beard under my jaw.

I've never grown it out before, and it's long enough that it's passed the itchy stage. I've seen myself in the mirror, and it's not a full beard, either. I'm only seventeen, after all. Her fingers explore my chin, then move up my cheeks. Her other hand joins the exploration, and I swallow, wondering if she's going to slit my throat next. Part of me thinks I can take her down. The other part of me is unsure.

"Do you like it?" she asks uncertainly.

I'm going to assume she's talking about my beard, not her exploration of said beard.

"I don't know," I answer finally. I swallow again. "Do you?"

She cocks her head to the side, then leans in close. Her breath smells a little like the wind outside. She rubs her cheek against the stubble, softly. When she sits back, she touches her own cheek.

"I like everything about you, Hector." Her hand goes back to petting my face. Weird, weird, weird. "What does it look like when it's gone?"

"If I had a razor, I'd shave it off for you."

"I have one. I borrowed it from the camp store in Windigo."

Maybe I should tell her that there is no such thing as "borrowing" disposable razors. Unless people are trying to catch some sort of disease.

"It's only fair. You cut my hair," she reasons.

I'm a little afraid of saying no. "Okay. Let's do it," I say with more bravery than I feel.

She beams at me.

Inside the cabin, she digs up the disposable razor still in the paper packaging. I thought she was just quietly gobbling chocolate the whole time she was in the camp store. In the bathroom, I find a small bottle of liquid castile soap the color of olive oil and a cup of water to rinse the razor in. The bathroom is too cramped and small, so we move to the living room. Still worried about being spotted by boats near the shore, I light a candle instead of using the lamps and set it on the table next to the sofa.

I peel the razor out of its packaging and hesitate. The idea of a razor in her hands makes me nervous, even though the worst she could do is nick me.

"You're nervous," she comments.

"Yes."

"I wouldn't hurt you, Hector." She looks at the razor in my hand and frowns. Her hair resembles white silk. "On purpose, I mean."

"I know," I murmur. Without thinking, I blurt out, "Would you, though?"

"Would I what?" she asks.

"Would you hurt me, if I asked you to?"

Anda abruptly widens her eyes and moves away from me. I put out my hands, realizing what a fucked-up question that was. "I'm sorry. Never mind. Just ignore that. Sometimes I say things I shouldn't."

"Sometimes," she says slowly, "I do things I shouldn't."

We take simultaneous deep breaths.

She pours the soap into her wet hand and lathers up my face. I kind of feel like a puppy being shampooed by a toddler. She's really sloppy, and lather drips on my lap and shirt. But I don't say anything.

"Okay." I hand her the razor. "I'm all yours."

I lean forward, and she kneels in front of me. After guiding her hand with a few strokes on the flat planes of my cheeks, I let go and close my eyes.

She holds my jaw with one hand and slowly drags the razor across my other cheek. I make the standard, face-warping expressions so she can shave off my sparse mustache, and she has to stop because of a fit of laughter.

"I have to look like this, to make my skin as flat as possible. It's easier to shave that way."

"You look like a clown," she gasps, trying to catch her breath.

"That's nothing new," I comment, smiling.

She snuffs out the laughter and looks at me seriously. "What? You think your face is amusing?"

"Well, sort of. I don't know," I say, flustered.

She sits back on her heels and pauses, opening her mouth and forming her words so slowly, as if each one were created for the first time, only for me. "You are…the most beautiful boy…I have ever beheld."

My stomach does a three-sixty. "I'm sorry, what century were you born in again?"

"Pardon?"

"Never mind."

"Don't you think you are pretty?" she asks.

Pretty. Wow. "Not really. I might have lived with my mother forever if I didn't look so much like my dad."

"Do you look like her?"

I stare at my hands. Deep brown with pale palms. Long fingers. Just like my father's. "I do. Enough to keep my dad away. He hates her for leaving him and then dumping me in his lap."

"But you don't live with him?"

"No."

"So you're not on his hands?"

I shake my head. "I don't know what I am."

This is the part where my social worker tells me none of this is my fault. Where temporary friends would cuss out my parents for screwing me up, and curse my uncle for being such a shitty pseudo-parent, even without knowing my own suspicions of how dead-souled he really is. Words can't fix any of it; they just remind me of what's gone wrong.

So when Anda stays silent and goes back to shaving me, I mentally thank her and audibly sigh with relief. She reaches for my chin, tilting it up.

"Be still," she whispers.

She drags the razor up my neck, against the angle between my neck and chin, and then over the sharp-angled jawbone. Scrape after scrape, sweep after sweep. Swishing it in the water between strokes, like I showed her. I'm surprised at how good she is at this and how nervous she isn't. She keeps going until it's all done. I wipe down my face and neck with a damp towel. When I take it away, I see a tiny red dot.

"Oh! I did cut you," she says sorrowfully, and leans in to see the damage.

I feel the tiny sting on my neck, just next to my Adam's apple. "It's nothing. I'll just—*oh hell*."

Anda's leaned forward and has her mouth on my neck, her tongue gently probing the area where the nick is. She licks at it the way a child would gently suck a paper cut. It sends ripples of feeling through my chest down to my toes and I grasp her shoulders.

I want to push her away.

I want her never to stop.

Her hands slither up my chest and capture my neck, thumbs at the angles of my jaw on either side. I manage to push her away, just enough to see her eyes—dilated on a circlet of steel gray. I'm afraid she might just tear my jugular wide open and have a bowlful.

"Hector. Don't be afraid." Her eyes drop to my lips.

"Okay," I lie. Because I'm terrified of what she could do to me. Of what she is doing, right now. And it has nothing to do with death, or blood. Or even this stupid body.

She could tear me to pieces for all I care.

And with that, I close the distance between us and kiss her.

Chapter Twenty-Two

ANDA

I t is a peculiar and astonishing thing, kissing.

I never understood it. Lips are for speaking, for eating, and for conjuring the necessary turbulence and resonance for whistling. They split when they're too dry; they constantly invite my teeth for a bite.

But when I kiss Hector, it isn't just flesh on flesh. Hector tells me things he's never said aloud. How he appreciates the puzzle that I am, the question with no answer. How he wants to give himself to me, though I've never asked for such a sacrifice. How he invites me to something far more precious than he's ever given before. Something both holy and almost destructive.

My fingers tingle, and I've forgotten that they're around his neck. I pull so hard on the both of us that I slowly draw us backward. My spine soon drapes over the wood floor beneath me and Hector hovers above, sheltering me from the ceiling, the roof, the disapproving sky.

You will regret this. Stop—

But I don't want to listen to her.

I'd been traveling further and further away from this. Before, there was the path forward to convergence with the storms and no way to reverse it all. To be like my sisters and leave my father's side of me behind forever. I thought that was what I wanted; in passivity, in my search to avoid pain, I let it happen.

But now I've taken a step off the path. It is terrifying, this wilderness. And yet I'm not as lost as I thought I would be.

You will regret this.

Like you regret Father? Like you regret me? I ask.

She doesn't answer.

I've stopped kissing Hector, and he puts his hand behind my neck. "Are you all right?" he whispers.

I don't answer right away. His hand is warm, spare, and steady.

I want to stay here awhile. I want to stay.

So I ignore her and answer Hector's question by pulling the belt loops of his pants toward me. His body, though lighter and thinner now, is still taut and solid. I pull him close until we are hip to hip and his chest covers mine. I want the weight of him on me. It's such a delicious alternative to the heaviness of the airy sky on my shoulders. Atlas never was so burdened as I have been. It is one thing to hold up the heavens, another thing to resist their alluring call in November.

He stops kissing me long enough to complain. "I'm squashing you."

"Yes," I say, seeking out his earlobe to live between my lips. Perhaps for a few decades.

We kiss for hours, it seems. Hector envelops me in his arms as if I might disappear, and I appreciate feeling so precious. I am used to using my other senses—pressure, and temperature, and the rise and fall of the living beings on this island and lake. They're fine-tuned instruments in my body, though I don't understand how they work. They simply do.

So there's a relief—almost a guilty simplicity—in letting my human form explore this tangled knot we've become. My bare legs entwine with his. I pull his shirt over his head so my hands can touch his scars, the ridged and erratic turns on his skin. There are collarbones and gently pulsating carotid arteries nestled between the ropes of neck muscle. Acres of skin I've wanted to sense, but hadn't. And there is his mouth. He is endlessly thirsty for me, and it is astonishing, being needed in such a way.

Sometime when the moon has arced away from the window and the cabin has become pitch dark, and we've stained ourselves with hearth ashes from our tumbling, Hector pushes against the floor, creating space between our bodies. I frown.

"Are you okay?" he asks.

My lips are swollen and I'm half drunk on something that can't be bottled. I nod.

"Hungry?"

I shake my head. It's a partial lie; I can't bring myself to put words to what I am.

"Are you tired?" I ask, in return.

"No. Are you?"

I shake my head. "I don't need to sleep." His eyes crinkle in puzzlement, and I add, "But I should like to sleep every night if I could sleep with you."

He smiles. It's so genuine and unrehearsed, like some I've seen on the island. A slight panic rises within me, a fear that something might blight that smile forever. Something has tried to wrest his happiness away before. He hides whatever it is, though it's lurking there. I've seen it. And I don't wish for it to return, not yet.

A strange urge wriggles in my center. I have the oddest desire to give him something. A gift. For the first time in my world, I am worried. Perhaps he won't like what I have to offer. And the wriggling turns to fear.

Anda, this is a mistake. You don't really know what fear is. Don't invite it in.

I deliberately turn away from the window and the sky. "I want to take you somewhere."

"It's the middle of the night. Where do you want to go?" He pulls me up but immediately places his hands around my waist. I like them there. "Can you stop time?" he says. His smile is disappearing. "I wouldn't mind if this night went a little slower."

Slower. I don't really understand, but then again, time has always been on my side. I think to myself, where could I take him, where time stands still?

This is a mistake.

I pull him toward the door, leaving her warnings behind us. "I know where we can go."

Chapter Twenty-Three

HECTOR

This is the last thing I ever expected. I came to this island to survive until my eighteenth birthday. To get away from my uncle and Dad. To not die.

And I've just spent the last few hours rolling around with a girl I can't keep my hands off. Who I can't stop kissing. I swear to God, I'm not even the kissing type. Lord knows, I've had as much romance in my life as highway asphalt. But I get it now. The stupid songs, and Valentine's Day, and those idiot kids in the hallway mooning over each other and swallowing each other's faces between classes.

I've become one of the idiots. And I like it.

I put on my jacket and boots, and Anda pulls me out the door. She doesn't think of putting on boots or anything, so I have to reel her back in and remind her. She looks at me wonderingly as I choose an oversize man's down coat from a hook by the door.

"Is this your dad's coat?" I ask.

She nods.

"Does he know you're here?"

She nods again.

Anger curls inside my stomach. What kind of father would let his teenage daughter stay on an island alone like this? Especially one like Anda, who isn't exactly the most practical person in the world (she insists on wearing only a nightgown under the coat).

Anda looks up at me. "Does your father know you're here?"

"No," I say flatly. I turn to the door to open it. I don't want to think of her dad, or my dad, for that matter. Not tonight. She seems to be happy dropping the subject of absentee fathers, and steps ahead of me into the darkness. We go down the stone steps and onto the path by the house.

"Don't we need a flashlight or something?" I ask.

"I can see everything," she tells me.

She guides me with such assurance that I believe her. We stay on the path by the house but soon take a turn into the untrodden depths of the woods. To our left, between the tree trunks, I see water—it must be Washington Harbor. If I have my bearings right, we're heading farther west, to the tip of the island. We crunch over dead leaves, pine needles, twigs. Low shrubbery brushes against our legs, and we duck under branches. Anda seems to know this path well. Not once do we detour around any obstacles.

After a mile or so, I ask her, "Where are we going?"

She doesn't respond.

"Say something." Still nothing. "Anything," I add. The only noise is the sound of our feet crunching on the ground. Normally, I live in silence. It's a second skin to me. But after being so close to Anda these last few hours, the silence between us is alienating.

After what feels like five minutes, she starts to talk. "One-point-two billion years ago in the Precambrian Era, extrusive igneous rock formed when lava rapidly cooled after seeping up through the Superior Basin." She waits for a second, as if the history of this land requires rest, respect, and space. "This basalt formed the bedrock of the area, and through geologic syncline, the rock layers folded, forming the Keweenaw Peninsula and Isle Royale."

I reach for her hand, and she squeezes it. Her hand is remarkably strong. She goes on to talk about glaciers and pressure, melting ice and lake formation. Geology never sounded so epic as when it came from her lips. Plus, it's calming. It isn't about politics or human drama. It's so beyond everything in my life, it's soothing.

We walk on and on. Must be miles, and I'm growing tired. After all, we've been up all night long. Dawn starts to break on the horizon, and blue begins to seep into the indigo. The sound of water lapping on the shore is a little louder. Suddenly, the land ends. There's no rocky beach here. The trees grow almost to the edge of a rounded point of land.

"There." Anda points to the water.

In the growing light of dawn, a white cylinder sticks up out of the water, maybe two hundred feet from shore.

"What's under there?" I ask.

"The *America*. Born in 1898. It was a steamship and sank in 1928." She says this wistfully, as if it's a long-lost friend or part of a memory that makes her happy.

"Wow. It's pretty close."

"Let's get closer," Anda says, squeezing my hand. She has a slightly feral look in her eye, like she's suddenly very, very hungry.

She raises her foot, as if ready to step directly into the water, when I blurt out a protest. "Anda, we don't have a boat."

"Oh." She plants her booted foot back on the damp shore. "Oh."

I wonder how long we'll stare at that cylinder—I guess it's a buoy—when the water splashes a little louder far off to our right. There's a walloping sound of water hitting water, like someone just emptied a barrelful into the lake.

"What was that?" Waves ripple toward our feet. Thirty feet away, there's a big log by the shore that wasn't there before. Or maybe I didn't notice it. It has a smooth, pointy tip, and then I realize it's probably not a log.

"Is that a…"

"Maybe it is." She leads me along the shoreline. It turns out to be a really old rowboat. It looks like it used to be painted metal, but rust has taken over and it's covered with algae. It's dripping wet. If I didn't know any better, I'd think that the lake just spit it out onto the shore. Nearby, a single paddle floats in the water. The handle end is broken, and the shaft is shorter now.

"You don't want to actually get in this thing, do you? It doesn't look very seaworthy." I'm trying to be all casual, but my spine has gone stiff with worry.

"It's fine. I promise."

"But—"

"We're not going very far out. And the water is so calm." She gestures out to the lake, and it's true. It's glassily serene. By the dim morning light, I can see where the lake bed goes from brown to green to blue as the water deepens farther from shore.

I figure we can go in the boat and if it's not safe, we can jump out right away and only risk getting our legs drenched. I push it into the water and Anda sits in the middle, chin high and posture like a stately queen. The broken paddle is hard to use, but it works to get us closer to the little buoy.

It's ridiculously easy to paddle us forward. Anda must weigh nothing, and the boat has no drag. Soon, she's able to tether a waterlogged rope from the boat to what I now realize is a shipwreck marker for divers. Painted on one side of the cylindrical buoy is the word "WRECK" with an orange diamond underneath.

"Here she is," Anda says softly. "One hundred and eighty-four feet long, with a gross tonnage of four hundred and eighty-six tons. Rather accident-prone, she was."

The morning light is stronger now. Without any turbulence in the water, we can see several feet down. A greenish bow is only a few feet below the surface, eerily receding into the depths beyond where the lake bed falls away. The surface of the boat is nubbly and irregular, with feathery algae attached, wafting in the mild current. It's a big boat, which shouldn't surprise me, but does.

I've never seen a shipwreck before. There was the *St. Anne*, but I hadn't seen that one up close. I've only seen wrecks in pictures, and they've all been of the *Titanic* when we studied it in history class. But this one is so close, and seeing its bones beneath the water chills me. I think of the people on the ship and how they must have felt when it sank. My spine goes rigid once again, imagining swallowing and choking on gallons of water.

I stare at the hull. "What was the name of the ship again?"

"The *America*." She smiles faintly.

"Did anyone die from the sinking?"

"No humans," Anda tells me. "A dog was tied to the stern. They didn't realize it until it was too late."

How depressing. I should be happy that lives weren't lost, but the dog's death and the ship's death make me want to crawl under a blanket and hide from everything.

"Why are you sad?" She climbs over her seat to sit next to me.

"I don't know."

"You wanted to see time stop."

"I did. But this isn't…" I can't finish my thought.

"The ship is sad, too," she says. "She misses her captain. She misses docking at Snug Harbor. She misses her duty." Anda stops talking to chew on her hangnails. Her eyes are on the hull of the submerged ship. She seems on edge now.

I turn to her. "Are you clairvoyant or something?"

She stops biting and twists her head to stare at me. The hangnails on her right fingers are raw and smeared with pink. "If I was, would that be okay?"

"Fuck, yes." I say it seriously, then grin widely.

"Really?"

"Sure." I sigh. "I could dig a fairy tale right now. Lord knows I've never lived in one."

"I'll tell you one sometime. And you can tell me if you like it."

Silence hangs between us for a few moments. And then a wave bumps the boat. More like the water pitches under us. We bobble unsteadily.

"What the—" I start saying. I have to hold on to the side of the rowboat to keep from tipping out of it. Anda's eyes grow wide, and she bares her teeth like a dog. Waves seem to be rising straight out from under us. There are no other boats making a wake. I don't understand what's happening.

And then I do. Under the water, the *America* is moving. Metal groans and screeches against bedrock as it shifts, the bow rising steadily until the algae-covered metal breaks the surface of the water. It nearly hits the side of our little rowboat.

"What the fuck!" I yell.

Anda quickly unties the rope from the buoy that is now slack on its chain. She glares at the *America*, as if it were a misbehaving child. What good that will do, I don't know, because some sort of earthquake must be happening. I shove the broken paddle into the water and start digging toward shore. Anda keeps glaring, and the earthquake or whatever must be over, because the boat sinks right back down. A sonorous *thump* jangles my bones as the wreck hits the lake bed, and the resulting huge wake nearly tips us over one last time. I'm covered in sweat, and my stomach is lurching. My heart thumps a frantic tattoo. "Holy shit, what was that?"

Anda doesn't answer. She's clenching her jaw and looks pissed as all hell, as if the seismic event was an insult of some sort.

"Did you see how the wreck rose up?" I need to calm down. I'm breathing really fast, but Anda still says nothing. Her lack of reaction dumbfounds me. "Anda? Are you okay?"

Her eyes swivel in a split second to meet mine. She could be made of marble but for the glistening eyes. "No." Her voice is dead cold and her words, deliberate. "I'm not okay."

I try to push down my fear and think. I've been keeping track of all the weird shit that's been happening around her, but there's been a million excuses to brush them away. I mean, look at her. She's just a girl. She's only human. A really weird human with a really messed-up dad.

I don't know what to say, so I just row back to shore. This time, she sits in the bow of the boat and looks back toward where the wreck is. She gazes with that unnerving, unblinking stare. The reflection of morning light in her dark eyes moves, like oil on water. When we land, I toss the paddle firmly inland, so it won't float away. My pants are wet from the splashing. Anda is still chewing on her fingertips and starts walking back toward home, as if she's totally forgotten that I exist. The shipwreck and the quake have completely changed her mood. She doesn't seem like the same person who was kissing me for hours only a little while ago, or tugging on my hand like an impatient child.

I pull the boat a little farther ashore so it's solidly on land. That's when I see the gash in the corner, near the stern.

There was a huge hole in the boat, and I'd never noticed.

My sweat feels like ice water now.

I always thought I'd be in danger on this island, because of the cold and the weather, and simple, natural problems, like finding food and water. But it's the unnatural things here that are going to be the death of me.

Chapter Twenty-Four

ANDA

Seeing the *America* was not a good idea.

I did not expect Mother to threaten him in such a way, to threaten me through Hector. She's angry. But I'm angrier. I only wish more than ever to safeguard this precious thing we have, that I have remade for myself. Inside, a ferocity has arisen that I didn't know was there.

And I like it.

I think of Hector, and our kisses, and the scent of his skin that still rises from me, a perfume I've never worn before. I wanted to share with him something beyond beauty and time. Something near and dear to my faulty, human heart.

But there is a problem. The forlorn cries of the drowned ship did nothing but whet my appetite. It's November 1 now. How could I have lost track of the date? The sinking of the *St. Anne* was already too long ago. I find that I'm famished again, and the emptiness is consuming me. And Mother's actions have occupied my mind.

On the way back to the cabin, I forget several times

that I'm with Hector. He calls out to me and clasps my hand. I remember for a moment who and where I am. He steals a kiss and I give it to him, but the haze of his presence is wearing thin—not from irritation, but from a larger presence grinding away at my existence. Like sand and grit against a boulder, it will eventually thin me out until I can't resist any longer.

You knew this would happen. You can't ignore what matters. You can't ignore me.

Her voice is clearer now than before, and she's attempting to sound dulcet, not angry. I've been trying not to listen, but there are other things that force me to notice them. The creeping juniper that ought to be evergreen is browning. The old man's beard lichens, usually hanging aloft in the pines, have fallen in irregular tufts and blow along the trail closer to the cabin.

But then I think of how the *America*'s bones saddened Hector. How he sees death with an opposite polarity that I can't understand. All I only know is that Hector nourishes a side of me that has slept since birth. And I don't want Hector to hurt.

You can't ignore me.

I'll try and then some, I say savagely without speaking.

That week, Hector and I live at home. He's quieter than before, warier. He looks out at the lake as if expecting a serpent to arise from the depths and swallow him whole. But when it lies there in peace, he relaxes ever so slowly. He spends a portion of every day fishing. Sometimes he brings home a fish, sometimes he doesn't. But when he does, he fries it, alive only an hour ago, and presents it glistening on a plate for us to share.

This pleases me. I am so used to being the one who keeps everything nourished, or drags them back into the humus of the soil to disintegrate. Father used to try to care for me, and vaguely, I remember enjoying it when I was younger. But those needs had left me.

With Hector, he's awoken what I didn't realize I missed. Once, he feeds me with his fingertips, dripping with browned butter. I nearly tackle him to the ground, rewarding him with hour-long kisses.

I make things that might please him, like more rock cairns in the living room. He comes home and sees my creations, scratching his newly growing beard thoughtfully. He doesn't read their words like I do, but that doesn't bother me.

What does bother me is that I can sense his pulse from a mile away. It's an inviting river of blood, and when he asks me to shave his beard again, I decline. It's too much temptation. I try to feed myself with other things, but we are already running low on camp store candy bars and dry soup packets. I'm starting to notice that Hector doesn't cook enough for two people—only enough for me.

If he only knew how misguided his actions were.

So I eat very little. Unlike Hector, I don't grow thinner as the days go by, and he consumes my leftover meals like a ravenous Isle wolf. And at night, he feeds from a different kind of hunger. We tangle ourselves on the floor by the hearth until inevitably, Hector gently pushes me away. The riotous noise of his blood is so loud in my ears, I can barely hear his voice.

"No," he says, but I don't understand what he's saying no to. There's an invisible wall that I can't see, but he does, and apparently, we can't walk through it. "No," he repeats, before kissing me gently on the neck and walking outside, coatless and shoeless, to cool off his warm skin on the stone steps outside the house.

I don't follow him. If I did, neither of us might return.

Chapter Twenty-Five

HECTOR

It has been the best and strangest week of my life.

We've been doing these ordinary things—cooking, walking, messing around every night until I'm almost seeing red from wanting her so badly. But I have to stop myself. I worry about what she understands. I mean, she can recite the geological history of the Great Lakes region like she's got a PhD, but she doesn't know how to make toast. Some nights, she stays awake, and I find her in the morning still standing by the window, watching the lake's horizon as if she's guarding something. And some days, she falls asleep in my arms like a child. So I can't take our physical stuff further, because she never pushes for it, and I won't. I would never.

She still spends hours listening to the weather radio. That NOAA lady's voice is grating on my nerves, but only because she always seems so fucking neutral about everything. I've been listening to the radio, too. They don't talk much about the *St. Anne* anymore. The excitement of the wreck has faded into a vanilla memory, like all horrible events in the news. I listen for any bulletins about my own runaway status before I remind myself I'm a runaway teenage boy who isn't even white. Who the hell cares?

There's one thing that isn't fading into memory, and that's survival. We're quickly running out of food, despite my attempts to supplement with fish. Every time I go fishing, I try to scope out any other cabins that we could steal food from, but they're either too hard to break into, or there's nothing once I get into the tiny kitchens. Anda doesn't know I do this.

I'm getting really worried and start making mental plans about hiking to another part of the island for food, maybe the hotel lodge at Rock Harbor. I'm starving all the time, though Anda isn't bothered by hunger the way I am. And it's taking a toll. My throat aches a little, and this morning I was chilled in my sweatshirt. Goose bumps arise on my arms, though I'm wearing two sweatshirts. I hope I'm not getting a cold.

Anda is on the floor, listening to the radio. I sigh, watching her. Because none of this—her, me, this island—is rooted in reality. At some point, I'll have to leave. Or we might be discovered. Or her father might come back. At times, I wonder if all this is just one marathon dream, and I've been immersed in some raging fever since I rescued Anda.

I gather my fishing tackle and hoist on my coat. Anda doesn't move as I head for the door. There's something awesome about that. It's not that I need kisses and sweetly packaged good-byes. It's just Anda's surety that I'll be back and in her arms tonight that makes me satisfied.

Outside, a wind is rising. The sky is a gunmetal gray, and mist hangs in the air. Most of the leaves have already changed colors and fallen, so there are no lush gold and red views now. I guess the island doesn't save them for trespassers like me, since I don't deserve that beauty. Add it to the list of other things I'm unworthy of.

You don't deserve what you have. A good house. Family. This from my uncle only one month ago, all coming after my grades were less than stellar, and after I got fired from Walmart. Sometimes it's not words, just silence. A week's worth of quiet fury can be worse than a bruise. At least the bruise heals, but silence digs into your bones for days on end. And then there's the guilt. *I'm doing the best I can, Hector. Can't you see that? I never wanted this.*

I know what he meant by "this." Not the fighting. Not the unexplained, dark sickness that would overtake me almost every month. He meant just me. Only me.

It pisses me off that even now, he demands to be in my head, though I'm the one who left him behind.

I concentrate instead on the wild around me. It's unforgiving and amazing, and I've got a hell of a newfound respect for it. I see one ray of sun shining on Washington Harbor behind me, and through the trees, Lake Superior's wet horizon stretches widely.

In the middle of all this beauty, I think, this island is eating me alive, little by little. It's winning, and I can't lose this time.

The dark green of the pines and barren swaths of trees seem to be bracing themselves for the onslaught of winter. The mist transforms to rain, soft at first, before it starts to pelt me in the back and penetrate my jeans. Waves of chills run down my spine, and my sore throat is getting worse instead of better. A faint headache pulses under my temples. I'd better catch this fish, and fast.

Chapter Twenty-Six

ANDA

After Hector leaves, I look around the house. The sofa and the braided rug are empty and forlorn, wanting someone to touch them. The kitchen has crumbs on the counter from the granola bars we've eaten. A glob of jam smears the countertop, and I wipe it off with my finger and onto my tongue. The sticky gel of tart fruit and sucrose dissolves as I press it up against my palate. I close my eyes.

How could I have forgotten that I liked this? I mourn that I've forgotten.

While Hector fishes, I pace around the house. Something is amiss. What am I to do, to make this house into a home? I think of Hector's mouth pressing against the crook of my neck. Yes, this. And no, not quite. Maybe more food. More blankets. I gnaw at a fingernail.

Father knows. He brings food and things that he believes I ought to like, such as broken geodes and rare pieces of beach glass. He thinks I'll be bewitched by these pretty objects, by the lure of food laden with sugar or salt. Sometimes he brings flat, circular lake stones with holes he's chipped into the middle. He thinks these will keep me safe somehow.

But none of it fits. He only knows the human way to care. I am made of storms and corpses, of granite and paper-white birch. Trinkets and morsels of food haven't comforted me since I was a child.

I'm not the one who needs to be kept safe. It is everyone else.

Then why do you let this boy stay?

I don't know.

Why do you need food now?

I don't know that, either.

You need to make it stop. You are losing the balance, and that way lies despair.

I understand, but I wonder—did I ever have balance? Or did I simply veer so close to her axis that the pull nullified everything else? I'm terrified. And yet I'm too weak to banish it all, to make Hector go away. I need a storm, not calories. I know this.

It is November 7. It has been 348 hours since the sinking of the *St. Anne*. My body knows this, too, feeling light and airy as dandelion fuzz. I need grounding, the way lightning hungers for a good, tall tree.

I've stood in the middle of the kitchen for over an hour, motionless, just considering these things. Finally, I loosen the stiff air about me and reach for one of Father's cookbooks. Hector will be back soon, and the morsels of breakfast have since dissolved away into my blood. One book has a recipe for quick breads. It calls for flour, butter, and baking powder. Also salt. There is no flour left, but I crush the remaining crackers to use instead. I don't bother to clean the bits of dust on the floor, instead letting my bare feet push them around, here and there.

I turn on the NOAA radio to keep me company.

Temperature dropping to forty degrees.

Waves of eight feet or more.

Forecasts are for ice-free areas.

No, that can't be right. The NOAA voice is wrong. It's not that cool, nor are the waves that large. I go to the window and splay my fingers against the glass, startled at the coldness of the glass. Between the branches of dead, lichen-covered birch trees, I see the waves of the lake. They are far larger than I sensed.

I've always been finely attuned to the air pressure and moisture, the vectors of wind and penetration of the judging sun. A radio can be fixed, instruments recalibrated. What do I do with myself if I am already becoming so broken?

Well. I can make other things, I think. It's a practical thought, and I readjust my spine to this new sensation of practicality. I snap the radio off, turn away from the windows, and busy myself in the kitchen, taking the ingredients down. I'm wrist-deep in the sticky mixture when static begins to tug at the cut ends of my shorn hair. The chimney begins to moan, and raindrops patter the roof. Such wonderful, delicious music. My eyelids have closed, so I can listen with heavy intention.

My mind begins to swim. Deep within, my spine and long bones ache for the storm. My heart beats, and with every pulse, there is a yawning need.

My hands squeeze the dough, and it oozes between my clawed fingers. I scrunch my face, breathing long and hard, opening my eyes and concentrating. That's right. I'm making biscuits, aren't I? Hector will be hungry. I am hungry, too.

You need something else to feed you, Anda. Not wheat, nor butter.

"Shh," I hiss.

I wish I could distance myself from her. I'm almost out the door when I stop. I'm making food for Hector, I remember, and shake my head. I grab a handful of sticky, needy dough. I try to drop it onto the cookie sheet when the wind whistles for me. It creeps under the eaves, through the cracks of the wall, and circles my ankles, coaxing me.

"Stop it," I whimper.

I drop irregular handfuls of dough onto a metal sheet. Mechanically, I put the sheet of lumpy dough in the tiny kitchen stove, the insides glowing red as hell. My vision swims. I see blood, not the heating elements of the oven.

Before I can wipe my sticky hands on a kitchen towel, the tug inside my belly grows too insistent and irresistible. It's a rope, tied to my spine and pulling hard. It would pull hard enough to rend me apart, I know.

Sustained winds of up to thirty knots.

Small craft should exercise caution.

The last storm was "large in size." A rather bland way to put kinetic energy, wind speeds, rain, cubic kilometers, and vortices of current into one measure of size. Words never suffice for much anyway. This storm, however—it's far larger than the last, in that I can feel the pull deep in my marrow.

It is November 7. It has been 349 hours since the sinking of the *St. Anne*.

"No," I gasp.

Yes.

My hands twist the doorknob to exit the house before I know it. My feet fly across stone and pine needles. The water is so close, and the rain makes my skin burn with a fury. The shore coaxes as only it can. In a blink, I'm at the lake's edge. The stones of the lake dig into the soft soles of my feet. I don't ignore the pain. Instead, it makes me smile. The stones don't hurt me; they're crying out for having touched me.

The water is up to my knees when I see the white sailboat in my mind's eye.

It's no longer within sight of the Upper Peninsula. Everyone who touches the lake knows that the silhouette of Lake Superior resembles a wolf, and Isle Royale, its vengeful eye. The sailboat is in the throat of the wolf, about to be consumed. Through the splash of white water, I see the name on the boat.

The *Jenny*.

Thomas and Agatha are on board, panic showing as white rings their blue irises. The boat is named after their only daughter, safe in landlocked Colorado. They thought the storm would not come up so quickly; they were wrong. They thought it would be the last good day to sail before winter set in; they were correct.

It will be the last day they ever sail.

They are mine for the taking, if I'm willing to take them. My fingertips touch the lake water. To me, it is warm as new milk. Remotely, in my brain, I remember there was a boy. And that there is a stove turned on in a house somewhere, but I don't care.

Nothing matters when death is calling for me.

It is November 7. It has been 350 hours since the sinking of the *St. Anne*.

It has been too long. The *Jenny* calls for me.
Good girl.

Chapter Twenty-Seven

HECTOR

I carry two fish back with me, shivering nonstop. Now my thighs and shoulders ache, too. I'm definitely sick, and it's freaking me out how fast it's coming on.

The rain starts pouring. This storm's far more vicious than the last. The drops pelt my face over and over. My head has that blown-up, dizzy feeling. I haven't had anything to eat or drink today. That was stupid.

When I get to her house, I'm so thankful to reach shelter. My hands are shaking when I drop the fish on her back step. I'm too tired to clean and scale them. I need to rest first. I'm going to just sink face-first into the couch for a few hours. Days, maybe.

As soon as I touch the door, I realize something's wrong. It's open again. The wind is smacking it repeatedly against the jamb, chattering a warning. I smell smoke. I step inside, and my hand touches something sticky on the doorknob.

I look at my fingertips. Ugh. What is this stuff? I sniff the gluey beige goo on my fingertips and smell a yeasty scent. It's dough. But that's not all. I look upward to where faint wisps of dark smoke spread across the ceiling.

Something's burning.

"Anda? Anda!" I yell, barreling down the hallway toward the main room. Stinging smoke coils up to the kitchen ceiling from the oven. Coughing, I spin the oven dial to off and open the oven door. A cloudy black plume meets my face. Shrunken, burned lumps decorate a black cookie sheet. I run to the bedrooms, but they're empty.

Oh shit. Where is she?

"Anda!" I yell hoarsely, the words feeling like sandpaper in my throat. I tear out the door and spin around wildly, looking for her. But I don't see her anywhere. The treetops are bending and whipping back and forth and grit blows into my face. Maybe she just wandered off? Or maybe she went back to the lake.

No.

I forget about my exhaustion and run through the trees, heading for the water. You can see the lake through her kitchen window between the trees. The closer I get to the water, the colder the wind becomes. The clouds have darkened, fast. Sickening thunder rumbles everywhere. Sheets of rain fall near and far away, looking vaguely like the sweeping folds of a woman's skirt. I'm soaked when I reach the water's edge.

"Anda!" I yell, but the splashing is so noisy. The water's surface is sharp with a million points from splattering rain-drops. I see a white thing floating in the water. Something small, like the top of a blond head.

Oh my God.

She's too far out for me to wade in and reach her. Remembering how hard it was to tug her to shore in my clothes, I yank my coat off, and then kick away my pants and boots. I run into the water. The icy temperature causes my body to revolt, making me hyperventilate. I dive in and swim hard toward the last place her head was bobbing on the waves.

My limbs immediately stiffen like lead from the blazing cold water. My head is buzzing from panic and faintness. I lift my face. The white thing in the water rises just at the surface. It is her. A foot or so away, I see the tops of her hands near the surface. Her body must be deeper, like her feet are pulling her down.

You might die doing this, an inner voice says to me. It's so calm, so filled with common sense. But I ignore it, swimming harder.

I reach for her arm and grab it savagely, pulling her to me. Once again, her skin is scorching hot. It feels good inside my chilled palm. I need to grab her body and tug her to shore, but I'm underwater. There is nothing to anchor myself so I can pull, and my face goes underwater when a wave hits me square in the head. That old familiar panic hits my heart, and I kick in a frenzy to break the surface. I cough and sputter, gasping for air, and keep going. Anda's face is only inches away. Her white-cropped hair sways in the turbid water. Her eyes are closed. She's dead in the water. The most beautiful dead person I've never seen.

Really, Hector. Am I worth it? the voice says again.

Suddenly, her eyes open.

Alive eyes, seeing eyes. They bore right through me, like acid. In a way that tells me that I'm not supposed to witness this.

I would scream, but I can't. The Anda I know, she's not here anymore. A brutal tidal force pulls me ruthlessly away from her arms. She disappears in the greenish-black darkness of the water as I'm swept out toward the body of the lake. I need to breathe, but I don't know which way is up. The burning in my chest grows into a vicious, hard knot. I remember learning about rip currents in science class. But I don't remember what to do. Fight the current? Swim perpendicular? Ride it out and let it take you?

All I know is that Anda is underwater, and I can't help her anymore. I came to the Isle to steal my life back, and I'm losing it. But I won't, not without a fight. So I kick and kick, trying to find the surface, trying to exit the stranglehold of water that's pushing me down, fast, away.

When my heart almost bursts in my chest, I realize my mistake.

This time, fighting was the wrong thing to do.

Chapter Twenty-Eight

ANDA

I know what death tastes like.

It's sweet. Not like sugar, which coats the tongue with those cloying molecules—carbon, oxygen, hydrogen. No; death is not encoded in atoms or things you can touch. It's bitter to some, like a tincture that must be taken in an inevitable dose. But to me, it's an unearthly sweetness that I crave, that can't be satiated with anything but the resolution of life.

I could have three deaths. I can almost taste them.

Thomas still clings to his boat, hoarsely screaming for his wife. There is so much water on board that the bilge pumps are useless. He cannot tell the difference between the lake and the rain anymore. It is all gray, the strange color between night and day, life and death, the places where I exist best.

The water has become one powerful thing, so overwhelming that he wonders why he ever thought it was a good idea to sail, when such a force lay simmering beneath the surface all along. He knew the history behind

Lake Superior and me. He remembers only now the tales of the November storms so brutal, they're called witches. I've fooled him with his own tenacity and confidence.

It's a beautiful day, Aggie. C'mon. Just one last sail for the season.

His belly is full of lake water. He's vomited twice and keeps swallowing it down with every relentless splash. He screams into the void for Agatha. He continues to fight.

I like them like this.

Agatha, in her life jacket, is sloshing on the waves, lost to him. Her gray hair is plastered to her skull. I can see her skull so easily now. Her flesh is but a thin covering on what will soon be at the bottom of the lake. She stopped screaming a few minutes ago. Despair has set in, and her tears add salt to the storm. Agatha carries more peace in her heart than Thomas, or younger sailors, who lust for more years of life. Her death will not satiate nearly as well. When life comes with more to lose, it means more when I take it. When hope has trickled away, they welcome the inevitable. It would be effortless to take them then. There would be no beauty in that.

Next November, I'll listen for the bells tolling at the Mariner's Church. Three more sonorous noises, added to those I've already taken from the *St. Anne*. The music is written. It's waiting for me to play the tune.

I could tear the life jacket off with a sigh and let her sink to meet me. Thomas, I could pitch into the water with just a whisper.

And there is Hector.

He hasn't a breath left. But he fights so hard against the unnatural riptide I'd created to pull him away from me. He let himself come to Isle Royale. Every night, he has come into my arms. He could have been at home.

Ah, but that was not a home. It was never safe. He hasn't said this explicitly, but I know it. Because as terrible as I am, I am safer than what he had. What a sad truth. My conscience creaks at these thoughts. But he fed me. Didn't he? He tasted my lips. He saw me. No one ever sees me with so little effort.

Ah, take him, Anda. I know how hungry you are.

I am. So ravenous. I reach my hands forward and feel the lake water in my blood.

Thomas. Agatha. Hector.

This should be easy. I never have to struggle like this. But I can't fight the newborn feeling mewling in my chest. I don't want Hector's life to keep mine alive. I just want Hector. But if I let him live, I have to relinquish my hold on the whole storm. I could let go.

But I can't.

I cannot.

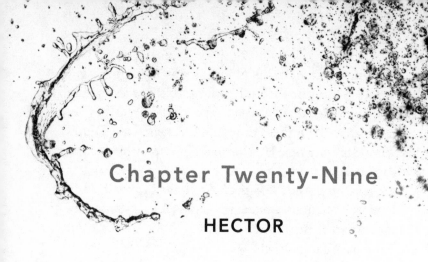

Chapter Twenty-Nine

HECTOR

A wave swallows me and I'm underwater, battered upside down again. And again. And again.

I'm going to die. I know this, but I won't stop fighting. I swim upward and gasp air, trying to tread water. Not that far away, I actually see a boat. I scream. I scream louder. It's no good—I can barely hear my own cries for help. The water is dark and green and churning, and I'm a dark dot bobbing too far away. They'll never see me.

And then I realize the boat has capsized. The boaters are in trouble, too. One is an old guy, white hair plastered against his head, clinging to the ropes on the capsized sailboat. I barely see a woman—in a split-second glimpse, she looks like someone's grandma—fighting the waves in the distance, her bright life vest marking her position too far away.

An enormous wave lifts me up, up, up, on a swell. I inhale hard, and together we crash over and I'm tumbling again under the waves. And then I see her.

Anda.

She's right there, an unmoving body under the waves. My vision is fuzzy underwater, but I know it's Anda. Her eyes are dark coals in her sockets. And the violent surges and waves don't move her an inch. It's like she's suspended in the vacuum of space, her cropped hair floating sweetly around her temples, her nightgown unruffled by the water, bare feet peeking out from the hem.

It's not possible. None of this is possible.

I've ignored the things I haven't been able to explain. The hole in the boat by the *America*. The earthquake, or whatever made it rise to the surface. The flower that grew and died in the span of a few hours. But I have a feeling I'm going to know, too soon, what I've been afraid to realize all this time.

Anda raises a single hand, and in response, the capsized boat is pulled beneath the waves. The old guy who's holding on to the boat is pulled down too, his arm tangled in rope. He'd probably wound it around himself so he wouldn't drown, and now it'll be the death of him.

Anda lowers her hand. The sailboat and the man sink like stones. The last thing I see is his white face, his open screaming mouth that can't scream underwater. Bubbles issue from the boat around him as he's pulled into the depths.

Chapter Thirty

ANDA

I sigh.

Exquisite, this feeling. This beautiful peace where the violence that is life is finally released.

Something touches me.

I turn and see Hector. He's swiping at my arm, trying to grasp my hand. In this state, all living things flee from me, but this boy is trying to get closer. I furrow my brow, not understanding.

Two more, Anda. Do not be distracted.

He's so tired, he barely has the energy to reach for me before his body bobs upward. Buoyancy is his enemy. He can't speak to me when he's underwater, but I hear him scream when he breaks the surface.

"Stop it, Anda. Please. Oh God, stop!"

God. He prays, but not to me. Nothing can help him, except me.

Me.

No, Anda.

I blink in the mist, and the rushing force of the water

whips my nightgown around my legs, tangling them. My vision blurs and I look up, seeing Hector's legs kicking. Fifty-two feet away, Agatha is not kicking anymore. She is weeping because she saw Thomas go down with the sailboat. She knows he's lost, and she's mourning him. It's a beautiful thing, her sorrow, but I cannot feed on sorrow. I see Thomas's fight in Hector.

But I see Agatha in me.

I begin to weep.

Hector's legs are kicking less vigorously. He doesn't have the power to dive down to me anymore.

"Anda!" he cries out. "Please!" A wave takes him under again, and this time, he doesn't have the strength to swim up.

The sensations war within me, tearing at my joints and sinews. I scream, for the pain. What have I done. What am I doing.

You are doing what is in your nature.

But no. I'll do what I want. Not what I need.

Anda, no—

I open my eyes in the water. I can feel Mother's fury and disappointment, but at a distance. I release my clawing grip on Agatha, softening the wind and waves about them so she can breathe without a lungful of wet. The *Jenny* is deep on the lake bottom; I have not yet broken her completely. Thomas's body has pulled free of the rope and his corpse is floating with the deeper current toward Grand Portage. I change the water pressure and let the remaining air trapped in the fiberglass hull of the *Jenny* do its job. The boat shoots up like a lost cork to the surface, only feet away from Agatha.

She gasps in surprise. It only takes the smallest effort for her to grab the metal ladder on the side and pull herself up. Her relief resonates as anguish within me.

I relax my hands, and the lake storm untightens its fist, opening up. The distress signal from the *Jenny* is received by the Coast Guard. It will take them at least an hour to find Agatha, but they will find her. I open a passage of rainless clarity between her and the nearest Coast Guard boat.

I release Hector, too. His desperate gasps are terrible to hear. I use an undercurrent to drag him closer to shore — it's painfully fast for him. The minutes unravel to nothing, and I meet him there, barefoot, dripping, with one foot in the world of death and one in the world of the oblivious living. Hector's body lies upon shore and he's coughing and gasping, turning over to pitch the water from his stomach.

You'll be sorry, Anda. This was a mistake.

Not now, I tell Mother. *Not yet.*

The hunger in my bones is partially sated by Thomas's death. It will have to last. Maybe forever.

Not for a witch like you, Anda. Look what happened to your sisters.

I think of my three sisters. The previous witches battled with their half selves, too. But their desire won out until they became wholly inhuman. Their histories are blurred because I've never been told how they began. But somehow, I feel their origin stories in my core. Somehow I know they were once like me, impossibly born of wind and flesh. Now they accompany the storms, three enormous rogue waves that consume ships almost as greedily as I have. Unconsciously, I have been falling into their destiny these last few years. How much time would I have left if I allowed it? Would I wake up and find my corporeal self gone? Would I even have the chance to say good-bye to Father?

My sisters wait for storms, their waves licking in hunger for work to do. Vaguely, I hear them hissing at me.

I ignore them and crouch down by Hector's side. My fingers touch his cold chest, which heaves with effort. He's so alive. It's a beautiful thing to see and touch. His eyes open, wide and wild, and meet mine.

"It's okay," I murmur. "You're going to be all right."

As the wind on the water begins to quiet down, a shadow nears us—a beautiful cloak of dove gray, softer than velvet. Mother is all soft, blurred edges and she touches Hector's forehead sweetly. I wonder if Hector's mother touched him with such tenderness. I don't want Mother so near me. So near him.

Hector's eyes open, and Mother disappears in wisp of moisture.

"Anda," he rasps.

"Yes, Hector," I say. I lean closer.

"Don't ever touch me again."

Chapter Thirty-One

HECTOR

I know what I saw. I know what I have to do.

Anda leans over me, dripping wet. Even now, she's so beautiful that I ache just looking at her. But I know what she is. I saw that old man's face as he was drowning. That man is dead, and Anda killed him. Suddenly, I can't see anything but his screaming face.

I turn to the side and vomit onto the stones of the rain-washed beach.

My body is sodden, and I have an exhaustion I've never experienced in my whole life, not even when I woke up after a night blacked out in my house in Duluth. I sit up, wiping my mouth and groaning. Anda watches me expectantly. Normally, I'd think we needed to get back to the cabin so she won't get chilled. So she won't get sick. But I know now that the whole time I've been worrying about her, it's been a phantom worry.

I'm the one who has something to lose, and I'm not going to lose my life over this…thing.

I stand up, my legs shaking beneath me. "Don't follow

me. Don't talk to me."

She opens her mouth, her eyes large and filling with tears. I wonder if she cries lake water instead of salt. She starts to say something, but I cut her off. "*Don't.*"

Fifty feet away, I find my boots and clothes. I stumble three excruciating miles back to the cabin. I don't look behind me to see if she's following. The truth is, I'm terrified that she will. That she'll be there smiling for me in that cabin, waiting to throw me back into the lake and drown me with a little toss of her head.

God. "This can't be happening," I mutter, but saying it out loud makes it all more real.

By the time I get to the cabin, I can barely stand. Thankfully, she didn't magic herself here somehow. Smoke stains the whitewashed ceiling. The couch is there, lumpy and soft, with the tossed blanket from last night. But I can't rest. I can't. I have to get out of here.

I take off my clammy, damp clothes and put on dry stuff. I find my backpack, and start stuffing all my belongings back in. There isn't much. The few sets of clothing take up most of it. I roll up my sleeping bag tightly. I wish it were thicker. There's my knife, which I attach to my waistband. One half-empty box of camping matches. My fishing gear.

I stand up to head to the kitchen, and white and black stars pop in my vision from dizziness. My mouth is dry and my throat raw and sore from screaming. Nausea hits me every few seconds, probably from having swallowed all that lake water.

Ugh. I gotta focus. *Get out of here, Hector*, I tell myself. *Run. You're good at that.*

I sift through the stuff we stole from the camping store. She probably doesn't even need food—God, it all makes sense, how weird she was about eating. But I shake my head. I'm not a dick, even if I'm going to die soon. I won't take all the food.

I divide the now-very-small pile of camp food and energy bars in half and put my portion in the bag. I fill a bottle with the boiled water we've kept in a big pot on the stove. I take one of the water purifiers and the fuel canisters for the tiny portable stove. She's got a propane tank and a cabin, after all. But the amount of food is laughably small. I could eat it all in one day, easily.

Maybe I can make it to the other side of the island. I'd been planning on going there with Anda, anyway. But now it'll just be me. Surely there's food in the lodge restaurant I can use.

Maybe Anda won't follow me.

Maybe then I can get off this island in a few months, a free adult, free from my uncle.

It's a lot of maybes.

Also, I'm pretty sure that I have a raging fever now.

I'm seriously fucked.

Chapter Thirty-Two

ANDA

I stay in the same position, kneeling on the shore at Middle Point. Mother stays silent—she knows how wrong my choices are. She has a glacial patience and will wait for me to return to my senses.

I will not.

Hours ago, Hector lay before me, alive, his heart beating so loudly in my eardrums, the most magnificent sound in the world. And then he left me.

I had forgotten what sadness meant, and human loss. The ending of one season, of one wolf—it brings about more life. Those endings are beautiful because of what might come next. But the ending of us, of Hector and me... nothing beautiful is born of this.

This is what you wanted. And now you see the consequences. It's not too late—

She's right. I've done this to myself, allowed myself to open a door I thought closed. I've invited in the possibility of an altogether different pain.

I weep, still kneeling on the shore.

Mother is coaxing me back into the water. There will be other boats. The whole month of November is still mine. But she doesn't understand the nature of my keening.

I *want* this agony. I want to know that I can bleed red like Hector. I want to miss biting his lip when we kiss. I want to miss him making me breakfast. I still want to discover the best and worst of him, a little bit every day.

I inhale the lake air hard, and it hurts my lungs. And I cry for the happiness of the pain.

The waves have calmed, not completely, but their energy is diminishing. I know that Agatha is being airlifted into a helicopter, and that boats are patrolling the area for Thomas's body, which they will find soon. I'm swirling the currents above the lake bed, and will lift his remains to the surface so Agatha may mourn her lover. Humans so adore lingering with their dead. I understand they even perfuse their bodies with plastic and preservatives so they can hoard their remains forever.

Finally, it grows dark. I think of Hector. I know he's left the cabin, and he's already on the Greenstone Ridge Trail to the other side of the island. He's trying to flee from me. Satiated on Thomas's death, I can think more clearly now, and my heart—my heart—it chafes and knifes at me on the inside with every beat.

I miss Hector.

But I must respect his wishes. Shouldn't I? We were a story with no happy ending, and deep inside, I knew that. Hector had yet to learn, but he did. And yet I made sacrifices anyway.

Sacrifice.

The word reminds me of another one Hector knows. "Scarify." To create scars. I think of the rounded burns on his arm, and I start crying again.

I miss Hector.

...

When I get to the cabin, it is empty. The ghost of his presence is the only thing lingering behind. His scent on the couch; the soap in the bathroom he probably forgot to pack with him. The food on the kitchen counter has been trifled with; only a portion of it is gone, as well as half of the camping equipment from the store.

But his clothes, his bags, his heart—gone.

I fiddle with the weather radio, but it discusses high pressure and sunshine. Not soothing.

I take the rock cairns from my bedroom and remake them, but their balance doesn't pacify me the way they always have before.

I know what Mother is thinking. It's better this way. Now I have November to myself. I have the cabin. Father will be back December 1 so we can hide on the island together until spring. He will bring with him packages and supplies to keep himself fed and taken care of. As for me, when I've tried not to kill in Novembers past, I've become wilder in some ways. Father says "less predictable," which, for a creature like me, is simple chaos. But maybe I can control this.

There is only one way to know.

I go to the bedroom and take my nightgown off. In the drawer, I pick out the things that Father bought for me. Jeans, a little too tight, but they're the only ones that fit me. A camisole, waffled long underwear, and a flannel button-down on top. Two pairs of wool socks.

I rush around the cabin, whose rafters practically hum with excitement at my activity. It's used to having me sit for hours, meditating on a piece of lint, organizing cairns. Now I'm sweeping all the leftover camp food into a backpack. I stuff other things in there, like scissors and a fish fillet knife sheathed in a kitchen towel. I bring the big flashlight, Father's store of batteries, soap, the remaining water purifier, and every box of matches in the kitchen drawers. Father has a tent rolled up in a sleeve of nylon, and I attach it and a sleeping bag to the back of the backpack.

I try to think like Father. What would he do to care for me? I make one last trip to the bathroom and put in toilet paper and the bottle of castile soap, and open the medicine cabinet. The bottles in there make my nose curl from their bitterness. There are so many that Father has needed—for pain that I never feel, for infections that I never get, for sleeplessness that doesn't bother me. I scoop them up and add them to the bag, too. I put in four tubes of toothpaste and several toothbrushes.

Finally, I root out the radio from its nest by the fireplace. My good friend. It has never been outside these walls, and I wonder what needs it has. Perhaps like other cared objects, like human babies, it might need clothes. I swaddle it in a towel before packing it safely.

At the door, I put on Father's warmest coat, three hats, two scarves, and hiking boots. The enormously heavy pack goes on my back, and I pause before leaving. The wind hisses from the outside. I ignore it.

I sniff the air, deciding on my path. I'll find Hector. And we'll go as far to the interior of the island as we can, away from the water. Mother will be quieter there, and her influence dulled. It will be much harder to tempt me back into the water this way, and I can concentrate on Hector. We've had a conversation that's only just begun. And I'm finding myself anxious, for the first time in my life, to finish it.

The cabin beams at me. It will be lonely without human occupancy, but the door lightly bumps my lumpy backside, as if to say, *Truly, the boy doesn't understand what you've done. What you meant to do. Go fetch him, Anda.*

So I go.

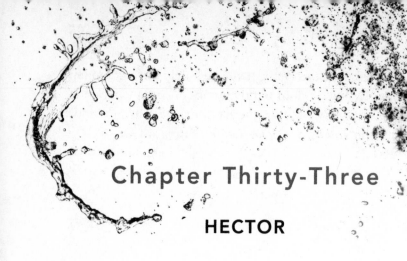

Chapter Thirty-Three

HECTOR

I take the Greenstone Ridge Trail toward the other end of the island, but I feel so awful that I can barely manage two miles before I have to stop and camp. I've already hiked close to six miles since this morning. I've eaten nothing all day. I almost died in the lake. My head is pounding, I'm dizzy and shivering, and my throat feels like I ate a dozen razor blades. I don't know how much more I can take today.

Just off the trail, there's marshland that's too wet to camp in. I look warily up at the gray skies darkening from the coming twilight. If Anda were going to follow me, she'd have found me by now. I'm glad she hasn't. I've tried not to think about her, and that dead guy, but it's impossible. Finally, I find a little area on a rise that should do.

The ground is still wet and it's going to make me miserable, because I don't have a tent. The next formal camping ground is miles away. There might be wooden shelters there that would keep me off the ground, but I'm too exhausted to take another step. I just pray that it doesn't rain tonight.

The wood and sticks around me are drenched. I won't be able to make the roaring fire that my chilled body is desperate for. My hands shake when I set up the tiny camping stove tripod and light the white fuel underneath. I have to start over again when the whole thing falls because one of its tripod legs bent in my bag. The fuel canister spills half its contents onto the mossy ground.

Great.

I try again. This time, it's stable. I put my hands around the flickering bluish-orange flame. It's warm, but I need an oven to get warm, not this tiny stove. I take some water and cook up a packet of freeze-dried chili mac n' cheese. It smells vaguely sour, like rotten cheese and old feet. I'm not hungry, but I have to try to eat.

When it's done cooking, I take a taste. It's actually not that bad, but it's not good, either. I've eaten about half of it when I puke again.

This is not good.

If I can't keep food down, I'll get sicker. I can tell my temperature is higher because I'm shivering like a wet dog. I knew when I came to this island, there might be a chance I'd freeze to death, but not like this. There's some Tylenol in my bag, and I pop that.

I get into my sleeping bag, boots and all, ten feet away from the messy, splattered pile of Hector puke. My teeth bang against each other like saved pennies in a jar. My mind is in a million places at once. What if I don't make it to Rock Harbor, the most likely place I'll find more supplies? What if Anda finds me and decides to drag me into the lake and finish me off? What if my uncle is out there right now, searching for me with the police?

I can't go back.

I refuse.

I need to focus. I need to shut everything out.

The knife is still at my waistband, and I unsheathe it after a few fumbling attempts. Luckily, I don't need steady hands for this. Good thing, since both my arms are trembling from the effort. My heart races in anticipation. I touch the blade to my left arm, near my oldest cigarette burns.

The pain is white-hot before it turns to a pulsating burn. My heart goes so fast that my eyes blur. The line of red on skin becomes harder to focus on. The knife drops to the damp soil next to me.

There is nothing but the pain.

It is a relief to have nothing but this one pure thing.

Chapter Thirty-Four

ANDA

It's dark when I find him.

He's lying in a sleeping bag just twenty feet off the Greenstone Ridge trail. The rank odor of regurgitated sick issues from nearby. The moon is low, rising quickly, as if to warn me that I don't have much time. His backpack is open, its contents spilled out messily. Hector is not messy by nature. In our cabin, he left things in neat piles, always very careful not to leave traces of himself behind. It was the actions of the fearful, keeping himself restricted and contained for the sake of survival.

And then I see the blood.

Hector is lying faceup, his knife a few inches away from his open fingertips. The edge of the blade is darkened, and dried blood crusts on the skin of his exposed arm. A line seven inches long runs from midwrist up to the crook of his elbow. The blood rivulets show that the cut was deep.

No. Not again.

I drop to my knees next to him in the darkness, the rain-drenched soil seeping moisture through my jeans. His unconsciousness is so deep that his eyes are unmoving beneath closed eyelids, and he does not stir when I touch his face. The blood on his arm is dried. He stopped bleeding some time ago. His skin scalds with fever, but his hands are icy cold. I slip my hand under his shirt, against his chest. His heart patters against his rib cage, a hummingbird's *tap-tap-tap*. It doesn't beat with potency anymore.

I don't know why I didn't see it before, but the island has taken its toll. Since the first day on the ferry, he's lost a lot of weight, maybe fifteen or twenty pounds. His cheekbones are sharper angles, his arms more spare and wiry. Malnutrition is making his skin color uneven, and there are ridges at the base of his nails.

The island has been consuming him.

I've been consuming him, and I couldn't see for my hunger.

I made my choice in the water hours ago. I won't have this happen. I'm used to getting my way, even with the alterations that Father has begged me for. But this time, it's different. In turning my back on that part of myself, I have to do things differently. Hector's way. Father's way.

My heart starts to hammer inside my chest, almost as fast as Hector's, because I have to fix him. I don't have brews and potions, like the fairy tales say I do. I only know the natural order of things. Chaos. Disintegration. Rebirth.

I glance at the metal camping things near Hector's tent; my mind goes blank. I don't know what they are or what to do with them. Metal and mechanical things, if they're not meant to be sunk, are not part of my language.

I rummage inside my pack and pull out bottle after bottle from our medicine cabinet.

Aspirin, 325 mg

Amoxicillin-Clavulanate, 875 mg/125 mg

Omeprazole, 20 mg
Triamterene-Hydrochlorothiazide, 37.5 mg/25 mg

I don't know what any of them are or what they treat. I look at Hector, whose breathing has become more shallow even as I watch him. I look at the orange pill bottles whose tops I can't manage to pry off, and the cooking camp set I don't know how to use.

For the first time in my life, I am terrified.

It takes a while to make the fire. I don't bother with the mysterious metal instruments for cooking. Instead, I gather several short branches, pile them together, and concentrate. I pull the moisture away until the wood becomes brittle, and then light a match to the curly pieces of bone-dry bark. A little wind gives the flames something to inhale, and soon the fire is crackling. I put a bowlful of water and salty beef soup powder on the center of the fire, upon two thick branches that won't burn through quickly. When the soup boils, I let the air flow calm so the heat is steady. The smoke rises, and I make sure that the wind tows it away from our camp.

Hector still doesn't stir. Food alone won't help him, not with this fever. I decide that the pill bottle labeled "amoxicillin-clavulanate" must be an antibiotic, because it sounds like penicillin—a fungus-grown medicine. It makes sense to me. So many things in nature will kill other things to survive. How clever to use that viciousness to fight other wars.

I smash the pill bottle open because the top refuses to be pried off. It says "PUSH AND TWIST" but nothing I do makes it budge. It says childproof. It is witchproof, too, apparently. It says to take one pill every twelve hours. I take one chalky tablet and crush it to a powder using a titanium spoon, then mix in a portion of the broth.

"Hector," I whisper. He's still quite a bit larger than me, but I manage to pull him into my lap so his head is slightly raised. "Hector, drink this."

His eyelids flutter, then shut. I take a spoonful of the liquid with the pulverized medicine and try to pour a few drops into his slightly opened mouth. It goes in. He doesn't swallow. I pour a little more in. This time, he gags, coughs, sputters. He grimaces at the bitterness, but he swallows some of it. I wipe his chin and try again. Some of it ends up in his stomach.

A few hours later, when the moon is high overhead, I give him the rest. This time, he actually holds a trembling hand to the cup and drinks the whole cupful down thirstily before sagging back into my arms.

When the sun rises, I take a cloth and wipe down his face. His breath is rank, and a sickness seems to ooze from his pores when he sweats, but his heart is beating ever so slightly slower. I give him another half cupful of medicated soup. He drinks most of it this time, followed by water. The clouds linger overhead, watching us, but I shoo them away. When night comes again, he will have gotten three doses of medicine. I suspect it's working, simply because Hector isn't dead. At least, not yet.

I eat and drink, too, because I must do something about my growling stomach and dry throat. We are down to only three granola bars and one packet of freeze-dried chicken stew, but I try not to think of what this means.

On the second morning, he wakes without me urging him to drink. His eyes are not as sunken into his orbits as they were yesterday, and his lips are peeling. The cut arm has a proud scab covering the wound now. There is a slight bloom to his cheeks that wasn't there before, and it's not because of fever.

"Hector," I say.

"Where am I?" he rasps, blinking sleepily.

"Here, with me."

His lips tighten and stretch, either a grimace or grin, I can't tell. The result is that his bottom lip cracks and a bead of red forms. Perhaps I answered the question wrong. He winces, and my nostrils flare at the scent of blood, but I push away the longing within.

"Anda…"

"I know you said never to touch you. But you were sick."

"I…"

"And I know that you don't want to be with me, but I wanted to help."

He struggles to sit up. I'm afraid to read his face and his revulsion, what he must think of me. He blinks hard, trying to reconcile himself to being upright instead of prone for so many hours.

I was terrified of losing him thirty-six hours ago. Now I find that I'm terrified of the words he's about to say. He exhales, as if there's too much already to be said. Weariness holds his shoulders down. After a few minutes, he finally speaks.

"Anda…"

"Yes, Hector." I look at him expectantly.

"I really have to piss."

Chapter Thirty-Five

HECTOR

It's not the most glamorous thing to say when you wake up in the arms of a stunning girl. A girl who does unspeakable things.

Anda leaves me so I can stagger to some trees and relieve myself. When I stagger back, I'm more than happy to be lying down again. My head swims and my mouth tastes like a dead fish, but I'm alive. Barely.

I close my eyes, and she sighs, as if relieved that I'm going back to sleep. But I can't let it go.

"You sank that ship, didn't you?" I say quietly.

She's quiet for a long time. I wait. I have nothing but time, after all. Finally, she whispers her answer.

"Yes."

"And that man, you drowned him."

Another long pause. "Yes."

"There was another person in the water, an old lady. What happened to her?"

"I let her survive. The Coast Guard rescued her."

My eyes quickly snap to her face, searching. "You did?

Why?"

Several emotions flit over her face. Panic is the overriding one. But sadness and confusion are there, too. Her mouth opens to answer, but she says nothing, instead picking up an aluminum mug at her side. "You should drink more water, Hector. It will make you feel well."

I sag back onto my sleeping bag. There are a lot of things I want to say, but right now, none of them include asking Anda to go away. I love being alive too much for that. And as much as she may be a monster of some sort, she can't completely devalue life, right? After all, she just saved this pathetic one.

The last time I got this sick was five years ago. Strep was going around and gave me a raging fever and throat that killed so bad, I couldn't swallow anything solid. Dizziness forced me to stay in bed for days. I remember being fed oatmeal from a spoon. I remember the taste of the nasty, bubble gum–flavored antibiotic syrup, and my uncle on the phone with the pediatrician every day. He took a week off from work to make sure I didn't croak.

I remember these things, but I don't want to. Because it makes me feel like I'm doing something really wrong by running from him. But I have to run. All the other memories tell me to.

In the next few hours, my fever returns along with that warped feeling in my brain. Anda makes me take an antibiotic pill and offers me bites of a granola bar between her fingers. There's an aluminum cup of hot water, too.

I take the pill, but when she offers the food, I don't open my mouth. I don't touch the mug of steaming liquid.

Her face contorts with confusion, corrupted within my fever. It's a grimace. Before Anda, I refused to take drinks or food from people. I didn't trust them. Now I can't trust her anymore.

"It's only food, Hector."

But I turn away, feeling the sweat drip off my temples.

Anda leans closer. "It's not poisoned. Poisoning is complicated. There are far easier ways to kill people." She looks down. "I won't do that. It's why I'm here. I came to help you and to get away from her."

Her. I don't know who she's talking about, but I can sense that she means what she says.

"I don't want to kill, Hector," she says. "Not anymore."

"I'm not afraid of dying," I whisper, eyeing the mug of water.

"I know that. So what are you afraid of?"

I close my eyes.

M y body is such a damned sellout. I get so delirious that eventually, I don't turn away the food.

I'm so used to taking care of myself. Of making my own dinners (frozen, but still), of earning money, of making my own scars. Being completely cared for is altogether alien. And wonderful. And awful, all at the same time. Awful, because it doesn't seem real, or that it will last. I keep thinking that at any moment, this will all disappear, and I'll be back in Duluth.

Or that I'll be back in that lake.

I dream of weird things. I see my father, my uncle, and my mother, all discussing me while sitting around the fireplace. When I yell at them to shut the fuck up, they ignore me. Even in my dreams, some things don't change.

Anda wipes the sweat from my face and chest. She's

dressed in filthy jeans and a sweatshirt big enough for a linebacker. There are smudges of mud in her white hair. It doesn't matter. Funny how clothes and hair only matter when you don't know someone, when they're all you have to judge someone on.

The silvery color in her irises is muted, maybe because it's dark now. Her eyes concentrate on me and are small with worry. I miss that wide-eyed look she had before. Care and concern have brought her back to earth. She's closer to me now, and yet something is missing, too.

I remember once flying a kite in school, the day before summer vacation started at the end of fourth grade. It was sunny and gorgeous, and the June wind was strong. My science teacher took us out to fly kites, and he'd flown a red-and-orange butterfly kite up in the sky when he handed me the string. The wind began to die down, and I had to reel it in more and more to keep the tension strong so it would stay aloft. But all the while, I was desperate to hold that kite in my hands, to feel the balsam wood parts that kept those wings wide and stiff, and to touch that fluttering tail of red and orange stripes.

Before long, it was in my hands. That kite was incredible to hold, but I was acutely aware that half its beauty was gone now that it wasn't flying anymore.

"You're the kite," I tell Anda. Like it's obvious that she should know what the hell I'm talking about. She looks at me quizzically, and then understanding shadows her face.

"Yes."

She rubs my back, as she's often done since I've been sick. It reminds me of my mother. When I was ill, she'd do the same thing—rub my back in endless, comforting circles. No matter how cold our apartment was, or how sad she was, her hand was always warm and strong. It showed the strength of her love. But it wasn't stronger than other things, like hate. And fear.

During my few wakeful moments, I catch Anda staring out at the horizon with longing. Like she actually wishes the gales were back, or that she could run back into the lake and sink more ships. I don't understand why anyone would crave that kind of awful. Then again, I have my own scars to prove their worth.

"You want what's possible," I say to her, inside one of my fever dreams. Or am I awake? I can't tell. The fir trees wave merrily above us, or maybe dancing in anticipation of our doom. It must be nighttime, until I realize that my eyes are closed. "Pain is so easy. It's what we do best."

"Yes, Hector," she says. "Yes."

Little by little, I get better.

I wake up one morning, the most clearheaded I've been since I got sick. Anda is squatting by the campfire, cooking something. And in my memory, I can clearly see that boat sinking, and that lady screaming in the water when it pulled the man into the depths.

"Why did you do it?" I ask.

She stops stirring but won't meet my eye. She knows exactly what I'm asking. There's silence for a long time.

"I needed it. It was part of me," she explains.

"Can you really stop?"

She goes back to stirring the pot on the fire, and her eyes well up. "I'm trying now." And then another long silence. "If I try hard enough, will you still run away from me?"

I imagine what it would be like to have a lover kill for you. It's asking the unaskable. And I realize that's what Anda is doing, only the opposite. Maybe it's just as awful, though in my world, it's so obviously right.

I look down at my arms. They're starting to heal again, a process that circles around to a fresh cut, inevitably. I'm so damn sick of inevitability. Anda stares at me, with patience, not expectation. It gives me enough energy to tell her, "I'll try if you try."

She smiles shyly at me. "All right," she says.

The more I improve, the worse off I realize we are.

Two days later, before dawn and after a long and deliriously good night of sleep, I look around. Peachy-gold colors the horizon, slowly brightening the sky. A yawn nearly cracks my head in half, and I sit up and stretch before groaning. My whole body feels creaky and very, very old. Geriatric at seventeen. Excellent.

Anda is taking a bowl of something off the campfire a few feet away. The embers crackle and snap; the scent of smoke is soothing. She offers me an antibiotic pill, and then a sip of hot, steaming, delicious…water?

For the first time in however many days I've been sick, I'm ravenous.

"Do we have anything else to eat?" I ask.

She shakes her head. Her hair is really dirty. Mud is caked on a few locks, and some twigs have tangled in there, too. She must have been sleeping on the bare ground.

"None?"

"None."

I think for a minute. "How far away are we from Rock Harbor?" I ask her.

"About thirty miles."

I pause, and her eyes say exactly what I'm feeling. Fear. Isle Royale might kick our asses in a very un-royal way.

Chapter Thirty-Six

ANDA

Hector moves slowly, but he's only able to walk in small bursts that day. Without food, we can't go too far. Washington Creek is a short hike away, and I can sense the cool slither of life, sinuous in the water. Much of the green around us is dulling to a brown in anticipation of winter. The urn-shaped flowers of the bog rosemary have all disappeared, and the carnivorous sundew have retreated into their sleeping buds for winter.

Water is dangerous for me to be around. Temptation simmers in the liquid, its connection with other living things that ought not to be aquatic. Boats. Humans, especially. But luckily this little stream is hardly a danger. I am relieved that we are planning on hiking the Greenstone Ridge Trail to the other side of the Isle Royale. In the center of this island, I'm least tempted by the lure of the lake, by Mother's influence.

Hector shows me how to cast the fishing rod a few times, and then I practice while he rests on a rise of drier land. He lacks confidence that we'll catch anything, but we must.

Thirty miles of hiking will take several days, especially in Hector's state. He must eat.

The lure plops into the trickling water, and I gently urge the undulating water to tickle a trout from beneath a deep stone toward the dancing rubber worm. I yank on the rod with a jerk, responding more to my own knowledge than the nibbles on the line.

With a spray of silver water, the fish lurches out of stream and arcs over my head. It lands squirming and wriggling beneath the shadows of an ash tree. Hector gasps with surprise, then jumps up to grasp the fish in his hands, deftly removing the hook. He strings a forked stick through its gills. It's only just over a pound.

"Wow. That was pretty lucky."

I smile. It has nothing to do with luck, but he'll figure that out soon enough.

Within twenty minutes, we have four fish. Hector's look of surprise is replaced by awe, then relief.

"Looks like we won't starve after all," he says, holding up the catch of trout.

I beam at him.

We eat trout, pike, and perch for breakfast, lunch, and dinner. Not to my liking, but the fish do their job. Hector gains strength back slowly, though not with the vigor he'd had when he first set foot on the island.

The weather is strange as we walk eastward on the Greenstone Ridge Trail. At times the wind tries to sting my face, and when I rebuke it, it listens to my commands less and less. Usually, the weather and the lake move through me, or I move through them, just as they do with Mother. It's hard to discern. There is a word for it in physics: *resonance*. When an external force (me) drives another system (the weather, the lake) to something far larger.

But ever since I kissed this boy, ever since I decided to stop taking lives, the weather has become an altogether separate entity, chiding me. Pleading. Punishing me. It's acting like a castaway lover. I'm finding that I can't prevent the wind from roughly slapping at our backs. I'm losing my grip.

There are other signs, too. Dead birds show up on the trail, sometimes denuded of feathers, sometimes with their eye sockets eaten away by vermin that ought to be dead or insensate this time of year. We see anemones and columbine blossoming as if it were May, not November. And the radio tells me tales of rogue waves hitting shipping vessels on the calm, clear days recently. My sisters are not happy with my decision, either. I'm spending so much energy keeping my hunger at bay that the island is suffering.

It's not the only one suffering, though.

My body hungers for loss. Letting Agatha go free, and Hector, too—it's taken a toll. Weakness snakes into my limbs, wearing me down. I think through the shipwrecks dotting the island shoals, like memories of past desserts savored: the *Emperor*, *Chester Congdon*, *America*, *Algoma*, *Glenlyon*, *Monarch*, *Cumberland*, *Henry Chisolm*, *George M. Cox*, *Kamloops*…the list is a nautical graveyard lullaby for my dark heart.

As I walk, the quiet sounds of nature don't soothe; they warble noisily in my ears. The dulcet whispers of the wind grate on me. I've never felt the weakness of thigh muscles and knees, or the need for oxygen, and I'm becoming a servant to them. I need nourishment to keep my energy up. And yet roasted campfire fish and endless cups of spruce tip tea don't bring the same energy that I need. It's a fire made from paper, instead of a good, seasoned, hardwood log. It burns fierce and bright, leaving me with nothing but ash far too quickly.

It takes all my concentration to keep the wind from pushing us too harshly, and to keep the ambient temperature around Hector level. It's actually far colder than forty-five, with the wind, but he can't tolerate that in his state. Later, it will be harder to keep him safe while we sleep, but I'll have to try.

I understand. But I had to let your father go. You will have to let go, too, or it will be your undoing.

What Mother doesn't understand is that I toy with the idea of my undoing. What would it feel like to be utterly unraveled? I imagine that it would be terrible and beautiful at the same time, but that in the end, I would disappear like a rising ember into a night sky.

I fear oblivion.

Instead, I focus on what I can. It takes every effort to keep the wind and low temperatures at bay around the two of us. I remember the taste of Hector on my tongue. I watch his lean, sturdy legs climb in front of me. And I start asking questions, because I'm finding that his voice is a balm for me.

"What's your favorite color?" I begin.

"Gray. Because depending on how you look at it, it can be every color."

"Have you ever broken a bone?"

"Three. My left fibula, my left pinkie, and my right collarbone."

I surreptitiously lick my lips. I love bones. Broken ones, especially.

"Tell me about your father," I say.

He stops walking and turns to me. His eyes glitter, and not in a merry way. He says nothing, just searches my face—for what, I don't know. Maybe he thinks that knowledge comes with a price.

"I will tell you about mine," I add.

Hector turns his back to me and wordlessly continues walking.

He stays silent for the next three hours.

We take a break every thirty minutes, taking a few bites of dry roasted fish or a long drink of water, and stare in opposite directions. Normally, I can live with silence for vast amounts of time. But the quiet between us is a thick, sticky thing.

When we hit Sugar Mountain (for the first time since I was five, I am disappointed that sugar doesn't await us in glistening, snowy piles), we're too tired to go farther. Island Mine campsite is nearby, and we unload our packs. Hector puts up the tent, though it takes a half a dozen grimaces, a few growls of frustration, and two "fucks" to get it right. I thought doing such normal things would come naturally to anybody but me. I'm finding that I am not the only person who isn't loved by the trappings of even semicivilized life.

It's not a good thing to learn, really.

Hector lights the portable stove (ah, so that's how you do it) and boils a canister full of chicken noodle soup. He'd found a lone packet hidden at the bottom of his bag, and whooped in triumph at its discovery. I'm fascinated by it, now that I have a moment to consider what it is. First it was a chicken, then murdered and plucked, then cooked, pulverized and dried into powder with desiccated onion and chives, but now reconstituted back to brothy life. Hector eyes me skeptically as I attack the globs of powder sticking to the sides of the cooking can with an aluminum spork. He sets out a few strips of roasted pike with the skin still on, bubbled and crisp. The sun is departing past the horizon and it's growing colder. Cloud cover quickly spreads over the rest of the inky sky, blotting out the moonrise. Hector feels the chill. I'm so tired, and it's taken a lot of effort to battle the wind.

The wind is not your enemy, Anda.

I turn away from the south and face north. My movements are an insult, I know. I watch the simmering soup instead. The flames licking the bottom of the boiling can are lovely. I wish I could eat them, or wear them like starflowers in my hair.

"Tomorrow we'll reach Lake Desor. I can try to fish then," Hector says.

"There's no fish in Lake Desor."

"Well…" Hector studies a map. "Uh, Hatchet Lake then."

"There's no fish in Hatchet Lake."

He stares at me, waiting. For what?

"So what lakes have fish?" he asks, huffing. I know this tone. I've heard it before in Father's voice. I believe it is called exasperation.

"Ahmik, Angleworm, Beaver, Benson, Chickenbone, Dustin, Epidote, Eva, Feldtmann, Forbes—"

"Basically, every other lake except the two I mentioned." I nod.

He shakes his head. What have I done wrong?

We slurp the salty soup as nighttime takes a stronger hold. I don't like the soup nearly as much as candy. I should like more sweet things. I wonder if consuming a pound of chocolate in a day is bad for a body. Surely not. I am, however, happy that the granola bars are gone. They tasted like pinecones glued together with sap. And it's dark, so dark.

Hector goes about carefully tossing away the fish remains far from camp. "I don't want the foxes or wolves to come near our stuff," he explains, when he sees me watching curiously.

"They won't come."

"How can you be so sure?"

I glance over my shoulder into the depths between the trees. I listen for the moose, the wolves, the foxes. Nothing. "They always stay away from me."

At this, Hector stops rinsing his hands with water. "Why?" he asks quietly.

"They don't like me."

I put my palm flat on the ground, near some browned strawberry leaves and tangled grasses. The soil around my hand trembles, the little clots of dirt shaking as if a tiny earthquake has hit. Worms and centipedes and pill bugs erupt out of the soil, fleeing in an outward wave, desperate to get away.

Hector's eyes are large with astonishment.

My father's home is not hermetically sealed from the outside, but not a single spider or ant ever trespasses. There are no cobwebs in the corners, and it's not because of my nonexistent immaculate cleaning.

"Did you learn to do that?" he asks.

I shake my head.

"Can you...not do it?" he tries again.

"I don't know. It's hard to not be myself. When I try, bad things happen. Up until now, I forgot that there was more than this one part of myself."

This time, Hector nods. "Tell me about it." He chuckles, but he's not happy. "I've been half of something my whole life. Too Korean or too American. Too Black, or not Black enough. It gets exhausting sometimes."

"What do you do?" I'm desperate to know.

"Oh, there's no good answer. I try to stop forcing myself into neat little boxes that people want to corner me in. They never stop trying, though." He shifts uncomfortably. "It never feels right when I try to ignore half of what I am."

I nibble my rough cuticles. Boxes. I think of what it's like to place parts of myself in them. My need to shatter, submerge, bleed. I think of how my warring sides of agony and relief bring more balance to the seasons. How that balance only happens when I allow myself the mercy of death, every November. How I weep for weeks in springtime, when living things on the island emerge to exist with excruciating pain, only to be relieved by death.

And then I think about licking butter off my fingertips. Of melting chocolate on the roof of my mouth. The delight of Hector's weight crushing me when we tumbled in the cabin that bashfully regarded us. I look at Hector's handsome, worried face and think of his hungered kisses—a completely idiosyncratic human action that means nothing in the clockwork of nature. His kisses had been an opiate for me—the girl, Anda Selkirk—and I returned them just as ravenously.

Can I redraw a line that's cut me in two for so long?

"Look, I'm no expert. I'm still trying to figure it all out," Hector says after a minute of silence. "So what are you fighting, exactly? I don't understand."

"If I told you, you would run away again." I frown. The insects and worms have since left the earth around me and once again, I'm alone. I can't stand the idea of Hector leaving, too. "I'm so tired," I say. "I'm not used to being tired."

Hector pauses. "You said you'd tell me a fairy tale sometime. This is what you were talking about, wasn't it?"

"Yes." I hesitate. "I'll tell you mine, if you tell me yours."

Hector bristles at my words. He turns away from me and goes to the tent. "I'm pretty tired, too."

I furrow my brow. His words have no relationship to my last words.

Ah. This is evasion.

I stand up and crawl inside the shelter. It's so small, this tent. It's a nylon tomb. Next to Hector, the whole sides of our bodies might touch. But there is only one sleeping bag here. A small clip light hangs from the peak in the roof, casting a dim glow inside. I look up at him, and he's poised to walk away.

"Listen," he says. "It's not as cold as I thought it would be. So I'll sleep outside, and you can sleep inside."

Oh. Sometimes, I'm too good at what I do. I loosen my fist, ever so gently. The wind picks up immediately and brings with it the real temperature I've kept at bay, somewhere around thirty degrees of good, late October Isle weather. It hits Hector square in the back and he shivers violently.

"Whoa. Brrrr. Holy cheezits, where did that come from?"

I open the door to the tent a little wider and smile. "Come in. There's just enough room for the two of us."

Wicked witch, I am.

Chapter Thirty-Seven

HECTOR

She can't possibly be inviting me in for that. Memories issue forth, as if they happened a million years ago— from the first night we kissed. A lot of kissing. Is this what she's inviting me in for? Turns out, what she wants is way more intimate.

She wants me to talk.

She'd asked me about my dad while we were walking. And now that we're squished in side by side, she asks again. "Tell me about your father."

I don't know why she cares. All I know is that the reason I'm here is so that I can leave him, my uncle, and my mother behind. Far, far behind. I can choose to talk about them on my own terms, or never ever again. Which is why I'm pissed that she's insisting on this. I don't want to be the thing that distracts her from herself. I don't want to be the magical, broken boy who heals all her own problems. Maybe it'd be better to be in the freezing cold out there.

I stare at the tent seams, being puffed tight by the wind outside. "Why do you want to know?"

"I don't know," she says, which is also infuriating. Satisfying her idle curiosity is not my responsibility. I already told her enough as it is, about how I'm constantly feeling torn by who and what I am. I cross my arms and close my eyes, hoping she'll drop it, when she says, "No, I do know. Because you're wearing this thing, like a cloak. It's so heavy. Sometimes, it looks like you can't even breathe."

Silence, and then...

I exhale loudly.

The silence cracks with hoots and laughs, from both of us. After we catch our breaths, she sighs.

"I won't hurt you." She pauses and thinks. "I won't hurt you like *that*," she adds. God. What does she mean? That she won't tear me to pieces or drown me in my sleep? Or psychologize me to death? She closes her eyes. "I'm sorry. I've no right to ask. I've no right." She turns onto her side to face me, and the curve of her hip makes her sleeping bag rise in the middle. She uses her hands, palms together, as a pillow. Just like a child. "Good night, Hector."

"Good night, Anda."

Her breathing becomes regular, and I feel the warmth of her body next to mine, while the bitter cold seeps in through the wall of the tent on the other side. A weird gradient of death and life.

And in the middle of it is me. One guy, trapped on an island with a beautiful girl who's willingly one millimeter away, and he's just given her the emotional Heisman for the night.

I suck.

"Come with me."

"Wha—?"

I only now realize I finally did fall asleep. It's still dark out. Pitch-black. Anda is nudging my ribs insistently and tugging at my wrist.

"Come," she says again. "The clouds are leaving. I want to show you something."

My body feels like it's been squashed by a Mack truck. My legs are sore, and I'm still so exhausted. After all, I'm barely over being sick, and we just hiked all day. But Anda won't take no for an answer. She tugs and tugs, and I wipe my sleep-heavy eyes and crawl out of the tent, groaning. She leads me slightly out of the campground to a higher elevation. She's taking me to the peak of Sugar Mountain at what, midnight?

"Look," she says. Her head is back and she's gazing at the sky. I look, too, but it's still wispy with a film of gray.

"It's cloudy."

"Oh, wait."

She sweeps her arm overhead, as if she were polishing the sky with her palm. When I look up again, it's clear. Holy shit, not just clear.

A wave of incandescent green and purple is smeared across the sky in a thick ribbon.

"Is that…?"

"Yes. The aurora borealis. It's caused by a collision of solar wind and magnetospheric-charged particles in the thermosphere."

"Right. *That*."

"Have you ever seen one?"

"Once," I say. "When I was a kid."

We just stare at the unearthly color for a long, long time. She slips her fingers into mine, and I tighten my grip on her hand. It's so small, so thin. She shivers a little, and I pull her closer. Seeing this thing reminds me of how alone

I am. Of how alone I could be, if I wanted.

Out of the corner of my eye, I see the aurora shift. It reaches the horizon, and the ribbon of color changes just so. It looks like a figure, standing on the edge of the universe.

It's absolutely stunning.

I glance at Anda, wide-eyed, giving her an *Are you seeing what I'm seeing* look.

Anda sees it. She frowns. It's not beautiful to her, whatever it is. When I look back, it's just the same thick ribbon of light in the sky again. I rub my eyes. What the hell?

"Did you—" I begin, but she cuts me off.

"It's getting colder. You're tired. We should go back."

We crawl back into the tent. It doesn't seem quite as cold now, so we lie on top of our sleeping bags. Anda throws her leg casually over mine and closes her eyes, once again using her sandwiched hands as a pillow. I watch her until her breaths come shallow and regular. She's dead asleep.

I wait for what feels like another ten or fifteen minutes, just watching her. Her eyelashes are a dark fringe, and her eyeballs zigzag occasionally as her slumber deepens. I wonder what she dreams of. Then again, maybe I don't want to know.

I take a few huge, deep breaths. And then I whisper, "My father is six feet, four inches tall. He loves sportfishing, building model airplanes, and criticizing Hollywood war movies." I lower my voice. "And he hates that I was ever born."

Anda doesn't move. She's still unconscious, and I don't know whether to be glad or sad that she didn't hear me. But just as I start to drift off, I take one last sleepy glance at her face and see something shiny.

A wet streak on her face. And yet she's still sleeping. How odd.

I don't wake her.

Chapter Thirty-Eight

ANDA

Something in him broke open that night. I felt it as I slept. As we continue to hike the Greenstone Ridge that day, we barter back and forth. I tossed him the first morsel, climbing the dirt trail flanked by browning ferns. Casual as it seemed, I had aimed with a sure hand.

"My father was born in Canada, of Scottish and Spanish descendants. He came to the Isle in his forties. He met my mother and fell in love."

And then Hector, tentative at first, offered this.

"He sends me one letter every six months. He always uses a fountain pen with blue ink."

Every taste of information, I swallow whole. I start to know the seams of his life, the scents and textures of what it means to be cinched into his skin. His favorite cigarettes (Pall Mall, because they were always at the corner store near his mother's apartment in Seoul). How he thinks macaroni and cheese has the unfortunate texture of glue. How he hates his thick, unruly curly hair.

The only things he seems to like are those most likely

to kill him. I neglect to say that the things I like are the ones most likely to kill everyone else.

Sometimes the truths we shared were half hidden. Like mine.

"Father's fingernails are always dirty. He hates to kill fish. He always forgives me." But I don't tell him what I'm being forgiven for. And Hector hides, too.

"He refuses to discipline me."

Then who does?

"He trusts my uncle."

But Hector doesn't.

"He thinks he's a good parent."

He's ruined this boy.

In Hector, there is something bitter, oily, and bubbling deeper below. A poison that he hasn't mentioned yet. Neglect only partly injures; it's what takes its place and fills the void that defines the impact. It has bloomed in the scars of his arms. I'm afraid to touch them, because I fear the familiarity. There's a darkness that simmers deep within me, too.

Three days into our hike, Hector fishes in one of the streams off the trail. I think of his scars. In the shade of some spindly red oaks, I watch him cast and bring in our lunch. He motions for me to wait, so I squat under the shade and regard the knife he left there with his other tackle.

It is a large blade, with a jagged, toothy edge near the hilt for sawing branches. The tip is getting a little dull from usage. Perhaps it isn't sharp enough. I push my palm against the edge to test it.

"Stop!" Hector rushes up to me, his face distraught. He's tossed the fish and gear behind him. "What are you doing?"

This upsets Hector. I should stop. I move to drop the

blade, but in standing up, the jagged edge skitters against my wrist by accident.

The pain is sharp, almost an itching sensation. I watch the red seep through the thin line, brighter than the bunchberry clusters by the trails in the summer. It's beautiful, the scarlet against my smudged skin. Life, rising up against all odds. It is destruction and creation, all at once. And then I understand something that I didn't understand before. I drop the knife to the moss. Hector kneels at my side.

"It's only a shallow cut. It'll heal okay," he says.

"I know."

He rinses the cut with clean water from his bottle, which stings. Hector stays quiet afterward. He's troubled by my small wound.

It makes him think of himself.

Hector and I don't speak of my cut for the rest of our trip. We've been dancing around the darkness of ourselves this whole time, like fingertips over a flame, promising a burn but always just out of reach. But not for long.

I'm learning this now. The less of myself exerted on the lake and the island, the more they fill the void—asking, needing, wanting. And lately, acting. The next morning, I sit down after breakfast and tune in to the NOAA weather station on the little radio.

Temperatures dropping to thirty degrees or less

Storm-force winds are expected, with winds forty knots or above

Very high seas on the coastal waters

I did not know about this storm coming within two days. It's a big one. And it frightens me that I'm being kept in the dark now. I've seen other signs, too, that Hector's all-too-human eyes haven't. Ruddy *Russula* mushrooms sprouting monstrously from a dead fox that was perfectly healthy and shouldn't be dead. Blue flag irises growing when the temperature is dropping. Splashes of warm summer rain in the middle of a night with freezing temperatures. And a murder of ravens—bare-fleshed, tangled in the skeletons of black ash trees.

This is all my fault. But this is what I wanted. It is what I chose, isn't it?

"I guess we better hike a little faster," Hector comments casually, but concern fills his eyes. The sky is thankfully still benign, with a loose, stippled pattern of clouds in the troposphere. "Those don't look very dangerous," he says, pointing.

Mother enjoys making these for me. She knows how I love them.

"Altocumulus *stratiformis translucidus undulatus*," I tell him.

"Gesundheit? I'm sorry, what?"

I smile. "You're right. Those clouds won't bother us." Though the sky is everywhere, I can't help but feel like it's trying to sneak up on me.

Hector and I don't need to be told that a flimsy tent is not much shelter in a storm. At night, we cling to each other for very unsentimental reasons. He hasn't kissed me since before his illness. We have, however, been chilled to the bone. Over the last two days, the cold has been seeping in through the protective wall I keep around us. Like water dripping inevitably between the crevices of a cupped hand, it finds its way through.

I know now that it is the inevitable result of being more human. There is so much less under my control. How do humans stand being tossed about so by nature, like ants in a deluge? And here I am, becoming one of those ants now.

It would be better if I could speak to Mother about this, but we'd both know what I was asking for. Bargaining. You can't bargain with such things. Trees and clouds and lakes make no exceptions, ever, for anyone.

Finally, we are only hours away from reaching Rock Harbor, our destination. Hiking along Tobin Harbor's rocky trail, we're filthy, hungry, and exhausted. Our limbs have hardened from the walking but are slimmer and sparer, like spindly, strong moose legs.

"I can't wait to find out what the camp store there has," Hector comments. "I'd be happy if I never saw another roasted fish for the rest of my life. But I guess we'll find enough packaged food to last until May."

"Why May?"

"That's when I turn eighteen. It's when the first ferry comes back here. No one will be looking for me then. My uncle can't claim me as his foster kid anymore. I'll be an adult. I'll be free."

He says it so simply, without restraint. He's forgotten that he never told me this plan. The world shrinks down and becomes very, very small. It takes Hector a full minute to realize that I've stopped walking.

He jogs back to me and searches my face. "Hey. Hey. Are you okay?"

I look up. "You're leaving the island."

"Well, yeah. I can't live here forever. Neither can you. We're barely surviving, and we could be arrested if they find us here, anyway. I'm leaving as soon as I can catch a ferry back to the mainland." He adds, only too late, "We can go together. If you want."

"I can't leave."

"Sure you can."

"My father…" I gesture helplessly. "The island…" I add,

which doesn't help.

"Well, how old are you? Do you have to stay with him?" And then it arrives, the question he's been holding carefully, ever since I first saw him on the island. "What are you doing here?"

How do I answer this, if at all? It takes a monumental effort to push the air past my throat, shape the words like clay through my teeth, under my soft palate. I should be thankful he didn't stop at *what are you.*

"I have to be here."

"Why?"

"This is where I belong."

"But you don't have to do anything you don't want to." His hands form fists. "You can fight it, what you are. You already are."

"But you didn't fight. You ran away." I cover my mouth, shocked at the venom in my words.

He freezes, all but his face, which contorts with anger. "What the hell, Anda! You have no idea what it's like to be me."

I stop myself from the obvious reply: *You don't understand what it's like to be me, either.* But all that comes out is a muffled cry of discontent. The wind rises to meet my cry. It revels in my misery.

Be upset, Anda. Be unhappy.

"I don't need this," Hector says. "I've been punished enough."

"No." No, no, *no.* It's me. It's only ever been me who deserves punishment. But even now, I can't say it out loud. I raise my eyes to him. His hair is so thick and curly, his dirtied face hurt and filled with exasperation. Off the right of the dirt trail, Tobin Harbor lies quietly, listening with quiet acceptance over my unsaid transgressions.

Something white reflects the sun. A boat in the harbor. "Oh!" I exclaim.

Hector reels around, looking for what's startled me. In the harbor, the boat is cruising a hundred meters away. A forty-one-foot Hatteras. My mouth waters.

They are looking for Hector. I know it.

"They must be searching for you, Anda," Hector says. "Why else would they be here?"

"Looking for you?"

"I didn't leave a trail here."

"Everyone leaves a trail," I say, and he withers at my words, like I've struck him, backhanded. I try to settle myself down. Reason. I need reason. "Anyway, researchers come by sometimes to count the moose and wolves, or examine any dead animals. They go to Mott Island, or stay in Windigo. Maybe it's them."

He still stays silent. Finally, he starts down the dirt trail, letting his words find me in his wake.

"Well, we have no food left. We can hide off-trail when we get closer to Rock Harbor and see if they're looking for us. Maybe you're right. Maybe they're just researchers."

"Yes. Just researchers." I love how easy it is to say the words that don't tell the truth.

The truth is, it is November fifteenth.

The truth is, I'm struggling to live within Hector's reality, as it has been on the island. I've forced and fit myself into his world. But more people means more realities smothering me. I don't know if I can conform into their neat categories. The boxes, as Hector calls them.

I know who is on the boat.

And I know what else is coming.

I've felt the cracking of my edges. A craving has been boiling just under the surface, after being shushed like a dog at her master's feet. So as Hector walks quietly ahead of me, I close my eyes for a moment and listen to the voice I've been desperately trying to shut out. The air around me caresses my cheeks, telling me to do what I must.

Yes, yes. Come back to Mother, Anda.

And my father would fear me. As he always has. Fear is tiring.

So is deceit.

Stop trying so hard, Anda.

Anda Selkirk doesn't exist. At least, not in their world.

I trot to catch up to Hector, who's already so far ahead, I can barely see him for the trees.

Chapter Thirty-Nine

HECTOR

We hide in a grove of trees fifty yards away from the Rock Harbor main dock. The buildings stand there quiet and deserted, and the white boat we'd seen is now moored. At first, there's no one in sight. Anda is acting twitchy and weird, and I remember our recent conversation with a sinking feeling. I don't know what she's running from, but I shouldn't have been so hard on her. I don't need her explanations. I never did. I don't know why I demanded them.

No, I understand. It's because I feel the noose tightening. We both do.

Anda is biting her nails and not even facing the harbor. I hear voices and clanking noises. A dark head pops out of the door that goes to the interior of the vessel. It's a tall guy. Middle-aged, and big.

No.

"I think my uncle is on that boat! Shit," I hiss.

Anda just gnaws her nails and stares into a small shrub at her knees, as if it were a crystal ball. "There are two men.

They're looking for us."

"You're not even looking." She turns to catch my eye with that unnerving, unblinking stare. The reflection of light in her smoky pupils glimmers with an odd iridescence. "Right. Never mind."

Soon, she starts working on her fingernails again, clicking on them with her teeth, and she bites off little bits here and there. She goes back to staring at the bush. She actually cocks her head toward it, as if it were transmitting a radio broadcast only she can hear.

Suddenly, the boat's engine groans back to life and water bubbles beneath the propellers. The guy who I think is my uncle starts the engine.

Wait. My uncle doesn't know how to drive a boat. I shield the sun from my eyes for a better look. This guy standing on the dock has a white beard and glasses. It's not him, and I sigh so loudly that Anda flinches.

The bearded guy undoes the lines tethering the boat. He's got a large backpack with him and a thick winter parka. Two other bags lean against his legs. A fisherman's knit hat covers his head, but there's gray hair peeking out of the edges. The boat purrs louder and quickly leaves the dock, trailing a white vee of foamy wake behind it. The bearded man watches it for several minutes as it grows smaller and smaller in the distance.

"Who is this guy?" I whisper to Anda. "He doesn't look like police or anything. You think he's one of those park researchers?"

Anda removes her raw fingertips from between her lips and looks back over her shoulder. She suddenly jumps to her feet and her mouth drops open.

"Father!" she cries.

...

I stay in the shadows. Anda runs right out and gallops down the shore, pebbles spitting out from her quick footsteps. She sprints straight to the dock, her feet thumping the planks. Her father doesn't freak out. Like it's the most normal thing in the world to encounter your extremely unnatural daughter staying illegally on a deserted island. No exclamations of joy or yells of anger. As she closes the distance the last few feet, he reels back, as if hit by a wall of air. She stops and they just regard each other.

I hold my breath.

Thank God the boat is far away now, which means hopefully they can't see Anda. I watch them talking a little, and her dad leans over to look where I'm squatting in the trees. My heart pumps a little faster. I've never met any girl's father, and this is not ever how I imagined the circumstances would be. Anda turns around and motions for me to come out.

There's no running away now. I have to trust her.

So I force myself to stand up and start moving my legs.

As I walk along the shore to the dock, I notice that Anda is shifting her weight from one foot to the other, like she's standing on a red-hot grill or something. She's not smiling. Neither is her dad. Ah, shit. He stands there and watches me approach. He's got that white hair like Anda's, but more wiry. His face is weathered and reddish, with deep lines in his forehead. He looks like he could be her grandfather, rather than a dad. And he's got those tiny circular wire-rimmed glasses that people from old-fashioned movies used to wear. As my boots creak against the dry boards of the dock, Anda comes to stand by my side.

"This is my father, Jakob Selkirk." She gestures awkwardly to him, like she's only just met him recently.

I extend my hand to shake his, but he doesn't take it. He stares at my hand for a moment, like he's not sure I'm altogether here. I clear my throat. "My name is Hector."

"I don't need to know your name." His voice sounds like gravel and burning coals mixed together.

Anda and I immediately exchange glances. This is not good. He looks at me, not unkindly, and rubs his white beard. "You're not supposed to be here. Your parents and the police are probably looking for you. You need to leave this island, and you need to leave my daughter alone."

My stomach bottoms out and lands somewhere on the other side of the world.

Parents.

Uncle.

No.

I drop my eyes to the dock. God. It's suddenly oppressively stuffy, like I'm in a coffin, which can't be possible, surrounded by all the water and trees and sky. He's going to turn me in. I'm going to have to go back soon. I've been here for almost a month. Hungry. Cold. Sick as a dog. Confused as hell, particularly when it comes to Anda. But it's been paradise.

I don't want to go back.

Don't make me go back.

But I don't have the balls to say it out loud, or to beg. To everyone in the world, I'm just a brat teen who ran away from a generous family member who's taken me in. There's no evidence that he's hurt me. In school, with my social worker, with my foster agency, with Dad—I'm always the bad guy. I'm ungrateful trash.

Mr. Selkirk turns to his daughter, his eyes taking in

her hiking clothing and her newly shorn, mud-caked hair. Worry melts into resignation, and he sighs. It's like he's already given up, but I've no idea about what.

"Come on. You both look half starved and dirty as hell. Get your bags."

After I run back to get Anda's backpack she left in the trees, he sets up this portable hanging shower thing so Anda and I can take turns washing off the grime from a week of camping. I guess we're funky enough that he won't even get in a boat with us yet. It's icy cold, but I don't care. It's not as bad as diving into the lake, and I've done that too many times. Afterward, we walk to the dock.

"I've got food with me," Mr. Selkirk tells us. "We have to get Anda someplace safe. There's another boat I can use."

We make our way to a smaller boat docked alongside several others farther down shore. After several tries, the engine grumbles to life and he makes me—not Anda—wear a life jacket of blinding fluorescent orange. He steers us out of the bay, then turns up the engine. We hang on to the sides of the boat as the coastline zips by and the lake water sprays our face with an unrelenting, chilled mist.

Only after we leave the harbor far, far behind, do I realize my mistake: Mr. Selkirk said nothing about keeping me safe.

Chapter Forty

ANDA

The water's been tempting me, electrifying my skin and inviting me in with an irresistible welcome that's hard to ignore. But I can't. Not yet.

I don't know what to tell Father. He's full of questions—I can see it in the wrinkles of his face, driven deeper by concern. But how do I explain it? How do I explain *me*?

I could let Mother explain. But she never shows herself to him anymore. She is a memory to Father.

Luckily, Hector asks questions while I cling to the side of the boat.

"Where are we going?" he hollers over the engine drone and splashing.

"Menagerie Island. It's one of the smaller islands around Isle Royale. The Isle Royale Lighthouse is there, but the house itself has been abandoned for decades. People aren't allowed to visit. It's private and out of the way. No one will find you."

"When you say 'you,' you mean only Anda. Right?"

"Right," he hollers. But he doesn't glance at Hector

when he speaks. Father's eyes meet mine, and I know what he's thinking. No one sees me, usually. But because of Hector, everything is uncertain. All the rules about me may have changed. Father is afraid. After an hour of the boat bumping us up and down endlessly, I gather my courage. I have to shout my words.

"Why have you come early?"

"I heard about the *Jenny*. One survived." He clamps his mouth shut, afraid to speak within earshot of Hector.

"He knows," I tell him.

Father's shoulders slump. I may have given him the worst news of all. He finally looks at me, his eyes almost hurt.

"You never leave a survivor on a wreck that small. Never. Something was wrong. I came as soon as the Coast Guard cleared out and the news died down. He has to leave, Anda. He's a distraction, and he's dangerous."

Dangerous. Father doesn't mean that Hector might hurt me with a knife or a slap. He's worried about a different kind of danger. Visitors and park people are on the island half the year when I'm there, and it's never a problem. They've never really seen me. But I have never, ever had meaningful interactions with any human except for Father. I have never been emotionally...compromised.

Father knows how to be around me. But he can't know how Hector's been, or how I'll react. And by react, he means possibly creating a glacier in a lake that hasn't seen one for ten thousand years. Or killing an island full of vacationers if I suddenly weep in June.

"He has to leave," Father says again.

Hector doesn't even try to fight Father's wishes. He turns away from both me and my father, and stares instead at the shoreline in silence. He's already miles and miles away.

It takes almost another full hour before our destination comes into view. By then, I'm boat-weary and my arms are jelly from holding on to the rails for so long.

Menagerie Island is a small, isolated sliver of bedrock. The jagged, reddish rise is sparsely decorated with a handful of stubborn evergreen trees. An octagonal whitewashed lighthouse proudly juts into the graying sky, next to a two-story brick house.

Lighthouses make my skin crawl.

I wonder at why my father brought me here. There are lots of lone islands sprinkled around Isle Royale. Perhaps he chose Menagerie Island because of its particular remoteness, knowing that no one comes here anymore. You even need a telephoto lens to see it from the nearest passing ferry. Or…maybe my father is trying to punish me somehow. He knows how lighthouses and I get along. Which is to say, we don't.

"Why Menagerie Island?" I ask him.

Father quiets the motor and we drift over shallow aqua water in the gathering dusk. The water is so clear, you can see the architecture of stone beneath it, solid and unchangeable after a millennium. The boat bottom scrapes against stone as Father heaves a plow-shaped anchor overboard.

I climb out onto a stony beach only fifteen feet long, flanked by boulders coming straight out of the lake bed along the edges of the island. Hector and I carry our bags and climb the hill up to the red house, only twenty feet away. While Hector carefully steps back down to help my father with the rest of his satchels, I introduce myself to the buildings.

The lighthouse is still working. I know this, because I've seen its bright beam penetrating ten miles into the night's darkness. No lighthouse keeper is needed anymore; the weather and isolation successfully pushed them away. No hearts beat here to keep ships from crashing. Only a solar-charged battery. But this doesn't quell my bad feeling. The lighthouse itself is a mighty force. After all, good intentions were mixed into the mortar and laid with each red sandstone brick.

When I tread around its base carefully, I repeatedly trip on nothing. And when I touch the painted brick, a thin curl of peeling paint tries to slice my fingertip. It's unhappy with my presence. It doesn't care that I've kept things alive on Isle Royale for much of the year. It only knows what I've done in November, what my sisters have done. To the lighthouse, I am the enemy.

"Let's go inside," my father says as he and Hector carry the bulk of our bags with them. For a moment, Father stands silhouetted against the setting sun, a melting, oozing yolk around his shoulders. He sees me hesitating. "Don't worry, Anda. The house won't bite."

Ha. *Don't be so sure*, I want to say.

Before I step forward, he looks over his shoulder to make sure Hector has rounded the corner. He drops his voice.

"Are you okay, Anda?"

I blink. I don't know how to answer that.

"Did he harm you?"

My eyes flicker up and I study Father's face. There are visions in his head that I can't get to, but I sense the sick, unchaste thoughts that worry him. I don't have words for them, but whatever they are, those particular evils have not touched my skin. As if Hector were even capable of such things. As if anyone had that kind of power over me. "Of course not."

But I wait for the rest of his question, fearful. *Anda, did you harm him?* But he doesn't ask. Doesn't care, perhaps. I'm relieved that I don't need to answer.

We round the house on the east side. A metal shack rests against the narrow passageway from the house to the lighthouse, where the acetylene used to be stored, back when the lights burned on fuel. Half the windows are covered up with white-painted metal, and the house looks like one of those old-timey cartoon characters, with dead white circles for eyes, all agog as we attempt to break in.

"How are we going to get inside?" Hector asks. "I have a knife. We can use a rock, maybe, to knock off the doorknob."

"Or we could use the key," Father says dully, and fishes a ring of keys from his pocket.

"Where did you get that?" I ask quietly.

"This island belongs to Isle Royale. The park management keeps a set of keys for emergencies, and I volunteer for them every year. I took it from the office safe."

He unlocks the door and opens it with a creak. The smell of dust and dampness frowns upon us, and Father leans down to turn on a portable lamp. Dim light shows we are in a hallway that leads to four small rooms. Dust is strewn over thick, warped wooden floorboards underfoot. None of the rooms is furnished, and the bare brick walls ooze with coldness and anger.

Keeping my hands and arms close to my body (I'm afraid I'll get nipped if I reach out too far), I find the only staircase. I take a few tentative steps up to see the half story above, claustrophobic beneath the gabled roof. I don't like it, and scoot back downstairs quickly.

"C'mon. Sun's going to set soon. We should try to eat and then go to sleep."

"And then?" Hector asks.

"Right now, you're the last person who should be asking questions," he says gruffly, and shuts the door behind us, encasing us in gloom.

There's a working fireplace, so we put the tiny cooking apparatus there and Hector gets to work making a pot of reconstituted beef stew, while I make sweet tea for everyone with the first pot of boiled water. Father watches me set the enamel plates and pour the tea—not too bitter, not too light. He seems shocked at the things I've learned in such a short period of time. Almost hurt.

When I hand him a steaming cup, he says, "Thank you."

"You're welcome," I say back, pleased at my good manners. And once again, Father stares like he doesn't recognize me.

At first, nobody speaks the questions we all have. We know the answers will come in time, but I'm terrified of them. Of what Hector might learn about me. We sit around the fireplace for a long time.

The truth is—I'm not really that hungry. Not for food. But I want my actions to soothe Hector with normalcy, and I want my father to see what I can become. Acting is a respite, somehow. Not having to be myself. I'm trying to convince anybody that I can be like this, or stay like this. The truth is—I don't know what I want.

I do.

"Shhh…" I say.

"What is it?" Hector asks, reaching to put a hand on my back. Father sees every movement we make, even in the low light of the flaming cooking fuel.

"It's the wind. It's rising."

From outside, it begins as a low, shuddering moan. It shivers through the eaves of the roof, winds its way down the chimney and curls around my feet, like a lost kitten. It's missed me, as I've missed it.

Now that I'm no longer in the interior of the island, now that I'm sitting on nothing but a rise of rock in the lake, it's become impossible to ignore Mother. My vision blurs a little. I can't concentrate and be the Anda I've been lately with Hector. There is insistent buzzing in my ears. I shake my head, but it refuses to be ignored.

Father cocks his head, listening to the rising wind. "I think there's a draft coming in from the roof. We should try to fix it, in case a storm comes." He clears his throat. "Anda, I would love some more tea. Maybe you could make us some, while Hector and I check it out?"

I nod, my eyes wide with understanding. As they exit the room and their footsteps creak up the groaning staircase, I wrap my arms around myself. My teeth chatter uncontrollably.

I know what's coming. Father is going to tell Hector everything. Hector will tell Father everything, too.

And then I'll lose them both.

Chapter Forty-One

HECTOR

When I follow Mr. Selkirk upstairs, I know it's going to be bad.

What I want to hear and what I'm going to hear will be so different. The fact that I'm not already with the police is a good sign, but reality has been slowly shoving itself under my fingernails, forcing me to notice. Mr. Selkirk knows I'm here. And time is not on my side. Nothing is ever on my side. Every day that goes by could be the day the police figure out where I am, a day that my uncle will have me under his thumb again. I think of Anda, but how long can all this last? I already know the answer. And it makes me greedy for every single minute I have before it's all gone.

The upper floor has an annoyingly low ceiling, and cobwebs shroud the beams above, undulating from an unseen force. I hunch over to avoid smacking my head on the beams and put my hand out to feel the air current.

"There's definitely a draft here," I say. Because I have to say something.

"Yes. It's an old, old house. Built in eighteen seventy-five. Good bones, though." He walks to the window, barred with metal, and runs his thick, scarred fingertips against the welded edges. "Like many things on Isle Royale, it will outlive us all."

"What things?" I ask, warily.

But it's a long time before he answers me. "Tomorrow, I'm going to clean up the mess that you two left on the island. I'll take the blame for any damage or stolen goods. Anda will stay here, just in case. And then you'll go back to your parents."

"I don't have parents." The lie is easier than the truth, and it has the same effect anyway. Pity.

"You must have left someone behind."

"My uncle," I say, without looking him in the eye.

"Your uncle, then. He must be missing you."

I bite my tongue, hard enough to feel pain in the core of my stomach.

The month my dad arranged for me to live with him, my uncle sat me down and patted me on the back. This was when I was easier to take care of, when he was easier to love. Before.

"We're alike, you and me."

My English wasn't too good then. I just stared, wide-eyed, at how a guy who could pass for white could be anything like me. He'd told me about his white mom, who'd died of diabetes a few years ago. How amazing my grandpa was, though a stroke wiped him out around the same time. How weird it was, sometimes, to be half one thing, half another, and neither at the same time.

"Half, half," I'd said.

"Yeah. Two halves don't always make a whole."

I didn't understand, but it didn't matter. He never brought it up again. I wish he had. It might have offset his tirades about my mother. The more problems I caused, the more he'd curse her for doing such a shit job of being a mother and dumping me on him. He never said anything about Dad being at fault. I always thought it was because he loved his brother.

I don't think it had anything to do with love.

"Hector? Did you hear what I said?" Mr. Selkirk asks.

I remember where I am. "Sorry. What?"

"I can't risk someone finding out a person is hiding here."

My shoulders sag. "I can't go back to my uncle." How can I say why, without having to actually say it? After almost five minutes of silence, all I can manage is, "I can't go back."

His boot digs at the planks by the wall, but he's been listening intently to my silence. He sighs. "Where are you from?"

"Duluth." I don't have the heart to lie this time.

"I'll take you to Michigan instead." He points at me. "That's all I can offer. If anyone asks me, I'll say I thought you were an adult. I have to make sure they don't find Anda."

"Then why did you leave her here?" I shoot back.

He spins around. "I didn't leave her here. She chose to stay."

"You shouldn't have let her!" I almost yell, before I realize that Anda is probably listening through the floorboards.

"Let her? She chose this. And you chose to stay on the island, too."

"I had no choice!"

"Neither did I," he growls back.

"That's pure and utter bullshit."

Mr. Selkirk rounds on me and for a second, he's

absolutely terrifying. "You have no idea what you're talking about. I would do anything to protect her. *Anything*. If that means dragging you back to Duluth and handing you to the police, then I'll do it. So don't push me. I may not know how best to care for her. God knows, I've tried. But I know some things. And I know you have to leave."

"But—"

"Stop!" Mr. Selkirk points at me. "God in heaven, you don't understand. It's not just about her. I'm protecting you, too. Don't you see? She isn't the only thing on this island—on this lake—that can kill you."

What am I not seeing? What is he not telling me? He starts to descend the stairs when I call out. "Wait. Tell me, then."

"No."

As he takes the rest of the stairs down, I realize his words don't quite fit together in my head.

I think of the visions of things I've seen, but not seen. The figure in the aurora borealis. The skull in the water.

I think of the wind pelting me with rocks ever since I stepped on the island. The fact that Anda seems to be listening to someone else all the time, and it's not me.

The air is even colder in the stairwell as I run down the steps. Wind is rattling the shutters. Anda squats by the fire, her eyes huge and fixed on the flames. She looks terrified. She must have heard everything. Her father is sitting in the corner on an overturned storage box, watching the shadows from the flames dance across the floor.

I head for the door and open it.

"Where are you going?" Mr. Selkirk barks at me.

Anda's eyes take me in and she inhales, as if to capture a breath to last a lifetime.

The wildest theory pings around in my head. Maybe

all the starvation has made my brain malfunction. But if this is the only way I'm going to get answers, then so be it. And if I end up on Michigan's shoreline, maybe that's meant to be, too.

I run out the door and down to the rocky shore of Menagerie Island, while Anda's father yells at me to come back, what am I doing, have I lost my mind?

Anda says nothing.

The boat is right where we've left it. I pull the anchor in with a huge swing of metal and clanking chain, and turn on the engine. I don't know a thing about boats, but I'm going to learn.

Right now.

Chapter Forty-Two

ANDA

I know exactly what he's going to do.

It's a test. An offering.

He's looking for the truth beyond us alone. He's searching for Mother.

Ah, take it, Anda. Take it, or I will. How can you say no, when it's bestowed so willingly?

Father runs out the door and brings the lamp. I move to follow him and he stops me with an outstretched hand.

I gaze at him with my eyes wide open, seeing everything. Knowing everything. "Don't pretend to stop me. You know you cannot," I remind him.

Father shrinks in my presence. The terror that he always hides behind his eyes comes forth, a watery, soft energy that's far too easy to push aside. I step past him and into the dark. I hear the boat motoring away. Hector is no sailor; he hasn't turned on the navigation lights so there is nothing but darkness and sound in his wake. Father can no longer see him.

Mother, however, knows exactly where he is.

And I know, too.

I've stayed away from the water for so long that the lure of the boat is almost too much to endure. The buzzing in my ear that bothered me before clears as I turn my full attention to the water. The lake is alive with life, pulsing in hearts afloat, all scattered across 31,700 square miles of Lake Superior. My blood hums with the purity of knowing.

Winds at twenty knots. Eight-foot seas on the coastline.

Twenty boats are alive on the lake. Two tugs. Three lake freighters holding forty thousand tons of goods between them—two lakers and one saltie. The rest are crumbs, little powerboats and sailboats taking a foolish night ride to enjoy the stars on the lake.

Romantics. Easier for the taking.

That's my girl.

But I don't want them.

I want Hector.

I know exactly where he is. The small powerboat is tantalizingly close by. He's running away yet again.

He doesn't know exactly where to go, except away from the spinning beam of our lighthouse. He has no idea what risk he's put himself in.

Even now, he's already thinking his own decisions that brought him to the island were wrong, and hasty, and everything the matter with his life has come to this. Testing a girl and the greater unknown, using his life as bait. He's realizing how much he doesn't value what he owns, the very lifeblood that pulses like syrup through his wind-chilled limbs.

He knows, Anda. He suspects all. So sink him, or I shall do it myself. He's only a pebble in your shoe.

I nod. I know what I must do. He's looking for Mother, for answers, and she'll do worse than reveal herself if I don't stop him. I could stop him, too. I could end this boy, end everything that brought him here. Like blinking in the sun, it would be too easy. I take a deep breath of the November air. There's incoming rain skulking across North Dakota, gaining momentum. The shoreline comes to meet me as I step down toward the ink-black water slapping against the rocks under my feet.

I splay my fingers out and feel the current thrumming in my arms. I can make an undertow with a kiss on the wind. This has to stop, because he knows.

Father has always said that he's the only one who can carry the burden of the truth. Anyone else wouldn't understand. They'd try to hurt me. They'd try to destroy me. People always destroy what they fear. But Hector isn't doing that; he's trying to hurt himself. I remember when he was sick, so sick, that everything that came out of his mouth was a puzzle.

"Pain is so easy. It's what we do best."

Hector hurts himself. I hurt others. But pain doesn't have to be the only thing we are capable of creating. It cannot be.

Mother is pulling him out farther, trying to keep him out of my reach. She has stalled the motor, and Hector curses with despair more than anger. He looks around to the dark void, the lighthouse winking too far away in the distance. Rapidly, she tows it. Now the boat is moving on its own accord, away from me, and away from the safety of land. Mother pulls downward at the same time, and gallons of icy water pitch into the boat, half flooding it.

Hector is terrified.

He gave himself. It's over, Anda. There is no choice.

Choice.

It's what humans possess, and buy, and sell in both

vast and minuscule quantities. And nature? A tree doesn't choose to be burned, nor does it choose to fall and kill the life beneath it in an instant.

There are no choices in nature.

But half of me is born of my father.

I raise my hands, palms up. Extending my fingers just a little, I reach far, far into the lake water and try to force the cold air away from him, but something's wrong. The air around him stays too cold. Mother's watery fist is curled around the boat's bow, but I try to slither under her grip to take the boat for my own. She tightens her hold and pulls the craft away from me, too easily.

Anda, don't.

I don't understand. I can't seem to get any sort of purchase on the boat, and it's filling rapidly with water. My eyes shut, squeezing tight with concentration. It takes every muscle of my body, tensed, to grip the waterlogged vessel. Even so, panting with exertion, I feel like I'm on the cusp of it slipping away.

I twist the tide into a rope to help me. But where I was once a conductor in such a scenario, it's as if I must play all the instruments now, simultaneously, and it's exhausting. I'm still so weak; the hiking and food and Hector have changed me, so much. But not for the better, and not forever. It's only introduced new ways to weaken me.

Anda, don't!

But there's enough of my old self to firm my grip and pull him the final hundred yards to shore. She can't fight what I've already won, though barely. When the waterlogged craft lands with a crested wave onto a flat stone of the beach, my father hollers. This is enough to free him from his fear, and he carries the lamp with him as Hector trips and falls out of the boat onto dry land.

He just kneels there, gasping. He's been hyperventilating since the motor stalled, and with good reason. Triangles of light through the punched tin partitions of the lamp mark his wet skin and soaked pants. He shivers violently. After a few minutes, he stands up and refuses Father's offer to help him up.

He won't look at either of us. We stand there, a trio on the brink of something that will change everything, waiting for his sentence to ring out.

"I'll go back to the mainland without a fight," he whispers. "I promise. If you swear you'll tell me everything."

Mother brings a soft breeze that caresses us all.

Do you understand the worst thing about making choices? There are consequences.

I wait outside while Hector and my father go in the house. I think of the ordinary tasks that must happen. They comfort me, almost as much as a soothing low barometric pressure.

He's changing out of his cold clothes.

Father puts on water to boil for a hot drink.

They find two crates to sit on, flanking the fire.

But that's all I can imagine. These are the limitations I have; the bit of normal life I've had only carries me so far. Want and need grate at my heart, making it beat erratically. It's not in tatters, not yet. But it's growing more ragged by the hour. What do I want? Still, even now, I'm not fully sure.

But I do know that I'm not capable of hurting Hector.

That's a lie. Now you're capable of more hurt than you can even begin to fathom.

I stare out at the darkness of the water, the oily black sky. I know she isn't trying to upset me. She only tells me truths that I need to hear.

After a stretch of fifteen long minutes, I knock on the door. It creaks open, and Hector's face meets mine.

"May I come in now?"

"He wants to talk to me, alone. We're going to the lighthouse for a while. We'll be back soon."

Of course. No one could explain it better than Father. He was there in the beginning, before there was an Anda of flesh. He can tell the whole story, without me and my clumsy attempts at kneading words into useful sentences. And it makes perfect sense to go to the lighthouse—the one place on this island that I'm loath to follow. It hurts my teeth just to know they'll be climbing that iron staircase soon.

I wait another hour. Then I open the door to the house. They've already gone. The room inside is empty, and the light from the camp stove is dead.

I shed the boots and the clothing that were never anything but a disguise. I find a white eyelet nightgown in my bag—one of my favorites, with the hem so frayed and worn that its softness lulls me with familiar comfort.

And then I walk to the lake. It's been too long. Any energy I had, I used bringing Hector to shore. I've never been so drained. The jealousy of the wind and air has settled into neutrality that relieves me. They'll let me pass without more bickering. The coming storm hasn't arrived yet, but there's enough energy in the depths to nourish me just a little. I've spent entire weeks in the water in November, but during this month, I've never spent so much time on land before. It has taken a toll.

And I'm finding that it's a toll I simply can't pay.

I've been trying to ignore the consequences of turning away from my witch side. But the island tugs and heaves with rot where there ought not be decay, wheezes in unblinking awakeness when it should be resting. And my own hunger is becoming something I'm terrified will be uncontrollable. Around Hector or Father, I might commit something so monstrous, it would fracture me forever.

I have to be one Anda. I cannot live in halves or quarters or broken pieces. How? How am I going to do this?

Come to me, Anda.

I hate her. I love her.

But I cannot say no, not right now. And so, with water in my eyes, I answer the call.

Chapter Forty-Three

HECTOR

Teeth chattering, I change into a spare set of clothes. Mr. Selkirk unzips my sleeping bag so I can wear it as a blanket around my shoulders. He pours out two steaming enamel mugs of hot tea and hands one to me. When I stop shivering, he grabs the lamp and tilts his head to the darkened corridor. "Let's go."

I follow him through the house to the back. A narrow covered passageway leads to the door of the lighthouse. Inside, a metal spiral staircase climbs the interior of the octagonal walls. As I start up the steps, my hand goes to touch the sandstone bricks. Two crowded windows of thick glass reveal nothing outside.

"How tall is this thing?" I ask, wanting to say something. Anything.

"About sixty feet or so. Walls are double-built. Pretty solid."

We've only gone about ten steps, but my legs are already fatigued from climbing. The lack of food has taken a toll. I try to hide my huffing and puffing once we're halfway up. The staircase spirals narrower and narrower as we climb, and it's just as cold in here as it is outside. Must be barely forty degrees.

"Seems like a miserable place to live," I comment between heavy breaths.

"Yes, well. The second lighthouse keeper was warned it was lonely, so he got himself a wife before he started working here. Stayed on from May till December for thirty-two years. Had eleven or twelve kids, too."

What a life that must have been. I can't tease out if I'm jealous of that lighthouse keeper, or glad that wasn't my life. But I'm no one to judge.

We finally reach the top and it's open to the air, with nothing but an iron railing to keep us from falling sixty feet down. At the center is the light, pulsing into the darkness. It's housed in an octagonal chamber built of iron and fitted with glass. The thing inside is blindingly bright as it goes on and off. I have to shield my eyes from the flashes.

"God. This thing is on every night, all year long?"

"Yes. Runs on solar. It changes its own lightbulbs when they burn out. It's not even glass."

"How far out can you see it?"

"Eh? Maybe ten miles or so." But Anda's dad doesn't seem to want to talk about the light anymore. He invites me to sit down with my back to the powerful beams. We stay silent for a long time, and the sound of the water hitting the shore rises up to us. It's windy and freezing cold, but I'm not budging until I hear what I need to know.

Mr. Selkirk fishes around in his pockets for something. "Did you mean what you said? That you'll go home, without a fight?"

"I said I'd go. I didn't say I'd go home." I won't meet Mr. Selkirk's eyes. "But I'll be off the island, if that's what you're asking."

The truth is, I don't want to hurt Anda. And if my presence means she might get in trouble, or something… else…can hurt her, then I'll go, come what may. The idea of regular people trying to make Anda do anything she didn't want to—it freaks me out and makes me want to hit things at the same time. "So…you said before that I had no idea what Anda was. You didn't say 'who.' You said 'what.'"

"That I did," he says, staring out at the darkness. He seems to be concentrating on something specific, somewhere south of us, but everything is awash in pure black right now. His hand pulls out a package, and I smell an earthy scent wafting on the air.

"So what is she?"

"To be honest, I don't exactly know myself." Anda's father holds up a wooden pipe and opens the small drawstring bag of tobacco. He starts taking pinches of the stringy stuff and poking it into the bowl.

What? "Well, where's her mother?"

"She's gone. Left even before she was born."

I chew on that one for a while. "Wait. How could she… before…" I shake my head. "That's not possible."

For a few minutes, he concentrates on packing the pipe with the yellow-stained tip of his pinky until it's just right. Then he takes out a tiny box of matches and strikes one. The spark brings with it the familiar, sneeze-worthy scent I love. He inhales so hard with the match that it makes bubbling noises until it's lit. The smoke is enticing, brown and earthy. I'd ask him for a drag, but somehow I doubt he'd share with a kid. After a few good puffs, he starts talking again.

"I grew up in Canada. Dwight, Ontario, to be specific. Had a real love of water. I couldn't get enough of it. I dreamed about spending all my days boating and got myself a regular obsession with Lake Superior. I read about the geology of how it came to be, the maritime history, everything. Finally moved here in my forties and spent every day on the shore, or in a boat. Then one day, a November storm hit me while I was chartering a ship full of tourists. We sank about three miles south of Isle Royale."

"But you lived."

Anda's dad peers at me sideways. "Yeah, you're a smart one." He laughs roughly. "I shouldn't have lived, though. I knew about every shipwreck that ever happened on these waters. Pored over them since I was a boy. I'd map them out, wrote tables and coordinates and saved the newspaper clippings. I think, in my heart, I wanted to die in this lake. Had an unnatural love of the Lady, if you know what I mean."

"Lady?" Was that some sort of designer drug?

"The Lady. It's what some folks call Lake Superior. She called herself a different name. Gracie."

This. This is the other thing that's been whispering in Anda's ear, what she's afraid of. Gracie? It seems like such a wrong name—too cute, too…religious, maybe. I'm not sure what to say, so I say nothing. Mr. Selkirk puffs on his pipe, and the bluish smoke rises into the sky.

"She's a beautiful thing. Even when she's angry. Even now, when she don't have much to say." He closes his eyes halfway and just listens to the water splashing in musically over the rocks. "I asked her for death when I hit that water. I said I'd like nothing better than to die in her arms. I had no friends. No real amours in my life. And so…she spared me." At this, he turns his face away from me, listening to something beyond me.

"What is it?"

"Nothing." He opens his eyes and smiles sadly. "I can't

hear her no more. Never stop trying, though. Back then, I did. She let me live, and I started to hear her voice. I'd dream about her. I'd see her in the trees, in the wind. I spent all my days talking to her, and she'd show me she'd been listening. Little things, like sending a little mist my way, or a wave of water at my feet. She'd even come visit my bed." He shook his head, and I swear that if he didn't have a beard and it was daylight, I'd see him blushing. "And then one day, Anda showed up."

"Where?"

"On the beach. November first, it was. Freezing cold, and there she was, bare as newborns are, on the shore not thirty feet from my house on the Isle."

"Wait, wait, wait." I put my hand out and stanch the urge to jump up and run away. I've *got* to calm down. "Wait."

"I'm not going anywhere, son. I'm in no rush. So stop telling me to wait."

I want to laugh, but it's not hilarious. "You're telling me that…Anda's mother is…the lake."

Mr. Selkirk nods.

Whatthefuck. "So what does that make her?"

"Look. The shipwrecks on Lake Superior aren't like others. I would know; I'd forget my own birthday before I forgot those dates. When the November gales come, they're a special breed of storm. And they're hungry and vicious and take ships like an island wolf could shake a coon pup. They have a name for this kind of storm. The Witch of November."

I swallow, but my throat is so dry I could choke on the air. The light from behind my head pulses into the gloom. This can't possibly be real. It just can't. I stare out in the darkness, as if it could tell me that yes, I'm hearing what I'm hearing.

He looks at my unbelieving face. "I know you think

it's not possible. There isn't a book in the world that'll tell you what I know now."

"That Anda is the Witch of November?"

Mr. Selkirk nods. "Yes. She's my November girl. It's not always November, but November's always inside her."

I grimace at him. "How do you know she isn't…the Lady?"

"Aw. No. Anda and the lake aren't the same thing. They need each other. Speak to each other. To the wind, and the storms, too. She has the lake in her blood, to be sure." He splays his hand apart, showing me his coarse palms. "See, there are moments when Anda is in this world." He shakes his left hand. "Human. But not often. She's like a spirit, snagged on earth, I suppose. Most of the time, she can't make sense of anything civilization has to offer."

He shakes his callused right hand. "And the lake, and the wind and storms, they communicate with her. Or she controls them. When the season is just right…" He clasps both hands together. "You can't hardly tell them apart."

"You mean, in November."

He nods.

"Which is why you left."

He nods again. "She's dangerous. Less human than any other time. She's nearly killed me more than once. Sure as day is day, she can sink a ship anytime. But the storms in November, they've an energy like no other time of the year because of her."

"Can't she just stop it?"

"Stop sinking ships? You can't hold down her nature, not with chemicals, not with ropes. Sooner or later, the dam breaks. Half of what she does is life, the other half is death. The living part, it bothers her the most. But she needs it."

"What if she tried?" I persist.

"It can't happen. Her sisters were the same way. Don't know who the fathers were, but legend says her sisters were like Anda. And they kept killing every November, tending to the Isle until their human sides just faded. I don't think there is 'trying' in this scenario, Hector. There is no good end to this story. But there could be one for you, and that would mean leaving." He pauses. "I'm not being selfish about Anda. Truly. If you don't leave, she'll swallow you whole and spit out your bones. She'll forget you meant anything to her by December."

All this time, I've been hanging out with something that could kill me, but I thought it could end. That she could change. What was I thinking? Should I just get out of here as soon as I can? But then again, she didn't kill me. She did the opposite. But how much longer can she hold out until I get hurt? Until I die?

I digest all this for several minutes.

"So why did you come back?" I finally ask.

"I knew something had affected Anda when she allowed that survivor. I didn't expect it to be you. You've changed her, somehow."

"You say that as if I've done something wrong."

"You have." He stands up, slowly, hand on hip as if his joints ache. As if the conversation just aged him ten more years. He starts to descend the metal staircase, lantern in hand. The light blinds me as I follow him.

"Wait. What have I done that's so bad? She would have killed people. She's a murderer, you're telling me, right? She sinks ships for breakfast. So why the hell is it so bad for her to…not kill people? To be more human? Maybe none of her sisters ever tried hard enough."

Mr. Selkirk turns around, and the lamplight shines upward, casting eerie shadows on his chin and nose and eye bags. He looks straight out of a Halloween horror movie, but when he lowers the lamp a little and the harsh shadows soften, he transforms back into a sad old man. Loneliness has carved out his cheeks, his temples.

"There ain't no life without death. Always has been, always will be." He shakes a finger at me. "And it's not just that. Boats aren't natural, Hector. Trying to use a hollowed-out hunk of metal to command something untamed like a lake, it isn't natural. Men take and take of nature all the time. Oh, they think they're being good and fair, lording over everything. That they deserve it all. But witches have been taking payment since we first started to challenge the Lady, back in the seventeenth century, the first time a schooner ever touched the water. And she don't take much, to be honest. It isn't up to you or me to decide the balance of things we don't really understand."

"But—"

"I find it curious that a fella running away from humanity wants someone like Anda to be more human."

I shut my mouth.

"Anyways," he adds, "time to sleep."

Without another word, he descends. When we make our way back to the house, Mr. Selkirk helps set up the sleeping bags. Only two. I explore the other small rooms, but they're empty. I run up the stairs, but the upper floor is empty, too.

When I come back down, I ask, "Where's Anda?"

"Never you mind."

I head for the front door, but Mr. Selkirk beats me there with a crooked few steps. He slaps his gnarly hand on the doorknob. "She'll be fine. She can take care of her own." He lies down on his sleeping bag and shuts his eyes. "You won't see her until morning."

Eventually, I fall asleep. And I dream of black waters, of my uncle looming in the recesses of my mind, sad and weary, but with a strange, starved look in his eye that I can't wash off my skin. I dream of Anda, peering at me with her tireless, wide-open stare.

And behind her, a watery shadow that watches us all.

Chapter Forty-Four

ANDA

I'll stay away all night. My presence is unwanted at the lighthouse, and there's nothing like a lighthouse and closed door to drive me far, far away.

The sky is carpeted with a thin film of clouds. Layers, actually. Cirrostratus fibrous *duplicatus*. I love the names of every species of cloud. I'm thankful that science has categorized them like the living things that they are — each with their own temperaments and life cycles.

I have already reached the shore, only twenty or so feet from the door of the house. The water laps at my toes and begins to climb my ankles, coaxing me in.

I walk step by step until there is no need to walk. Until gravity falls away and there is nothing between me and the water. The surface of the lake climbs through the strands of my hair and cradles my scalp with icy fingers. And then I succumb to the liquid, letting it carry me into the deeper, darker depths.

Mother.

I want things I cannot have. I want to be something I

cannot wholly be. I feel things that I could not before, and they gnaw at my untouchable heart.

I have done some terrible things that, perhaps, I should not have done.

What once was a simple question—how must I be with this boy?—is drowned by something far larger. What am I?

I don't know. Oh Mother, I don't know.

I'm afraid of what she will think of me.

I sob with my eyes closed. The lake is just a reservoir for my tears now. She's cold at first, but like all mothers, she welcomes me back into her arms.

Welcome home, my dearest.

I stay the whole night, drifting in layers of silken, blanketed currents above and beneath me. Father understands my need for immersion; he's seen me disappear into the water for days at a time.

The water soothes, but doesn't quell my mind.

In Hector, I see what I can take, mercilessly, and what it would cost. There is beauty in keeping him alive. It also means keeping his pain aloft, perhaps forever. Death has always been a pretty thing to me. A relief. An exhalation. But I don't want this. Not for him, or for us.

He's broken you.

No. He handed me the glass; I let it shatter. Hector brought me closer to the other reality in my life that I've never been comfortable with.

Do you miss Father?

Yes. And no. I feel the loss of him every day, though he tries to stay close to me. But I am content to be, without him. It is our nature. We belonged to this world before we ever belonged to anyone else.

This is the price I paid to love a man. The pain. You are a price I paid, too. I knew you would inherit this legacy. Are you willing?

I don't know.

Oh, Mother. I don't know.

It takes a while for the morning temperature to penetrate the surface of the lake. It holds energy and releases it so sweetly. Just as it's releasing me back to my father.

The stones of the lake bed touch me underfoot and I splay my hands out, balancing myself. My feet take one step after another as I rise out of the water. My body is drenched and so awfully heavy. So clumsy, this body on land. Eyes still closed, I let my face find the warmth of the risen sun to my right. East. The wind begins to dry the beads of water on my eyelashes and cheeks. The lake water leaves behind a film on my skin, an ancient perfume. I inhale the cold air and let my lungs fill, the first breath I've had in almost twelve hours.

"You aren't even cold, are you?"

My eyes fly open. Right on the dense, wintering foliage of the island, Hector sits. He's fully dressed, with a coat and a sleeping bag loosely draped over his shoulders. His expression is inscrutable.

He's spoken to Father. They've spoken of me, of Mother, perhaps all night long. But I recognize the dark gleam in his eye.

He knows it all.

And here I stand, naked beneath my sodden nightgown

after a night with Mother, who in the end, still left me with questions I must answer on my own. She left me the questions because we both know what the answer must be.

Oh, Hector. What must he think of me? Why doesn't he run? Why doesn't he attack me?

I don't know what to say or do. I've forgotten his question already.

"Come inside," he says impatiently. He stands up and gathers the sleeping bag in his arms in a gentle hug, and I suddenly know that maybe my life would be happier if I were such a sleeping bag.

I follow him obediently into the little house, though I know I don't have to. The lighthouse glares at me, its eye within the octagonal chamber now dead for the day. I bare my teeth at it, before entering the darkened house.

"Your clothes are here. I'll step out while you change."

I spin around to watch him go back to the door. "Where is Father?"

"He went back to the island. He's cleaning up the house and Washington Creek campsite where I stayed."

"Oh." I stare at my feet, afraid to ask the next question. It's not necessary, though. He answers it for me.

"I'm leaving tomorrow morning."

There's a tumble of thoughts in my mind, but none of them make it to my lips. He hesitates, and when I say nothing, he leaves me in the dark and shuts the door behind him.

I should have said something.

It's better this way.

"Is it?" I ask, aloud. But there is no reply. So I listen to the voice of my half-human heart.

Run. Run after him, Anda.

So I do. I reach for the door and bolt outside, where the

sun's light is already gaining muscle and warms the bracing breeze trying to nip at my ankles and wrists.

"Hector," I holler. "Hector!"

"Geez, I'm right here, Anda."

I spin around. Hector is leaning against the wall of the building, next to the iron acetylene shed. There is so much distance between us, growing rapidly even as the seconds tick by. My damp nightgown sticks to my legs and belly as I step closer. Hector crosses his arms in front of his chest and won't meet my eye.

When I'm only inches away, I see that he's breathing fast. I have this effect on him, and it warms me to know that I still matter. Perhaps it's pure fear, but perhaps not. I put my hand on his chest and he freezes, as if I'd put a cold pistol against his temple. His heart beats so fast. I know the current of blood within it, the dance between valves and chambers, the laminar flow and miniature eddies that sing to a creature like me.

"Don't," he whispers, still looking away. He begins to tremble.

"I won't be ignored, Hector," I say steadily.

"But you aren't real. And I have to leave." His voice is hoarse, and he's got purplish shadows beneath his eyes. He didn't sleep well.

"My father said you have to leave, didn't he?"

"It doesn't matter what he said." Hector can barely look at me. "I need to go."

"Look at me," I command him.

He does, but it takes a year and a day for his rich brown eyes to finally meet mine. They see me only superficially, not like how he looked at me before last night.

"I'm still here," I whisper. My body leans into him, and I put my cheek against the hollow of his throat, listening to him breathe. I let my fingers skim up his arms and hook over his shoulders. And still he stays frozen.

"I know what you are. I can't…" he whispers. "You aren't real to someone like me."

"I am. Right here. Right now." I stretch up on my toes and let my hands follow the curve behind his neck. He closes his eyes, and I pull his face closer.

He is so beautiful. His tired eyes, dark eyelashes, his defeat, and the terrors of a life that drove him into my arms. The arms of a murderess.

I kiss him gently, warming his cold lips beneath mine.

Kiss me back, Hector, I beg. *Please.*

Look who has the power now. Is this what you want?

This is what I want. I want this strange, broken boy who could see this strange, broken girl. Even when he didn't know what he was looking at.

I can linger forever, if need be, with my mouth waiting for his to speak against mine. I could wait a century, even as his bones crumble against my skin.

Slowly, as if melting drop by drop, Hector's arms unglue themselves from his sides and encircle my damp waist. He embraces me and lifts me up, angling his face so he can fit my lips more perfectly. I hold his face in my hands, wishing I could control the kiss, when I know I have no power.

It is nothing like our first kisses. The ones where we stepped cautiously into each other's sphere for a few short hours, testing the solidity of the plane between us. Now we've found that the ground is riddled like a honeycomb and we've fallen through.

Fallen. Falling.

After too short a time, he breaks the kiss, but not his hold on me. The embrace is so tight. He'll be gone tomorrow, and his embrace says so. Finally, we breathe. Not a sigh of relief, but of something far more complicated.

"Oh God, Anda," he whispers against my neck.

"No gods here, Hector. Only us."

It's a prayer, of sorts.

Or a curse.

Chapter Forty-Five

HECTOR

How many ships do I need to sink to stay here forever? What sins must I commit to unmake myself?

I don't move a muscle, conscious of my hands absorbing the warmth of her back. Her cheek presses against my grizzled one. I hear her inhale, ready to speak.

I don't want her to say anything. *Please don't talk. Let's just stay like this and pretend there isn't any future. Ever.*

"Do you really have to go back?" she whispers against my chest.

Anda already has me waking up before I'm ready. I squeeze her hard, but I know I have to answer eventually.

"Yes. I made a promise to your father. It's safer." I don't say for who, her or me.

She nods. "How much time do we have, then?"

"He's coming back tomorrow morning. He's taking me to Rock Harbor. The same friend who dropped him off is going to drop me off in Michigan." At least I won't have to go back to Grand Portage. He's giving me a chance, even if I don't have one with Anda.

The water laps at the shoreline in a quiet, hypnotizing rhythm. The sun, though briefly out for the morning, is now gone. It's already darker, and the ominous weather makes me shiver. Everything around us seems to be waiting on our next words.

She looks out at the lake. "I thought we would have more time," she says.

I slip my hand into hers. "We have now."

When she turns to me, her eyes are swimming. "So you don't hate me."

"No." I pause. "I don't completely understand you, but I don't hate you. You're complicated. You're not one thing." I close my eyes for a long second. "I should know. I'm not one to judge."

"But it makes you run," she says quietly.

Running. I don't know how to explain to her that I always, *always* feel like I'm running. Running toward something, running away. I'm a moving target, I'm in pieces, I'm never whole. Sometimes velocity and trajectory are better than the mass itself. So yeah, it feels natural to run.

"Will you ever stop?"

"I don't know. I can learn to. I have to unlearn some habits, I guess," I say quietly.

"I should unlearn some habits, too." She hesitates, then adds, "I've only ever valued one half of myself over the other."

I look at Anda. "Can you do it? Can you stop the whole ship thing?"

"I am right now." Her face looks calm, but her hands are tight fists, as if the reminder itself is work.

"Can you do it forever?" I ask.

"I don't know." She looks worried. "I can't stop death. You know that."

"But there was already a natural cycle."

"I took myself out of the cycle."

"Why?"

"It upset Father."

"Maybe we shouldn't worry too much about what other people think," I say. "It gets tiring, doesn't it?"

I sit down, and Anda promptly sits in my lap, wraps my arms around her damp waist. I like the way she doesn't ask. People tiptoe around me all the time, all except the ones who should. I love how she thinks of my body as an extension of hers. No one's ever done that before.

"I'll weigh you down so you can't run," she says. But my body is still tense, and she feels that.

I shake my head.

So she gets up, turns around, and sits on my lap so we are face-to-face, her legs wrapped around my waist. My heart immediately starts to gallop as she entwines her arms around my neck. Our noses are an inch apart now, and all I can think about is whether or not it's possible to kiss someone for twelve hours without breathing. Speaking of which, I'm breathing really damn fast now.

"Feel like running?" she whispers.

"Maybe," I lie.

She takes her hands and pushes my shoulders so I fall backward on the broad stone beneath us. She pulls my arms above my head, holds my wrists down, and straddles my waist. Her eyes bore into mine.

"How about now?"

I don't answer her. I just let her kiss me.

Chapter Forty-Six

ANDA

I could do this forever. Trap this boy and make him mine. I would let his marrow bones crumble beneath me and I would still sing and kiss the splinters of him until he was nothing but dust. But I do not say such things aloud. I am learning that my sentiments aren't always…well received.

We kiss for a long time. The air is cool, and I'm too preoccupied to keep the temperature at bay. So our hands search out pockets of warmth—under his shirt, the nape of my neck, the narrow of my waist and his.

After what seems like an hour, he surfaces to breathe. I pout, still sprawled over him.

"C'mon," he says, sitting us both up. "This rock can't be comfortable. Let's take a walk." He leans back and pulls me to my feet.

"You want to walk?"

He nods.

"We've walked a lot already. Over forty miles," I remind him. I'm still staring at his lips.

"Fine. Then I'll walk." He crouches down and pats his

shoulder. "Get on. I'll take you on a tour of the grand Menagerie Island."

I climb onto his back. He shows me how to wrap my legs around his waist and drape my arms over his shoulders. Oh, this is worth relinquishing my position of pleasantly crushing him against a rock. This is very good.

He treads carefully, his boots looking for each secure step with thoughtfulness. There are a dozen ways to trip and fall, even on this tiny rise of land, but he never falters. I squeeze his broad, angled shoulders tighter and kiss the back of his neck. I could do this all day.

"I could do this all day," I tell him, realizing that there isn't a point to keeping anything to myself anymore. Especially when it doesn't involve crumbled bones.

"Good."

"Are you tired?"

"No. Are you?"

I shake my head. He pauses, before asking, "So...do you need sleep?"

"Sometimes." I think for a while, and then explain. "My body needs sleep sometimes. I don't always know what I'm feeling, when I need it. Father recognizes it better than I do. I get...angry. And irrational."

Hector laughs as he carries me around a cluster of lacy cedar bushes, fragrant with their oil. "You are always irrational, Anda."

I nod. It's true, after all.

Hector stops walking and turns his head so he can see me. "You know, I haven't had many bad dreams since we've met. Most of the time, I dream of rain, and the lake, instead."

"Tell me about your bad dreams, Hector."

He gently lowers me to the ground. Menagerie Island is so miniscule that we're already on the east end. I slither my hand into his, but he won't look at me. His eyes are on the distant horizon where the sky is clearer. The clouds behind us are pushing closer. Already, a slight mist moistens the air. I can taste the heaviness of rain coming.

Hector shakes his head. "You don't really want to know what my bad dreams are about."

"I do."

"No. Because then they'll become your bad dreams, too. And I don't want you to think of me like that."

"Hector." I pull him closer and bury my face in his neck. He smells of sweat and shame, and I'd make it into a perfume to wear every day, if I could be so lucky. "Take me with you."

He encircles my wrists in his hands, the same way he did when he found me in the lake, trying to pull me above water. Instead of forcing him away with a riptide, I pull him down, down to the ground. I sit in his lap and wrap his arms around me, as if they were the harnesses of a rocket ship. I offer him the nape of my neck to hide his face against.

"Tell me everything," I whisper.

And he does. Slowly, carefully, unfolding like an ancient letter. He'd never told anyone, because he's never been sure of the truth. It started when he was eleven. His uncle often left a half-drunk beer in the kitchen, forgetting which bottle he'd finished and hadn't. With his uncle snoring in his recliner by the TV, Hector would chug it down, wincing at the bitterness. Knowing and hoping that it would make him feel unlike himself, because being Hector wasn't pleasant.

Soon, he got used to getting drunk once or twice a week and stumbling to his room to sleep it off. It made getting in trouble with teachers and his uncle tolerable. It made him forget that his mother never bothered to contact him after he moved in with his uncle. He and his uncle were fighting a lot then. Sometimes his uncle would try so hard to show he wasn't angry all the time. He'd buy him a nice T-shirt, or make him his favorite breakfast—bacon and cheese melt sandwiches. They'd rent videos and watch them together. Anything with spies or espionage. Those were the best. Then they'd spend the evening picking apart the plot holes.

But it wasn't enough to stop the fighting. So he took the bottles and more from the fridge, guzzling them to forget. He'd forget about Korea. He'd pretend he'd never tasted the sweet cakes of *tteok* stuffed with red bean paste, or heard his mother laughing while he'd clumsily bow to her on New Year's Day. He'd forget about his dad. In his dreams, he'd burn the letters that promised everything and delivered nothing.

And then one day, he woke up in bed on a Saturday at noon. His body ached like he'd had the flu. His brain pounded like gravel had tumbled within, scraping the insides of his skull. There was dried blood inside his pants, and there was pain, the worst pain he'd ever had. He figured he'd hurt himself by accident, somehow, while he was out of it.

Two weeks later, it happened again. No memory of anything, but the pain and the blood, again. Terrified, he thought maybe he had some sort of cancer. Could someone his age get cancer like this? He stopped drinking the leftover beer. But the blackouts happened anyway. Again and again. His suspicions went in a different direction, darker still. Until he finally stopped eating any food or drinks in the house, unless he'd brought it home himself, saved from the lunch he'd bought at school. But then he started losing weight.

His uncle fussed at him, worried over Hector's disappearing appetite. He gave him antacids when the vomiting started, too. Coaxed him with a new pair of sneakers if he'd just start eating again. Life got a little better.

And the blackouts came back.

Every morning after he had awoken, confused and nauseated, his uncle would be kind. So kind. So forgiving, and generous, and there would be gifts. A new video game, a new coat. And then inevitably, he'd stop being kind. The rage would return. And then the next blackout.

The last one was two nights before he'd left for Isle Royale. This time, he wouldn't be found. This time, he wouldn't go back.

My mind is murky with thoughts as he tells me this. I don't understand what happened. I open my mouth to ask a simple question, then don't. Does it matter? Does it matter beyond that it agonizes me, knowing there was pain and a violation of trust and an evil that's so awful that Hector won't say exactly what he thinks happened? So instead, I ask another question.

"Why didn't you tell anyone, Hector?" I whisper.

"Because I couldn't remember anything. I had no proof. And I was…" He tries to control his breathing, which is coming low and jagged. His hands are shaking so hard that he's an earthquake against my skin. "Anda. I was so ashamed."

"But it wasn't your fault."

Hector is far taller than I am. Heavier, too. But he starts to wither away from me, pushing me off his lap. I turn and capture him before he can flee, and he crumples into my lap and soaks my nightgown as his angular shoulders shake. I know what he would say. That nothing I can do matters, because I can't change the past. I can't make any of it go away.

So this is why he ran. He ran away from terror, and I run toward it, every November. How can two such people belong together? How will we survive?

"I don't want to talk about this anymore," he finally says, pulling himself up and messily mopping his face and nose. "We don't have much time. I want to know more about you. I want to know everything. How you do it. When. I want…" He takes a deep breath, about to burst.

I understand. He wants to fill up with anything else, so full that there isn't room for nightmares. This is how I know he's so fractured inside, that even a nightmare like me is a relief in comparison. If I can banish the viciousness of his memories, I'll try. Because I can't make them not real.

You could. You could take him down to the depths. And then there would be no more pain. There would be no more feeling.

I turn and hiss. "Ssss…I won't!"

"Why not?" Hector asks, visibly hurt.

I turn back, and remorse melts the anger in my face. "Oh, Hector, no. No, no. I wasn't talking to you."

"Who, then?" Hector wipes his eyes. Then understanding lights his face. "Oh. You're talking to her, aren't you? Your mother?"

"Yes," I admit, extending my hand out and sweeping it around us. "She's everywhere. The sky. The clouds. The water. The storm."

"What is she saying?" His curiosity is pushing away his sadness. It's already working.

"Do you really want to know?"

"Yes. Everything."

"But it's not pleasant."

He laughs ruefully. "You know my secrets now. Tell me yours. I don't care how awful. I want to know."

"You won't like me anymore."

"That's not possible."

I try again. "You'll be afraid of me."

"I already am."

This time, it's my turn to be hurt by words. "You are?"

"Well, wait. Not afraid. But I respect what you are. What you can do." He thinks for a moment. "And what you haven't done."

He's thinking about Agatha, and himself. I am capable of restraint. Or at least I was, once.

I stand up and offer my hands to pull him up, which he allows, gamely. He doesn't need me to stand. We look westward, where a low cloud is coming quickly to meet us, so drooping that it almost seems like a fog falling from the sky. Already, heavy drops are pelting us and splattering the dry rocks around our feet. Hector hunches his shoulders and looks ready to bolt back to the lighthouse.

"Rain's here," I say. Not so much to announce the obvious, but more as an introduction.

And this is Hector, I would say. So please be nice.

He is owed to me, and to you. You know this.

I ignore her words. She's been saying and hinting at such since the first day he went into the water.

"Should we go back? Do you want to listen to the weather radio?" he asks.

"No." I turn to him. "I don't need it to tell me what's here, or what's coming. This won't be bad."

"How do you know?"

"Because I'll make sure it's not bad," I say firmly, speaking more to Mother than to Hector. Usually I'd come out to the shore and welcome it with mouth open to the sky, ready to drink it in. But I don't want it. Not now, not yet. "Don't touch me for a minute or so, okay?"

Hector nods and steps away, his face replete with careful fascination.

"Oh, and don't touch anything metal," I advise him. "And don't touch the lake water."

"Okay."

Now he sounds truly scared, but it will all be better soon. I close my eyes and feel the depth and fullness of the cloud. Yes, it's low. Nimbostratus. Not a big one, not a dangerous one, but substantial enough to cause rain for a while and promise swells enough to make boating a choppy affair. I stretch out my fingers and sense the intentions of the cloud. It wants to stay for days. I could wind it tighter, coax it into inviting in a cold front and turn it into the storm predicted by the radio yesterday, but I won't let it. I carefully pull it out taut, like a tablecloth being smoothed of its wrinkles. I push the cold front back, keeping it at bay.

The pressure rises. The storm would mew complacently if it could.

When I open my eyes, the gray above isn't as dark and the rain is smaller caliber, soft and gentle.

"I can't believe you did that," Hector says, his palms out and collecting the light drops on his skin. "That was amazing."

The word—"amazing"—sloshes around inside my belly. Astonishing. Surprising. Stupefying. "You say it as though it were a positive thing."

"It is."

"But I can do things that are worse. Far worse."

"I know." Hector takes my hand in his. "I could do amazing things, too. Horrible things, if I wanted." A grimace passes over his face, and for a split second, I see what he could do. Translate his own pain into horrors for others. I wonder how many people have this inside them, this whispered potential for violence. Those with enough reason to do so, but choosing humanity over nourishing that destruction. Hector shakes it off, so splendidly. He squeezes my hand, and I look at our fingers clasped together. Twenty fingers. All able to do such damage.

So we stand there, two terrible people capable of terrible things.

But not today. It will be a détente of sorts, where we leave our miseries and propensity for unhappiness outside ourselves.

Until tomorrow morning.

Then I will go back to being myself. November will be mine once again, and Hector will not.

I should be relieved, truly. But if I am, why do I ache so much?

Chapter Forty-Seven

HECTOR

We eat a little, though neither of us is hungry.

We drink a little, though neither of us is thirsty.

We do these things, because everything ordinary is extraordinary when the time is ticking down really fucking fast.

That night, when the sun sets and the air is misty, we take a walk outside after being indoors for hours. Maybe kissing, for hours. Maybe talking. I don't need to count the minutes of anything we do. That would mean that time was passing, and I don't want the reminder.

Outside, the temperature has dropped, and the sun is a gold crescent on the horizon. The lighthouse winks on, and its beam fills the fog with a dull light. Anda eyes the tower like a sulky kid.

"Come on. You should go up there," I urge her.

"Why? The light hates me."

I could ask exactly how she knows that, but I don't. I can see it in how she carries her body. Withdrawing into herself, as if being pelted by acid instead of rain.

"C'mon." I take her hand and bring her back inside. She drags her feet all the way, but not so much that she's not willing to come with me. I take both sleeping bags in my arms and lead her through the house and the back corridor to the interior of the lighthouse. Anda sucks air between her teeth as soon as she touches the iron railing.

"Really, I don't think this is a good idea."

"Why?" I say, several steps above her. From here, she looks up at me, and her eyes are huge in the darker light inside. Her skin is luminous, as if she can channel the unseen moonlight.

"Because we are opposites. I can feel its hostility for me. And I despise it, too." She narrows her eyes. "Why are you so insistent on bringing me up here?"

"Because. I never thought I would tell a single soul the truth about me. And I did. And…" I close my eyes, taking a huge breath. "I feel better. Not fixed. Not by a long shot. But better." I open my eyes and stare at her. "I don't know, Anda. I have a feeling that if you tried to make peace with it, it would be…good." She waits for something more, knowing I'm holding back. Finally, I smile sheepishly. "And also, I want to see you in a light, bright as day. All night long."

Anda smiles a little, but she doesn't seem convinced. She carries her worry with her like lead weights on her feet, taking one clonking, heavy step after the other up the spiral staircase. Her breathing comes with more effort, a slow rasping sound as if she's harboring razor blades in her throat. The closer to the top we get, the larger her eyes get, wide with fear and apprehension. When we finally reach the iron gallery, she squeezes my hand so hard that her nails bite into my skin.

"It's too…" she begins, but doesn't finish her sentence.

She shakes her head and crumples down onto the iron floor surrounding the glass-chambered light. I immediately drop to my knees to help her, but she hisses at me. I back off.

Her hands touch the metal below her and she snatches them away, as if they'd scorched her. She lets out a shriek of fierce anger, an almost feral noise. I take a few more steps away, giving her room. Something incendiary is playing out inside her head. I pray that the sleeping bags in my arms won't spontaneously combust. Was it a mistake to bring her up here?

"It's okay. Forget it. We'll go back down," I say quickly, holding out a hand. Anda recoils from my hand and grimaces.

"Stop. Just, stop."

In the slowest of slow motions, she lowers her fingers to the black metal beneath her. Her fingers quiver with pain when they make contact, and she shuts her eyes tightly. Her shoulders shake, and she drops her head, feeling whatever it is that the sandstone bricks of the building have stored up for over a century. A keening issues from her throat, a sound too much like wind against the eaves of an old building.

When she finally raises her eyes, they're bloodshot. Dark circles shadow beneath them. It's like she's mourned a thousand deaths in the space of a minute. I take a cautious step closer.

"Are you...okay?" God, that's a stupid question.

"No." She whimpers and wipes her wet cheeks. "But I would like to lie down now."

"Here? I didn't realize it would be so bad. I'm sorry. We can go back down."

"No. We'll stay here," she says miserably. "It's okay."

I don't ask again. I shake out the sleeping bags and zip

them together so we can lie inside together. She wriggles to get her feet to the bottom, and her body curves around the gallery as the light pulses above us. Anda shuts her eyes tightly.

"I can see the light even with my eyes closed." She frowns deeply.

I kick off my boots and scoot next to her. It's cold as a meat locker with the wind up here, but I don't care. I slip one arm beneath her head as a pillow and wrap the other around her waist. The air is still damp and misty, and I shiver.

"Cold?"

"Not much," I lie.

She harrumphs at my bravado. She can see right through me. "Well. It is November, after all." Anda smiles a tiny bit, and I smile back, and her hands move beneath the sleeping bag. The wind around us dies down and suddenly it's not quite as cold as it was only seconds ago.

Oh.

"You did that, didn't you? When we hiked on the island. You kept it from being too cold."

Anda nods.

Every once in a while, I silently freak out. *This isn't real, she isn't real, this can't be real, holy hell, what is going on.* And then I try not to hyperventilate and remember that she's here, and I'm wasting my time doing reality checks.

We lie there for a long while, not speaking. Just watching the light pulsing inside our eyelids when they're closed, letting it bleach the insides of our eyeballs when they're open. Finally, after a long time, I ask.

"So what did it say? The lighthouse?"

Anda's eyes are closed right now. I run my fingertip across her dark lashes, and she allows it. "It told me that

November was not the only answer."

"Huh? To what question?"

"I don't know. I have to think on it. But then it…it asked me for an apology."

"And?"

"It showed me exactly what I've done. So I apologized. And I showed it what men have done to the lake. And it apologized."

"Are you friends now?"

She shakes her head. "But we understand each other a little better."

I trace my finger down her cheek, then over the swell of her lips. I want to kiss her so badly, but I now have the distinct feeling that we're not alone. I pull my hand back, and she catches it.

"Don't worry about the lighthouse. It doesn't care about such things," she says, and puts my hand lower, against her collarbone.

"What things?"

"These things." Anda slips her hand under my shirt, her fingers touching the ripples of my rib cage and then down, drawing a line across my belly where the waistband of my pants is. My body flashes with heat, and I swallow, shutting my eyes.

"Anda." It's a million questions at once.

"Yes, Hector."

And that's the last thing we say for the rest of the night.

Chapter Forty-Eight

ANDA

The lighthouse does not speak again that evening, and neither does anything else. I'm glad of it. There is no room for any voices in my head.

Hector fell asleep when the cloud-draped moon was only four fingers from dipping below the horizon. I watch him by the light of the flashes until moonset. He will be angry when he wakes up, to feel like he's wasted time on sleeping. But his body has different needs than mine.

Well, except for last night.

Last night was so many things. Painful and clumsy. Instinctual and tender. And easy, far too easy, to succumb to a facet of myself I'd owned but banished until Hector was there to wake it up.

The eastern sky warms with lemon and peach hues as Hector stirs. His eyes blink sleepily, and his hand finds mine, still resting on his shoulder where I haven't moved it for four hours.

"Oh no," he groans. "I fell asleep."

"You did. You sleep beautifully."

He rubs his eyes. "Your father is going to be back soon."

"Yes. We should have some tea waiting for him. That would be easier for him to digest than seeing this."

I point to the area between us. Which is to say, the nonexistent area between us.

We spend a few more precious minutes just lying together. Hector's eyes are open and seeing, memorizing me in a quiet, frantic way. Neither of us wants the fairy tale to end. Every minute is a desperate last one, until finally Hector plucks my hands off his body.

"C'mon. It's time," he says, with as much regret in his voice as I feel in my belly.

The lighthouse pretends to sleep as we dress hurriedly and gather the sleeping bags. As we descend the staircase, it creaks. I swear it says something like:

See. You're more human than you think.

"I thought you weren't watching," I whisper back.

November is not the only answer, you know.

I furrow my brow. "I don't understand."

Hector turns around, arms full of sleeping bag. "Did you say something?"

"Oh, nothing."

He'd be upset if he knew the truth—that the lighthouse was probably laughing at us all night long.

We get ourselves into a semblance of dressed and normal, with reconstituted oatmeal cooking and three mugs of tea, when we hear Father's motorboat purring nearby. We go out to meet him as he throws the anchor onto the shore.

"Well?" Anda asks.

"All cleaned up. I couldn't hike the trail, of course. Not enough time. But I trust that nothing too bad was left behind there. I fixed the broken door on the camp store in

Windigo and left an IOU for the missing items."

Hector nods respectfully. "Thank you, Mr. Selkirk. I'll pay you back."

"Don't worry about it," he says brightly. Too brightly.

Ah. He's joyful that Hector is leaving.

"Do you have time for breakfast?" Hector offers, but Father shakes his head.

"I'm afraid not. The fellows will be at the harbor in two hours to bring you back, and I'm already behind. I'm going to fill the tank with gas. Only be a minute. I've got a few granola bars you can have on the way."

I go with Hector back to the house to gather his pack. Inside, he captures me in a hug so fierce, I can't draw a breath.

"It feels like a dream," he says. "Like it's all been a dream."

"Good," I whisper. "Keep it close. Don't forget me."

"Never," he tells me.

I can't believe he's going. And I can't believe I'm letting him leave.

It is the right thing to do. The other way would have been in a coffin.

Mother's voice oozes contentment. She acts as if this is the only way, as if she has forgotten it all. That once, she allowed a human's love in her life. That she allowed me to be conceived, just as I consciously chose not to kindle a new life last night.

The air around us grows humid, and spots of moisture begin to plink down on our faces as we grip each other hard. The door opens and we spring apart, wiping our faces. Father sees the pack on the floor and grabs it. "Time to go."

I follow them to the boat, and Hector climbs in, his lips in a grim, straight line. When Father starts the boat and pulls up the anchor, he doesn't say good-bye. I know he'll be back again to check on me. He always comes back.

Hector turns away from me and hunches over. He can't even stand to look at me.

I can't hold back anymore. I cry in earnest, feeling the loss of him. It twists and gnaws inside, and instinct tells me that I could take him back—piece by bloody piece, if I wanted. I could have him forever. But I can't.

I won't.

The sky above roils with low pressure, and the clouds descend closer to earth, trying to enshroud me with a mantle of comfort. Drops begin to fall with intention. In the distance, neither Father nor Hector does anything to shield himself from the downpour.

In the end, I can't stop anything. I'll go back to being Anda, only half of a whole that can't live with any peace, not without destroying something precious or losing something I can't afford to lose.

As the sound of the boat recedes and the noise of the rain slaps on the water in a rising discord, I lift my hand to my cheeks. My fingertips touch the mix of rain and tears there. I bring it to my lips. It's salty and the tiniest bit sweet. The beautiful and the broken, woven together.

It tastes like us.

Chapter Forty-Nine

HECTOR

She's upset.

The rain gushes down in frigid torrents and soaks me. I have one poncho in my bag, but I give it to Mr. Selkirk to wear, though he protests at first. I want to feel this rain. It's Anda. Even though it's chilling me to the core. It crushes me to know that I can't do anything to console her.

For two hours as we travel back to Rock Harbor, Mr. Selkirk and I barely talk. There's nothing to talk about, really. I know that Anda's father probably gave us that one day on Menagerie Island together to say good-bye. He certainly doesn't want to talk about that. When I get on that boat in Rock Harbor, it will take me away, with the hope that I never return. He probably doesn't want to talk about that, either, because any other option means putting Anda in danger.

And since he's doing me a favor by not turning me in to the police, I don't bring up anything in case he changes his mind.

So silence is the way to go for the whole trip.

The boat spends most of the time pitching and rolling, and I hang on to the slippery side rails as best I can. At some point, the rain lets up, and I wonder what Anda's thinking. Maybe she's already forgetting. Maybe she's entranced by some shiny rock and can't be bothered by memories of me anymore.

I lean my head down on my arm, trying to shut my mind off to everything but thoughts of last night. Miraculously, despite the bumpy ride, I must fall asleep, because Mr. Selkirk yelps at me to wake up. For a second, I'm lost to where I actually am.

"Hey. We're here."

The boat's already slowed down, and I shake the sleep from my foggy head. My bag is still by my feet, held down by a bungee cord. I look around, trying to see the land coming up quickly ahead of us. There's a white boat—the same one that dropped off Anda's father when we first saw him. Tiny specks of men stand on the dock. There are at least four, maybe five.

Five?

"How many friends of yours are picking me up?"

"One. Why?"

"Look."

Mr. Selkirk takes his hands off the steering wheel for a moment to dry off his misted circular glasses, then puts them back on. He frowns when he sees the dock.

"There are two boats there."

I let go of the railing and come to his side of the boat for a better look. He's right. There are two boats, one behind the other. The partially hidden one has a thick orange stripe running along the edge.

It's the Coast Guard.

"Fuck!" I blurt out.

What, what, what am I going to do? I can't pretend I'm someone I'm not. The Coast Guard is probably here for me. I tried hard to cover my tracks, but maybe not hard enough. Maybe they found my Isle Royale searches on the school library computers? It doesn't matter. My heart pounds so thickly in my head that my inner ears ache.

"Calm down, Hector. There's no point in making a scene."

He's right, of course. But I can't help but wonder if he's secretly happy that I'm going to be in custody soon, instead of freely wandering the Upper Peninsula of Michigan, drooling and pining for his daughter.

I try to control my breathing and prepare for what's going to happen. I might be cuffed and searched. I might not. There'll be another few hours of a nauseating boat ride back to Grand Portage. There'll be a radio into the police and my uncle will be contacted.

And then my dad.

And if anyone cares, my mom.

I have hours, at least, before I have to face my uncle. I imagine his fury. I imagine his eyes on me, the ones that are always wordlessly asking for forgiveness and silence. Nausea rises in my throat and I think of ways to escape. Diving off the ship? I'll just get soaked in freezing water before they turn around and pick me up. Running away deeper into Isle Royale? Well, that will last until I fall down from exhaustion. I'll have no food. No shelter.

I'm trapped.

My whole brilliant, idiot idea of staying here didn't work.

As our boat slows even more and the dock is only a hundred yards away, the four men grimly wait for us. One is wearing plain clothes—the guy that Mr. Selkirk was with the other day. The other three are in Coast Guard uniforms, wearing faces about as welcoming as a hypodermic shot in the arm.

They all watch us with steely eyes as our boat closes the distance, but seem relieved when Mr. Selkirk throws them a line. One of the uniformed guys grabs it and ties it firmly to a bollard on the dock.

I force myself to stand up and stare them each in the eye.

"Hector Williams?" the middle officer asks, firmly.

Hearing my name nauseates me. I never knew a name could sound like a judge's guilty verdict.

"Yeah, that's me," I say, finally.

The officer is my height but with salt-and-pepper hair and a two-gallon paunch. He frowns when he looks me up and down. Almost like it's my fault he's got to work on a dismal November day. Oh wait. It is my fault.

"How did you find me?"

"We found your online research about Isle Royale at the high school library after you went missing. You used a dummy login, but the search times matched your class schedule."

I sigh. Well, so much for not leaving a trace. I pick up my bag, and the three guards bristle. I narrow my eyes, sizing them up. One must be the captain. Next to him is a white dude with pasty skin, his hand resting on a holster at his hip. The other is a guy trying to do his best "I used to be a boxer" stance. I don't know what it is about them, but they irritate the hell out of me. "I'm not armed. I'm not going to shoot you with a goddamn granola bar."

The shorter, brawnier officer with blond hair waves at me. "Just give us the bag. We'll take that."

I throw it at them, not too gently. They part so I can

actually step onto the dock.

"Should we cuff him?"

"Hell, yes. He's trespassing."

"What about the other?"

"No. He was just here doing maintenance. We've got his contact info for questioning later."

They all herd me closer to the Coast Guard boat, and one of them takes out cuffs. Mr. Selkirk stands there by his little boat and watches me with an empty expression while they turn me around and crank the metal around my wrists. His friend murmurs to him, but Mr. Selkirk doesn't respond. He looks kind of…upset, actually. Maybe to realize that his daughter's been hanging out with a fugitive for a month without supervision. There's nothing like brown skin and handcuffs to steal away that temporary sheen of teenage innocence.

Their boat is medium-sized, with that broad orange rubber edge and junk on the roof—radar stuff that spins around, antennae, and horns. An inner cabin is large enough for half a dozen people to stand in. They walk me to the cabin, where the door is open and someone is sitting there, waiting for me.

Skin an even, light tan color. Hair shorn close to the head and lips pressed together in a frown. Broad shoulders expand beneath that old canvas jacket that smells like a bar. He belongs in that expanse of middle age where he's still strong enough to pin me down, even though pure youth has long since abandoned him.

My uncle stands up and stares me down with grim eyes.

"Hello, Hector."

Chapter Fifty

ANDA

I've never done this before—search the lake hoping for a person to be alive. But as he and Father travel farther and farther away, I find my mind has trouble remembering his face. His voice. The scent of his skin and the texture of his palms. The air scours my cheeks and swishes angrily against my ankles. It's trying to remove him. My memories of him are dissolving all too quickly.

Forget it all, Anda. People fade away. But I'll always be here for you.

I know. The best thing for me to do would be to sink into the lake and spill the contents of my memories. Wash out my thoughts and only keep what matters. This happens with my father, too. Come December when he returns, I often find myself staring at him for hours, because I've completely forgotten his face.

I stand on the shore and inhale the lake air. The rain slowly comes to a stop, as do my tears. I think of the clouds above and how they offer themselves to me. To become something larger, fiercer. But their call is distant, unlike in previous Novembers. And I want to give Hector safe passage. He deserves to have a life that doesn't end as a skeleton at the bottom of the lake. I extend my fingers and resist the scrubbing of my thoughts and memories. I settle the clouds into softness, keeping the precipitation low.

Keep him safe. Bring him to land.

Yes. That is what I'll do.

I walk to the lake and let it welcome me into the depths, forcing myself not to feel. It doesn't matter, anyway. The water hugs my waist, a gentle caress. It's cold, much colder than I expect. How utterly human of me to notice such things. How very interesting. I've changed since Hector arrived on the island. I wonder how long it will last, if at all.

I must concentrate on Hector while I can.

Outside the boundaries of the lake, he's lost to me. He won't be mine anymore.

Anda. He was never yours to keep.

Chapter Fifty-One

HECTOR

The Coast Guard officers stand behind me in the doorway, waiting. They don't want to get between us. God, please. Let them come in. Or say something. Anything. They might crack the frozen air in the cabin.

"Don't you have something to say to me, son?" my uncle says calmly, matter-of-fact. I can see that inside, he's boiling. His eyes glitter at the sight of me.

"I'm not your son," I say quietly. He takes a step forward and I flinch. The guards behind me move just a touch, ready to come between us.

Ha. It's about six years too late for that.

They watch with tense anticipation as my uncle comes forward and hulks over me. He opens his arms and bear hugs me, hard. I almost fall over from the force of it, what with my wrists pinioned behind me and all. The officers behind us exhale in relief.

"Okay. Let's go," the captain says. My uncle leads me to the bench seat behind us. Someone offers us both life jackets. I stare at them with a what-the-fuck look.

"I'm cuffed. I can't put that on."

"Oh." One guy fishes in his pockets for the keys and uncuffs me so I can put the jacket on. After, they motion to put the handcuffs back on.

"Really? Is it necessary? I'm here," my uncle says. "He's not going to jump in the lake."

I close my eyes. Best idea he's ever had.

Apparently, we'll be heading back to Grand Portage. The police are already aware; they're going to pick me up and question me. My social worker has been notified. The foster care agency has been notified. My father has been notified.

My mom…well. He never says anything about my mom, anyway.

The captain sets a comfortable cruising speed and glances up at the sky. It's still gray, with clouds closer to the water, but no rain. Hardly any wind.

"The trip should take about three or four hours, depending on the weather."

Depending on the weather.

That one phrase is a shot to the heart. It hurts just thinking about leaving Anda behind. I wonder how long it will take for her to get completely back to her normal self. A week? A month? A minute? With nothing but the lake nearby and no weird guys like me messing with her life, she could already be over me. Mr. Selkirk is probably dancing in his little boat all the way back to Menagerie Island, happy to be rid of me.

My uncle chats up the officers, like they've been poker buddies for ages. He thanks them for making an exception and allowing him to come to get me. Says he knew he'd help calm the situation. Secretly, I get the feeling that he doesn't want me to be alone with law enforcement. I ignore them, trying not to hear his voice, but it's impossible. Eventually, he sits back down next to me.

For half an hour, we don't speak.

The officers glance at us and give my uncle looks of sympathy. They have kids, too. Their kids aren't respectful, either. But they don't complain out loud, because really, there's no point comparing.

Ah, but *you* guys don't leave roofies in the kitchen.

It's so atrocious, it's almost funny. So I laugh. My uncle turns to me quickly.

"What did you say?"

"I didn't say anything."

The officers disperse to the windows to talk over some schedule or other. I fight the urge to get up and bolt to the other side of the cabin.

My uncle clears his throat. "You know, your father is coming to the States."

Shocking. I sneer at him. "Really? Why doesn't he send a letter instead?"

My uncle throws me a dirty look, and I immediately quiet myself, staring instead at my boots. This is the way he likes me, after all. More docile. Controllable and caged. The officers make some respectful remarks about Dad being in the military, and isn't my uncle such a swell guy for looking after a kid like me.

The conversation dies quickly, and the officers talk among themselves. For a full five minutes, my uncle sits next to me, wordless for a change. I steal a glance sideways at him. He looks sad. Something is preying on his mind. It can't possibly be guilt. So what is it? I muster up the courage to say something.

"Do you think…he's going to take me back with him to Germany?" I ask. I'm not even sure why I'm asking. Any answer is going to be bad. Living with Dad would just be another prison. No more letters, just him. He'll squeeze in a lifetime of fatherisms and daddy guilt and I'll hate him even more.

"I don't know. He might." My uncle rubs his hands before clasping them together. He hunches his shoulders over and studies his fists. The captain, with his back to us, straightens up just a little, turns his head just so. I know he's listening to our conversation over the din of the boat motor and splashes. "He might not, though. Yeah. He might not."

He almost seems to be convincing himself. I know he would miss me. He's gotten used to having me there. There were normal days, sure. When we'd watch a football game on TV, or he'd come home from the library and bring me three books I actually wanted to read, because he knew what I liked.

It's easy to think about those days when nothing went wrong.

But it's far too easy to remember the days when they did.

Right now, I see him differently, as if somebody sharpened a focus in front of my face that's been blurry for ages. He looks old and lonely. The idea of him by himself in that house with nothing but beer and cigarettes and cigars…it's depressing. I can almost see him staring at the TV set on static.

"I'll miss you if you go," he whispers. "I know I've been too hard on you. I'm sorry for that. I am." Quietly, so that none of the officers can hear.

My uncle slips his hand around my shoulder and pats my back.

It's not much of a gesture. Just like that dad who felt sorry for me because I didn't have someone to teach me how to fish. Like after my uncle would scream at me for screwing up, oh, everything—then pat me once remorse finally kicked in. Like he would when I was twelve and woke up after another lost night, again. A year's worth of pats on the shoulder. Apologies. So many apologies.

A million thoughts violently force their way through my head, a mudslide of terrible things. Nothing has changed. Nothing. I want the officers to see what's going on, but everyone's head is turned away.

Everyone's head is always turned away. No one ever sees. No one ever wants to see.

I want to hit him. But then it'll be me doing the hitting, with three Coast Guard officers watching me attack my guardian. Once again, I'll have no evidence. I'll have no proof. It's the word of a loser runaway kid who's already costing the state thousands of dollars to track him down. It's me with my bad grades and garbage attitude with too many near-expulsions at school.

I tear his hand off me and jump up, hyperventilating. *"Don't you fucking touch me. Ever."*

The captain whirls around. My uncle stands up too, his face ashen with surprise. His hands are out, a what-the-hell gesture.

"What is wrong with you?" he asks. Not angry, but hurt. Confused. Because I can't possibly remember what I wasn't supposed to remember. The officers stare at us. The uncle who can do no wrong, and the nephew who embraces all things wrong.

Oh, what a great actor. I'd applaud and throw him some fucking roses, if I could. The other officers come inside, and questions start pinging back and forth. They keep their distance from me, probably afraid I'll swing. One of them takes out the cuffs again. My uncle's face is sweaty, and he says something like, "I pat his back and he freaks out. This is what I have to deal with. Every day."

I want to cry and hide. It's never going to end. It's always going to be a story I'll never get to write, not the way I want to. The part of me that drove me to plan, sock away money, and escape to Isle Royale—I don't know where to find him. I just don't give a shit anymore.

A puff of damp, cold air hits my neck. The door to the cabin is open, and beyond, the lake waves are small and well behaved against the light gray sky. There's a space between two of the officers. Just enough.

I turn and run. The two guards grab for me, but only get a slight hold on my arms. I wrench away, falling on the slippery floor. My legs scramble to gain some footing and I kick one of the guards now reaching for my ankle. The other one moves to throw himself onto my back, getting my neck in a chokehold. The crook of his elbow crushes against my windpipe and I try to cough. I can't. I try to breathe, but that's not happening, either.

I can't reach the water. I'm going to get dragged back and there will never be an opportunity to escape again.

No. *No.*

I ignore the shouts coming from the inside of the boat and my uncle's yells to grab me. My hands ball into fists and I aim right at the guy's face over my shoulder and he howls in pain as my knuckles meet the crunch of bone under skin. The vise around my neck is gone and I kick away, pulling myself against the floor outside the cabin.

I make it to my feet and lunge between the open gap between the two railings. Someone grabs my whole torso from behind, pinning my arms. I try to throw him off, but it's so slippery that I can't get any traction. My boots squeak and slide beneath me as I try to kick. But I'm already so tired from fighting.

"Stop fighting, Hector. Just stop," my uncle begs me. "Please. It's over."

I stop struggling. Straight ahead, the lake water splashes with waves that are rougher and higher than moments ago.

Only ten feet away.

Oh, Anda. I was so close.

Two other officers grab my arms and they all throw me inside the cabin. I land on my knees, and my arm is yanked behind me, hard. The one with the smashed nose cusses loudly as another guy handcuffs my wrists to a metal railing against the back of the inner cabin.

Now the only way I'll escape is if the ship sinks.

Anda. Please.

Chapter Fifty-Two

ANDA

The water weighs me down, and I feel its strength against my legs. It reaches all the way from Menagerie Island to Isle Royale, and to the docks in Duluth and Copper Harbor. Gentle waves splash on the rare, frosted sea glass inside Whitefish Bay. It is calm. I'll keep it this way until he's safe.

There are more than a dozen boats afloat in the bay. So many others, along Marquette and Keweenaw Bay. There is a lone boat crossing the length between Isle Royale and Grand Portage.

Hector's on board.

I make sure that the seas are placid ahead of the bow, and that the wind stays reined in. If I could push it faster, I would. If I could—

Wait. The boat has stopped moving.

The engines are in neutral. The ship bobs gently in the water, but unusual vibrations and irregular knocks communicate to the depths below, frightening the fish. Shouts reverberate and send rings of sound through the hull and across the surface of the lake. My eyes close and read the tale, like a book open in my hands, illuminated by a noontime sun.

They are fighting. Three, no, four, subduing the one. He's fighting, not for life, but something else.

For me. For an end to it all. I squeeze my eyes shut, listening hard to the wishes of his heart. There is nothing but surrender and despair.

"Hector!" I cry out to the sky, panicked. And the sky answers.

There was a small storm that was due to come, but weakened. I gather its roots and glut it quickly with more moisture and warmth. The clouds above the lake condense with a roiling strength, moving and flowing across the lake, thickening into the troposphere. The storm drags its nails into the calmer air below, molding breezy puffs into muscular corridors of wind.

Waves rise quickly, from short swells into choppy, breaking crests. It will take time to grow them larger, but grow they will. Three-foot seas will turn to five-foot seas, and ten-foot waves will follow. I feel the energy from my skin to my bones, delving into my breastbone and spearing my heart. A heart that is now stuttering to a stop.

Hector.

Hector.

He isn't safe. He isn't free. He was supposed to go to Copper Harbor. But everything I sense under that boat—the boat heading for Grand Portage—is not dulcet or safe. Which means he's with the police. Or worse, his uncle. *What happened? What are they doing to you?*

Rage percolates like acid in my blood, thundering in my temples. I open my mouth and the screech of a gale emerges, blasting the water around me into more mist, becoming a powerful rain that spreads, viruslike, to the miles and miles around me. The water around my waist rises as I flow forward. I look down and see my hands splayed out and reaching above the surface. My nails have blackened to obsidian, and my blood vessels darken to ink-like vines that trail upward toward my neck. I taste a sweet, oily darkness in my throat.

As my body slips beneath the water, time and distance disintegrate, too easily. Nothing but crumbs crushed beneath a boot. I am flying toward the boat, beneath the waves.

No; I am the waves. I am the witch. My sisters sense me and beg for release. For the first time, my hunger isn't aimed at any boat, haphazardly chosen. Just this one. With surgical precision, I'll pluck the lives one by one. I center my energy toward the craft. It's only two hours away from the coast and one hour away from Windigo. One hour too far away. I laugh. There's no safe haven any more. Not from me.

This isn't your battle, Anda.

But it's hard to hear Mother in the chaos of my mind. She has strength, but I have something powerful, too.

Anger.

As the weather shrieks its obedience to my call, my mind falters. The hollowness from the lack of recent sinkings dilutes my thoughts. Fury and hunger tumble together, a roiling clot of frenzied sensations. There is no clarity between them, and soon, no divisions. Warm, panicked, beating hearts call out. Only one wants me, but I'll take them all in a single, yawning bite. There is nothing like the feeling of my watery hand, slipping around their throats and hearts, pressing down with the cold and impossible weight of my fingers. They will stop and be mine.

Somewhere in the recesses of my storming mind, there is a whimper. I cannot remember why I'm so angry. There's nothing but the pull, the need. It's so bitter and vivid, I know nothing else. I crave it.

I extend my arms. Soon, I'll touch the boat, as a child might test the icing on a birthday cake. I shall pull it down, wrap my fingers around its hull, and keep it tethered to the bottom until nothing but bones remain. And even then, I won't give up the dead.

Take them, Anda. It's November. There is no choice in being what you are.

Yes. Yes. It's time.

Chapter Fifty-Three

HECTOR

The rain comes suddenly, with a slap and a rumble.

"They didn't say the weather was going to be this bad," the captain says, twisting the radio knob to find the NOAA frequency. He switches on the windshield wipers to clear the glass in front of him. The waves, which were low and cresting before, have doubled in size. In minutes, they triple the amplitude.

"Do you always see storms come up this fast?" my uncle asks nervously. He's holding on to a side railing and scanning the dials up front, as if he has any clue what they're for.

"Sometimes," the captain says. His voice isn't reassuring at all. The other officer is attending to the broken nose of the guy I hit, casting me occasional glances.

There's nothing to look at. The cuffs are on, and I'm going back to hell.

The boat had been barely pitching up and down when we'd started the journey toward Grand Portage, but the soft gray clouds have morphed with frightening speed. They've thickened into a darker, sinister color—like smoke rising from burning wet wood or plastic, with a greenish tinge. The drenching rain that soon turns into a deluge.

I can't help but smile with pride. God, she's good.

"Should we turn back?" my uncle asks quickly. He fidgets with his life vest and tightens the strap around his chest.

"No. We're almost halfway there. If we run into trouble, we'd be better off being closer to Grand Portage."

"Well, can't you go faster?"

"Through those waves?" He points with disgust. "No."

I look forward and then sideways. The waves are so much higher now, cresting with foamy white peaks that dissolve into the water before appearing in another wave, bigger than the previous. They strike the vessel left and right. The spray constantly fills the air. The boat is heaving at extreme angles. To the officers, it's troubling. My uncle looks like he's going to shit his brains into his pants.

To me, the violent rocking is a lullaby.

The captain hands the radio to another officer, whose voice can't contain the worry everyone is feeling. The captain goes back to steering the vessel. He drives the boat perpendicular to each wave, so the nose of the craft bobs up nauseatingly high before crashing down on each valley. The windshield wipers are going at full speed now, but we can barely see anything past the next wave coming in. The sky and water are one mass of greenish gray. I can't believe how fast she's made this storm. It's absolutely incredible.

"Gale force winds. Experiencing a nine Beaufort, only five about ten minutes ago. Seas at least fifteen feet now," the captain radios in. "Crew is fine. We got one bloody nose we'll explain later. Our two passengers are okay."

Okay? Depends on who you ask.

"Are we going to be okay?" my uncle asks. When he says "we" I know he's not including me. He now seems to have completely forgotten that I'm sitting back here with a contented smile on my face.

"Well, if we can keep managing these waves, yes. She's a good, hearty ship. As long as it doesn't get worse, we'll be all right. She's handled this type of weather many times before."

Ah. But has Anda handled her?

Chapter Fifty-Four

ANDA

So pretty, this thing I've composed.

The boat is clawing its way up the steep waves and crashing over them. I've crossed impossible lengths, and its shuddering hull is within my sight. Soon, it will be within my reach. The captain has good control, but he's sweating profusely under his uniform. I smell his fear—sour and rank. It inflames me.

The rest of the passengers are holding on, waiting for the storm to abate. Under the surface, I open my eyes and take in the murky, churning water around me. The silt and stones of the lake bottom pelt my skin. They're fawning, and I kick them away. They'll never persuade me to be kinder.

I raise my hands a little and incite the wind, whipping the waves to twenty feet.

Twenty-five.

Thirty.

The captain is well seasoned, navigating the steep swells to let the ship's reinforced bow take all the brutal force of each eager wave. The boat is sturdy and will take the punishment according to the physics of its creation. She has good bones. It will be lovely to bite into them and spit them out.

But—this won't do. It's taking too long. From the depths of the lake, I hear a calling.

Don't be greedy. Share, my dear.

Others are hungry to partake in the coming feast. I hold up three fingers on my right hand, swirling them slowly above me, inviting the Three Sisters to rally forth. Rarely released but just as voracious, they had their turn in my place before evolving into a legend.

The three rogue waves travel one after the other; impossibly large, even within such a terrible November storm. People speak reverently of them. They've taken other ships before, far larger. My sisters are ravenous like me but cannot come forth without my call or mother's. They live only for destruction, tied irrevocably to one another's strength, and ours.

I kiss my first fingertip and release the first one. Made of wind and water and the disturbed depths, she comes from a slight angle, far larger than anything the captain has encountered before. The angle is off just enough that when the ship crashes down the deep trough, it sways dangerously from port to starboard. Lake water washes over the entire craft, and two glass windows on the cabin break. The boat takes on water and begins to list to the port side. It's survivable, yes. The men inside yell and shriek, all but one.

I kiss my second fingertip and send along the second sister.

The same size as her first sister, she will cripple the boat. The passengers can't believe a second rogue wave is coming.

It's enormous. Their eyes widen with sheer, frozen fear as they see it. They feel the inevitable in their hummingbird-fast hearts.

The captain hollers, desperately trying to steer her straight, but now her starboard side takes the worst of it as it presses her down, a weight and force she cannot bear. She lists so badly that her keel bobs above the surface for a second, and her hull cracks—ah, such an alluring sound. The passengers are finding their upright is sideways, their down is left. I hear a bone snap and skulls crashing against the inside of the cabin. There are more screams.

I sigh. This is the sweetest part. I kiss my third finger and send along the last sister, stronger and more willful than the first two, and at least one-third more enormous. She is the youngest and the most ravenous. Now the captain knows I am here. His eyes open wider with reverence. Inside his head, he says it to himself—the Witch of November. The Three Sisters. It's just like the tales of the *Edmund Fitzgerald*. He wonders if they'll sing a song about him, too, someday.

The third sister hits the vessel with pure green water, the thick of the wave immersing everything. She cracks the hull further, and water gushes into the boat. Two of the crew have opened up the door to the cabin, now the roof of their prison. The captain refuses to leave. He's a good man. I'll give him an honorable death and let him stay with his lady. As water rapidly fills the cabin inch by inch and the sighing boat begins its descent, I sense the other passengers.

One is praying to God and is in too much shock to move.

One is kicking to the surface and trying to climb out of the doorway. He's the most frightened, and his heart is black and heavy within his chest.

Another is treading water, holding a set of keys. He is panicked and trying to decide if another life is worth his.

Only one inside the vessel welcomes death. It speaks a name.

My name.

Anda, it says. *I'm ready.*

Chapter Fifty-Five

HECTOR

My head is barely above water.

The cabin is sideways and filling with lake water fast. So fast. I mean, this is what I've begged for, and yet— the real rawness of it drives into me with terror. My heart beats hard, almost within my throat, threatening to choke me. I pull on my wrists behind my back, and they swish helplessly only two inches through the water, tethered to the railing behind me. I thread my right fingers into my left, needing to hold on to something. I wish it were Anda's hand, but right now, I'm all I've got, and it seems like a shabby second-place prize. It doesn't matter; in a little while, I won't be alive anymore.

"Oh God," I sputter, the water splashing into my mouth. "Oh my God, oh God."

I thought this was what I wanted.

It is, isn't it?

The captain is yelling, trying to get his meager crew out of the ship. One of the officers is chest-deep in the moving water, pasty-faced and bleeding profusely from his forehead. He can barely see with the salty blood staining his eyes. The captain helps to push him out the flapping cabin door and he's swept straight out, as if swallowed whole into the lake. I wonder if he'll survive. But then I remember that Anda's out there. I know his fate almost as clearly as I know my own.

The other officer is hanging on to the side rail (now our ceiling), his fingers fumbling with slippery ring of keys to the handcuffs. He's breathing so hard that he can't speak. His hand is shaking. If he's not careful, he'll drop the keys. I watch the glint of wet metal shivering in his grasp. They're tiny and laughably simple, like a kid's toy keys. I'm surprised I can focus at a time like this.

"Give them to me!" the captain yells.

My uncle is about five feet away, freaking out and greedily gulping air. His eyes are so wide that the whites surround his pupils. He looks at the captain and me. He's neck-deep in water now and splashing hard to keep his body afloat, even with the life vest on.

My uncle's eyes lock onto mine, wild with fear and panic. But the way he clings to the door, I can tell—he's not afraid for me. He's afraid for himself. Somewhere behind those brown eyes, there's nothing. They're empty. There were times that I thought there was enough between us to keep us floating. Enough to make me feel real guilt for getting us in this situation. But it's never been enough.

Suddenly, a huge wave crashes over us and we all pitch to one side again. My head goes underwater, and I hear nothing but a roaring surge against my eardrums. I feel the ship pull my wrists down behind me. The metal digs into my flesh. Seconds later, we pitch to the other side. My head emerges from the roiling water. I've been given another chance at a few breaths.

"Get out! I'll uncuff him!" the captain yells at my uncle and the other officer. He grabs the keys from the other officer, whose face is an openmouthed expression of shock. When they don't move for the door, he screams, "Go!" The officer yanks at my uncle's vest.

My uncle doesn't hesitate. He and the other officer reach for the doorway. They start swimming through it.

My uncle doesn't look back.

The captain's hair is plastered against his forehead as he looks up and takes a huge inhalation. He dives beneath the water, his hands fumbling to search for the cuffs. I feel metal jabbing at my hands and wrists. He can't find the keyholes. He comes up for air, gasps a few times, and dives down again.

Another wave crashes over us, and I'm under the water. The whole ship lurches hard, so hard. This time, it doesn't right itself, and the metal groans like a sick whale. I feel the captain's hands still fumbling against mine. Suddenly, one of my wrists is able to pull free. There is a faint *snitch* against the metal around my other wrist, and it too is released. He grasps my hands to pull me up, but I don't know which way is up anymore.

Suddenly, his hands are yanked away.

I try to open my eyes, but all I see is boiling water, bubbles and confusion. I can't see the captain. I'm being pulled down with the ship as it recedes beneath the furious waves. Pressure squeezes painfully against my eardrums.

The captain is gone.

My uncle is gone.

I try to look above me, but there's nothing to see. So I shut my eyes, even as my heart wants to burst inside me.

Chapter Fifty-Six

ANDA

The two crew members are bobbing on the waves, bellies full of water. Already their lungs have liquid deep within their spongy recesses.

It has begun.

There is an unmeasurable momentum in the storm, and it's beginning to escape my grasp. Mother's energy anchoring it all, making it solid and unstoppable. Hector's uncle floats where the boat took its last gasp of life before sinking. He claws at the water, so desperate to stay afloat. He screams for no one but himself.

Hearts bleed their oily whispers of truth when I'm near. As victims die or face its dark mirror, their dreams infect me. So here is the truth. I have tasted all flavors of terror before, including the bright flashes of sweet regret, but his is nothing but acrid and corrupt.

Deep in the waters, Hector is still trapped within the ship. The captain has lost consciousness, his body cradled against the ceiling of the cabin. One more minute like this, and his mind will be beyond retrieval. But Hector is still alive. Barely. He's waiting for something.

Thunder rumbles and forces its voice into my head.

Anda. Why do you pause? Finish it.

I reach out with my hands, feeling the full power of the water, the wind, the sky, the air. They throb in my temples and heart, begging me to bring this to fruition.

End it.

Hunger and craving war with another sensation, raw and pulsating within my chest. The lighthouse. My father. Hector. All these have nudged this facet alive. Life, and the worthiness of the fight. The lighthouse had opened me to the thoughts and hearts of those I'd taken for so many years. It was always easy to smother their wails for mercy under the insistence of my own hunger. I hear them now with a clarity I never could. I feel them. It makes me cry out in agony.

Mary, one of them thinks. *Mary. I wish we could have had more time. I wish we could have had one more day.*

The other weeps for his captain. *Joe. Please be okay. Where are you? Let's have that one last beer, right? Joe. Joe. Joe.*

Hector's uncle slaps the water away from himself. *It's over. He's gone. He's gone. It's better this way. But his father. Oh God, his father.*

And the last one. Hector. At first, he's silent. Even his silences are exquisite. And then, finally:

Go ahead, Anda. What are you waiting for?

He is anger and despair all at once, daring me to claim my birthright, what I do best. But no—it's not just a challenge. It's a question.

What *am* I waiting for?

Chapter Fifty-Seven

HECTOR

The need for oxygen is excruciating, clawing at my ribs. The water buffets my body, even as I fall deeper and deeper. My throat constricts and spasms, refusing to let the water into my lungs. The pressure threatens to implode my eardrums. I curl my fingers into my palms and squeeze.

So this is what it's like to drown. It's far worse than what I imagined.

Is it, Hector?

My eyes fly open.

I would gasp if I weren't almost dead already. Even though blackness etches at the edge of my mind and my heart wants to burst from my chest, I can see her. She hovers in front of me. White hair, barely swaying in the water. The same pixie face, the same honeyed skin clouded by the swirling water. And yet I hardly recognize her.

Her eye sockets are black and gruesomely void, a complete absence of light or humanity. Her lips are closed, and black tendrils snake from her onyx fingertips, up her arms, to her neck, like some terrible disease has rotted her from the outside in. Her feet are black too, as if dipped into tar. She's terrifying. There is a purpose to her terror, too—she's showing me what she is for a reason. There is no poetry here, nothing vaguely romantic about this side of her, no matter what I've thought or understood. But I'm not afraid.

Go ahead, I say in my head. *Whatever I have, whatever was worth anything—it's yours. Some good can come out of this. You can have me.*

Anda's thoughts claw their way in, a razor scraping against steel.

Yes.

Her black eyes remain vacant. I can't see what's in their depths. Her hands extend toward me and wrap oh so gently around my neck. They're burning hot and sear my skin. She comes closer, and I see oblivion in her features.

The darkness of her eyes seems to expand, becoming larger than both of us. It fills my vision until there is nothing but nothing.

Yes. It's over.

I smile as the darkness fills me and annihilates my last thought.

Chapter Fifty-Eight

ANDA

I know what has to be done. It is nature. There is no choice, and there is no judgment.

My hands thrill to be around his neck, to feel the waning of his pulse. His eyes are half closed. He's lost consciousness. I salivate, wanting to consume what's left fluttering inside his body.

Distant memories shake within me. A palm against my skin. A kiss that tastes of chocolate. Cool scissors against my scalp. Scraping a razor against a sculpted male cheekbone, too beautiful to endure. An invitation to be hurt, offered willingly.

Hector.

I withdraw my hands to my chest. The ship above me is already half consumed beneath the waves.

Hector.

I scream so loud that the sky shudders with fear and the sisters cower, dissolving into infant swells.

What have I done?

But my heart. Oh, my heart. I miss him already, and

he's right here.

I see him with more clarity as darkness drains from my eyes. The tar-like, lifeless color recedes in my fingertips, and I recognize with full understanding where we are.

Hector.

I yank his arms toward me, and will the water to settle so I can ease us through the flapping door of the sunken ship. But it is hard. Even with my ability to change the pressure and waves around us, the boat continues to roil with anger at being taken. The deepwater surges don't respond to my command.

Let go of that boy.

I jerk in surprise. There is a strong, winding core of current that swirls around Hector, trying to pry him away from me. But I won't have him stolen. Never.

I grasp him firmly around the chest from behind and issue a command to the waters around us. The water concedes, and we lift upward. I push the door to the boat cabin open, but I have to kick with my human legs for the force to exit the ship. My body flails in the bubbling water around us. I have trouble seeing which way is up, knowing without instinct where to go.

You are making a mistake.

I want to scream at her. Mistakes are for those who *can* make a choice. It's mine to make. You can't stop me. This is what I want.

She doesn't answer me. Not with words, not this time. Her fury boils within the water and it scalds my skin—a sensation I've never felt. There has always been that energy within me, scorching with ability, but now it's outside my body. Huge, and expanding. And there's something else that's also changed. My hunger is still there, but it seeks its nourishment from a different source. Not to extinguish, but to kindle.

I want life.

I kick and kick, pulling Hector up with me. Luckily, we are buoyant and let ourselves shoot up like corks. As our faces break through the water's surface, I gasp for air. Hector's face is ashen, his eyes still half closed. Our bodies crest over the huge waves, up and down, and still he won't wake up.

"Hector!" I scream, shaking him. For an agonizing ten seconds, he does nothing but let the lake water flow over his face, into his throat. "Hector! Wake up!" I grasp him around the chest and squeeze him so hard that water pours out of his mouth. I squeeze him again and again, as if just embracing him could spark an awakening. Just when my arms are so tired they burn with pain, Hector coughs and sputters. He gasps a few times more, then pitches lake water from his throat.

I cling to him as the waves around us grow even larger. He coughs, a terrible barking dissonance, the most gorgeous sound of life I've ever heard. We cling to each other, hard.

"What happened?" he tries to yell, but his voice is bubbly and hoarse. "What are you doing?"

"I don't know!" I scream back. It's the answer to everything.

The storm rages on and tightens its hold over the area around us, as a fist squeezes a sodden tea bag. We kick and paddle, trying to stay afloat though the waves try to pull us down with each mighty wall of water. Hector is still wearing his orange life jacket. Were it not for that, we'd both have trouble keeping our heads out of the water.

My body is tiring, and I've never known this type of exhaustion in the water. My muscles crave air, and sugar, and rest. I keep kicking, though my calves feel leaden and tight with lactic acid. A wave of water crashes over us, and we spin beneath the surface, water forcing its way into our noses, burning our sinuses, blinding us. We fight again for the surface, coughing and sputtering for a blessed few seconds before another wave comes over us.

Hector's arms find their strength—what little he has to offer—and give it to me. For a second, his eyes meet mine and ask the other question he wishes to know.

Why can't I control it? Why won't I stop the storm?

Do you really want to know, Anda? Mother asks me. *Let me show you.*

Chapter Fifty-Nine

HECTOR

She's not the same.

The inky tendrils have fled from her body. Her body is cold against mine, not the burning torch I'd felt when she'd been in the lake before. Anda's got one hand on my life jacket and one around my shoulder, but her grip is flimsy. Her eyes are gray again, huge and taking in the storm around us. Exhaustion pulls her face into a scowl. We struggle to keep the water out of our throats.

"Can't you make it stop?" I scream, but Anda can't answer, because a huge wave pushes her underwater, and I have to use every bit of energy to pull her up. When her face surfaces, white hair plastered and splayed across her forehead, the landscape of her expression is unrecognizable. I've never seen terror in her face like this. "Make it stop, Anda!" I beg her.

Anda twists her head to face me, but there are no answers in her expression.

You really want to see what we are made of, Hector?

I've never heard Anda's mother before in my head. It

leaves behind pain that simmers across the seams of my mind.

I clutch at Anda, asking for answers, but she's silent. She's looking past me, far in the distance. At first, I think she's having another spell. But then I realize she sees something.

I turn my neck. A huge mound of water rises out of the lake. It's as if an unseen hand is pinching the surface, tenting it upward like a tablecloth. Spikes and spires poke out of the surface in the distance, around the pinnacle of water. I blink and paw the water from my eyes, but it's still there. All of it.

Only twenty feet away, something muddy and tarnished rises out of the water. At first, I think it's a piece of rotted log, pitched upward by the roiling lake water. But it keeps rising and rising. It's not a log, but a broken mast. Chunks of green-covered metal are attached to it and faintly, writing on the side of a huge wall of metal becomes visible.

Gle--yon

It's a sunken ship.

Holy shit. This can't be happening. Just can't. But even as I'm not believing anything I'm seeing, more spires and chunks of metal rise out of the depths. Wrecked hulls of boats, small and large, begin swirling around the mound of water that grows taller than a house. Taller than a building now. It's a cone of lake, ever growing, surrounded by the swirling skeletons of dead ships.

Anda is watching, too, but she's not aghast like I am. Her terror settles into reverence and cool acceptance. Whatever she's seeing, it's no surprise.

A chunk of metal swooshes beneath us, narrowly missing us. It would have chopped us in half if it were closer. Anda and I try to swim away from this hurricane of rusted metal and water, but the water swirls and pushes us closer. It's impossible to get farther than a few feet in a few seconds. It's hopeless to try.

Yes, hopeless. Some battles can't be won, Hector.

The voice leaves its acid marks inside my thoughts, and pain blossoms anew at my temples. Somehow, I know that I'm not meant to hear her words. It's unnatural, and I'm paying the price for it.

We watch as more and more wrecks rise out of the depths, traveling from the distance to join the others as they spin around the torrent of sickly green water. The water peaks and narrows before widening higher up. The clouds dip down from the sky and enshroud the hourglass of water, and lightning sizzles against the smoky sky. Two twirls of cloud spiral down on either side, like dancer's arms wanting to touch the wrecks.

"Holy fuck," I mutter, between coughs.

It's her. This gigantic vision of a creature, with her waist encased in mist, hair made of storm clouds careering down her shoulders, and a gown made of the skeletons of sunken ships.

I'd heard of her through Anda. I thought I'd never seen her. And then I remember the skeleton in the lake that disappeared at a second glance. She'd made herself known, and I'd tried to ignore the sign. She's always been there, waiting to show herself.

"Mother!" Anda screams.

Chapter Sixty

ANDA

She turns her massive body to look down at us, tiny as we are among the flotsam of the storm. Though tendrils of air and vapor surround the crown of her head, she has no face. No expression that I can read. But I don't need a visage to understand what's in her heart.

If you cannot do what's in your nature, then I will. For both of us.

Mother swoops an arm toward us, a waterspout of tremendous force that pulls us out of the water. Hector and I are over and above the lake, ten, twenty feet, before she lets go and we plunge, screaming, back down.

As soon as we hit the surface, Hector's hand is yanked out of mine.

No.

I churn my legs in the lake, trying to find the surface, trying to find Hector. When my head comes above the water, I see him, but he's already twenty feet away. It might as well be a mile.

"Anda!" he hollers. "I'm coming!"

But as he reaches for me, the jagged stern of a huge boat sweeps toward him. I see it come so slowly, knowing what's about to happen. Tons of metal, torn from the lake bed where it had been living for over forty years.

The *George M. Cox*.

As its broken stern slices through the water, it sighs, unhappy to be clawed from its resting place by the Rock of Ages lighthouse. It was happy there, an old man in repose on the lake bed. It enjoyed the curiosity of the divers that hovered about its wreckage, like children pawing at a grandfather's knee. Now the steel plates of its hull groan and creak as Mother throws it with precise care, tearing the watery space between me and Hector.

It's pushed too close to Hector. As it sinks back into the depths, it swallows the water nearby, sucking everything down with it, including him.

"Hector!" I scream.

But he doesn't surface. He's too far away, and I can't swim fast enough to get to him, not with this useless body. I paddle through the greenish foam anyway, trying to grow closer, trying to paw the water, a feeble attempt at finding him. But it's no use. I'll never find him.

I won't win, not like this. She's forcing my hand on purpose.

Mother turns to me with her petticoat of wrecks flailing around her, the storm clouds gracing her empty brow. She's won, and she knows it. This was always the plan. She would have me only one way, and she's willing to show herself to do so.

I've felt the warring sides within me. I've let them push me this way and that, never realizing that I could change the terms. Never understanding that there were choices that could be made.

I close my eyes and exhale, letting my body sink into the depths. I splay out my arms and fingers, feeling the water at my fingertips, welcoming the energy there. The darkness. The light. The beauty and the horror. My vision blurs into one that sees far beyond the murky three feet before me. I see the ships pawing at my mother's swirling skirts, the demineralized skulls skittering across the lake floor.

Black tendrils snake up my arms, and my heart ceases to beat. With a flick of a finger, the waters around me calm in an orb, and the winds above whimper in fear. I see her nod her head with approval.

Once you make your choice, daughter, there is no going back.

She thinks I've come to my senses. She thinks I've come back to her. She thinks I can divide myself, once and forever, when no division needs to exist. Hector has taught me this, too.

Deep within the water, I reach out and sense what I've often cowered from. The ancient lake sturgeon and hook-nosed trout; the mussels clinging with fierce tenacity to the lake beds; pines and cedars and birches that root into history itself. Always, their pain in fighting and living stung me; always, I ran away from it. But I'll entangle this colossal strength in my embrace now.

Mother doesn't realize that though I may be her daughter, I am not her possession. I never was. I am my father's daughter, too. Mother may be the lake, and she may be so for centuries. But there is one more thing that outlasts mountains, and lakes, and rivers.

Time.

I am November.

This is my time. I can reach down, and up, and into the

endless nothing in between, and take with me the strength of a million Novembers yet to come. I can stop splitting myself in two, and take strength outside of death, where life rouses itself in earthquakes, in cells, in seeds, in struggle. In my human imperfection, there is power that exists in no other being.

Time. Life. Death.

Human. Island.

All of it is me.

I am the Witch of November.

And Mother has made me angry.

Chapter Sixty-One

HECTOR

I can't get loose.

The back of my life jacket is snagged on a piece of metal, on this huge wreck that is falling into the depths of the lake. The pressure on my ears is excruciating. It's dark, and the cold is worse than anything, and I can't breathe.

I wish I could help Anda.

I almost wish that I'd never come to Isle Royale, but that would be lying. I always knew at one point or another, I'd run away and not come back. And I don't mean in the visiting sense.

I close my eyes and let the pressure squeeze harder.

No. You won't run away, not this time.

My eyes fly open. I see nothing in the water, only the black depths of the lake. But something pushes against me. It's powerfully strong, but doesn't snap my bones. I'm forced upward as my orange life vest is torn from my body, still snagged on the wreckage. Just when my brain wants to burst from lack of oxygen, I break the surface—and find that the surface is broken.

The lake looks like nothing I could imagine. It's frozen, rain locked into place as it hovers in heavy sheets above it. Large pockmarks litter the surface, which doesn't seem liquid anymore. It isn't frozen, or solid, or gas. It's nothing that can be defined by any textbook.

The ships are locked in place, half submerged. In the air, Anda's mother is still in her gigantic, unearthly form, but something's wrong. She's blurred at the edges, and she seems to be locked in a struggle with something I can't see. Until I realize I'm looking in the wrong place.

A hundred feet away from Anda's mother is a wisp of darkness, floating above the water. It's almost like a smudge of smoke, hovering there for no good reason. But it shimmers and sways, and seems to be sucking the light and energy from everything around it. I peer harder and see arms, legs. The dark blob of head swivels and turns to me. The eyes pierce right into me, seeing everything.

It's Anda.

Her mother notices me at the same time Anda does. Everything unfreezes with a roar. Her mother raises a mass of solid water that pushes toward me with terrific speed. I barely have time to inhale before the water hits—when it doesn't. The water pauses in a thick wall, like boiling glass only feet from me. Anda's hand is raised in my direction. With a twist of her wrist, the wall of water dissipates into a cloud of vapor.

A piece of stained wreckage floats nearby, a newer piece of boat with the fiberglass hull still intact. I grab on to the smooth surface, trying to buy myself time to catch my breath. Over my shoulder, Anda's tiny dark shadow of a figure continues to hover, while her mother's vast body of wreckage and clouds tries to pummel her.

Every assault that Anda's mother sends my way, Anda

blocks, almost too easily. But she can't stop the storm, and I can't hold on for much longer. The waves are still high enough that they douse my head over and over again, and the burning in my forearms becomes agonizing. The cold is numbing my brain. My hands begin to slip, when I wonder. Why am I trying? What could come out of this that could possibly be worth living for? I think of my uncle, wonder if he's still alive. Wonder if there will really be an Anda for me to ever come back to. My fingertips make helpless squeaking noises as they lose purchase on the wreckage, and Anda's head turns toward me. Though a mile away, I can see her expression of hurt and fury.

Don't you dare, Hector.

I understand. This life isn't just mine to throw away anymore. She knows it, and I know it. I hyperventilate, trying to get oxygen into my limbs, then kick my legs anew to get a better hold on the piece of fiberglass. There's a broken chunk of metal above me, and I reach for it, dragging myself higher. I have a better grip. This time, I'll hang on for a bit longer.

I don't know if that will be long enough, but I'm not planning that far ahead right now.

While Anda fights off another enormous rogue wave that comes my way, I hear the faint buzzing of a noise, barely above the din of the rain and roaring wind that's buffeting my head. I think maybe it's a helicopter, which would be madness in a storm—especially *this* storm. But there's nothing overhead but gray swirls of condensation. Faintly, a single voice forces it way through the chaos.

"Gracie!"

I turn around. In the distance, a small boat is churning through the rough waters, headed toward me. It's Mr. Selkirk, with eyes on nothing but the unstoppable force that is Anda's mother. I scream at him when he's only forty feet away, and he slows the motor down, just enough to scan the choppy waves. Bobbing up and down, it's a miracle he sees me, stuck to this piece of junk. He steers closer to me, and my body sags with relief. I let my cramped hands slide off the wreckage as Mr. Selkirk draws closer.

I hold out my arm, but he doesn't reach for me. He doesn't throw a line.

His dark blue eyes are snapping with intensity behind his wire glasses. He still wears the old wool hat that encases his white hair. I sigh with relief when he bends over to drop anchor, but to my surprise he only tosses a big orange life vest. I catch it, but my face says everything I want to. Why won't he let me on board? My exhaustion is ten years old, my muscles cramping painfully, and even with this vest, I won't last long in the frigid water.

Mr. Selkirk yells at me. "You tell her why."

"What are you talking about?" I sputter lake water, clinging to the life vest.

"She won't understand. You tell her."

I try to yell at him to stay, to let me get on his goddamned boat, to make sense. But Mr. Selkirk drives the boat at full throttle toward the two warring elements—the mother, the daughter; the lake and the storm. He becomes a smaller spot of white and silver on the sine-like waves, appearing and disappearing between swells. He drives the boat—which wasn't small but now looks like a tiny white dash—right between them. Anda is still just a smudge of coal in the sky, her arms conducting the air and water around her, fighting to keep her mother from sending me to my death at the bottom of the lake, where her mother believes I deserve to be.

I don't think they even register that Mr. Selkirk is right

there until it's too late. He drives between two sailboat wrecks climbing the column of water on Anda's mother. The angle is impossibly steep, and the boat too large to turn quickly. Anda and her mother suddenly become aware of him at the same moment.

But it's either too late, or Mr. Selkirk knows exactly what he's doing. The boat can't handle the pitch of the wave, and I watch with horror as the bow of the boat climbs, climbs, climbs—until it can't go any farther. It hesitates and begins its descent in reverse, before flipping over. Mr. Selkirk's dot of a body falls through the air as the wall of water collapses on top of him and the craft.

Mr. Selkirk is gone.

Chapter Sixty-Two

ANDA

There is a rift torn into us.

Mother and I see it as it happens—the extinguishing of this tiny life between us, that sparks so brightly even we are blinded. A life that even we have no power to return to this world. Ever with the power to kill, neither of us has possessed the immeasurable force of sacrifice.

He has eclipsed us.

Father.

Gone.

Mother, the tower of water and swirling cloud, the shipwrecks still rotating about her in homage, shudders, as if the molecules of her being have forgotten why they clung together in the first place.

The thousands of tons of flotsam and wreckage begin to sink, forming huge eddies and whirlpools as they displace the lake water beneath them. The mountain-sized cone of water simply falls, at first in slow motion, then with the speed dictated by reality. A huge wave pushes outward in a ring, almost thirty feet high.

Mother doesn't weep. She has only ever taken when she needed to take, has only ever given when she needed to give. And her need is so great that this offering makes no sense—in a way that makes no sense in her order of the universe, when things happen according to the seasons, and the rotations of the sun, for survival and survival only. It tears her open.

Even as my own grief paralyzes me, I sense what happens deep beneath the waters. Mother has gone to Father's corpse. She's forgotten all about us. That is what she has always done—crash from one passion to another, leaving behind things of beauty and brokenness, like cracked agates on the shoreline. And sometimes, a baby.

But I know she'll eventually understand that sometimes, there are gifts. There can be these inscrutable items of beauty and horror outside the rules dictated by nature. But to me, it doesn't feel like a gift. It feels like robbery, like Father has committed a crime against those he loved. Father is gone. He is gone.

Mother envelops Father's slackened body with her watery arms. She will rejoice over the flowers that will grow from his corpse. She will fall in love, heartlessly, with the blooms, before bringing the icy winds of winter next year to kill them. An encore of death. And the cycle will continue. Her joy and mourning will be reborn again and again. She would have it no other way.

The huge wave of Mother's receding form reaches Hector, whose body is limp and tired, held above the waterline by a soaked, bobbing life vest. But even he can't handle the power of the wave that comes, larger than the Three Sisters, larger than anything I've ever made, because this is born of the fury of Mother and her retreat. Its bitterness reaches him, turns him over and over, forces him down so low in the waters that even I fear I might not be able to bring him back in time.

But I find him.

And I find that I can't touch him anymore. Not like this. Not like I am.

I push the water hard, below him, forcing him upward as fast as I can. As he breaks the surface, he gasps and flails, though his life vest will do the job of keeping him afloat and alive. More than I can right now.

Hector sees me, and in the glassy, perfect surface of his exquisite brown eyes, I see what he sees. A creature with darkness in her blood, sewn into her very bones, in so much of what she touches. Faintly, I know that the clouds have run from me as I've bidden, that a helicopter is in the air already. That the Coast Guard has launched three boats for the one that they lost contact with over an hour ago. They will search for the bodies that they hope are still alive in this world. They will find Hector, close to death, but still mercilessly, mercifully alive.

I look at Hector, and everything he has to live for. I think of Father, and his absence gnaws at my marrow.

I see myself, and there is no beauty in what I behold.

The water begins to envelop me and I recede into the depths, to a place he can't follow.

"Anda—" he begins. He's barely conscious now. This struggle and the cold have been too much for his body.

But I don't listen to him. He calls for the Anda he knew.

I sink back into the water. It's time to say my final good-byes.

Chapter Sixty-Three

HECTOR

Chapter Sixty-Four

ANDA

Chapter Sixty-Five

HECTOR

Death sucks ass.

That's what I had thought when I first woke up in the ICU. Every bone, joint, and inch of skin suffered its own brand of misery. Sharp things bored into my wrists, my neck. I choked on objects that burrowed down my throat and into my chest, gagging me into silence. My brain was a mixture of cotton balls and sand, and my thoughts were a gluey mess. The drug dreams were too freaky to be enjoyable.

But then I got better. My breathing tube was pulled. I got to sit up in bed and eat vanilla pudding and green bean puree, which I've discovered is a type of hell in food form.

For a long time, I didn't ask how I got there. I spent my recovery just thinking about everything that happened, up until the last moments in the lake. Someone says my dad visited, but I don't believe it. He wasn't here when I woke up. I didn't watch the news or read the paper. Every time a doctor, or nurse, or psychologist, or physical therapist came into my room, they'd meekly ask, "Do you have any questions?" I knew what they were asking. They wanted to know if I wanted to know.

Finally, I couldn't avoid it any more. Actually, it was the housekeeping dude who told me. He was dumping out the garbage in my hospital room late at night. I was busy coughing up a half pound of very nasty-flavored snot from my right lung.

"You're that kid, right?"

I gave him the shifty eye. "I don't know. Am I?"

"The runaway. The one who almost drowned in the lake."

I nod, looking for yet another tissue to spit into.

"Well. Hope you recover fast. Your uncle, too."

That's how I found out that my uncle survived.

And I wept.

At first, I was angry with Anda. She had come this close to being with me when she changed to save me. But she couldn't fix everything—and then I realized it wasn't her responsibility to solve my problems. Or kill them, either. I wouldn't want anyone I loved to carry that burden. Hell, I didn't want it myself.

If he'd died, life *would* be different. But he'd still be around, in my thoughts and memories. I spent so much time running away that without him, I'd feel a little unmoored. But now I have a reason to get better. I could have a trajectory that doesn't involve disappearing.

That week I found out about my uncle, I couldn't keep away from the news. I inhaled it all, as best as my feeble, fluid-swelled lungs could handle. They said that three people died. The captain's body was never recovered. One of the officers suffered a heart attack during the rescue and died three days later in the hospital. The other one went home already. And then there was Anda's father.

Mr. Selkirk's body was also never found. I shiver to

think of where it could be, on the bottom of the lake. I wonder if Anda's mother—Gracie—is keeping him as some sort of macabre consolation prize, or just using his bones as a toothpick. One day, the nurse was taking my blood pressure and temperature when she noticed me muttering as I scanned the paper.

"Gracie?" she said. "Who's that? A girlfriend?"

She was trying to be nice, but I winced at her comment. "Nothing."

"Aw, c'mon." She had that irritating tone of voice that said *Not leaving unless you tell me!*

"Well," I admitted, "I heard somebody call Lake Superior that."

"Gitche Gumee."

"Excuse me?"

"It's an Ojibwa phrase for Lake Superior. Didn't you learn that in school?"

"Oh. Yeah." I'd totally forgotten, of course.

I looked it up later. "Gitche Gumee" means "Great Sea" in Ojibwa.

Great Sea.

Gracie.

I find that my thoughts spiral around Mr. Selkirk, the moment he asked me to explain things to Anda. I try to remember them hard, play them back like a movie. That's where he lives now, in memory, and I'm sad that he's gone—and sadder that Anda's lost her dad. I feel terrible for her. Jealous, even, that she had a parent worth mourning.

I think of the captain and that other guy, too. It's a strange feeling, to be forever linked to death. The guilt weighs me down like an anchor. I know that much of this all happened because of me. Anda isn't completely to blame.

I wonder what she's thinking or feeling right now. Or if

she feels anything at all. I wish I could go to the lake and just touch the water, but I'm also terrified of it. Would her mother try to swallow me into the depths and drown me again, right there and then? Are we in a cease-fire? Would Anda know I was there? Maybe nothing would happen. But as long as I'm trapped in the hospital, none of these thoughts matter.

I search for news about Isle Royale. But I find zero search results about a girl hiding on Menagerie Island. There's plenty of stuff about how I hid there for longer than they thought a kid could manage, and how the Park Service is going to ensure that this never, ever happens again. There's even an article about how Mr. Selkirk, a park volunteer, died trying to save the capsized passengers of the boat that sank. But not a word that he left a daughter behind.

I'm surrounded by endings, but even Anda knew she wasn't capable of finishing this story for me. Not the easy way. Not the wrong way.

It had to be me.

It took a few days to decide what to do. While my lungs continued to clear out the muck from being near-drowned, I thought and thought. It felt like a jail term in my hospital room, knowing what I had to do but resisting. I thought about Anda, and how she could have done what was easy for her and obvious, but didn't. She didn't let me live just so I could keep hiding. Years of fear made it hard to even lift my stupid finger to the red buzzer tethered to my hospital bed rail. But I finally did it.

The nurse's voice commed in. My finger was still shaking from pressing the button.

"Yes? May I help you?"

I swallowed and forced the words out. "I need to speak

to the social worker."

I remember him walking into the room an hour later. I'd never had a guy social worker, and I'd never had a Black social worker either. I didn't even understand who he was at first. He looked for a place to sit down and I ignored him, adjusting the plastic oxygen tubing prongs in my nose. It was annoying as hell, but kept me from gasping all the time.

"I understand you wanted to talk to me?" He straightened out his plaid tie and sat by my bedside while I finished looping the tubing over my ears.

"Uh. Who are you?"

"The hospital social worker. I've been assigned to you."

"What happened to Pam?" I asked warily.

"Vacation. I'm covering." He extended his hand. "Jim Barton."

I didn't shake it. "You're a guy," I said, only realizing too late how stupid that sounded.

"Yeah. That happens sometimes." He smiled at me, but not too brightly. He took his hand back and picked up a pen. "So how can I help?"

I clamped my mouth shut. I was a little too freaked, and the idea of telling a guy, a stranger—I just couldn't do it. After a half hour of silence (this guy played chicken really well), I realized Pam wasn't going to magically show up. If I wanted to make things happen, I'd have to talk.

"I don't want to live with my uncle again," I blurted out. Even if it was only going to be for another few months until I turned eighteen, there was no way. Jim nodded and waited. And finally, it all came out. I told him everything. Even the parts about how I felt like I was confessing, though I'd done nothing wrong. He wrote it all down. He tried to keep a straight face. A professional face, even as he scanned the burns on my arms that I confessed were my own. But once in a while, I saw a flash of anger. I've never been more relieved to see an angry person in my life.

Someone was upset about what had happened to me. Someone, not Anda, finally knew.

He called CPS. The police got involved. The ball was rolling.

Living in the center of this juggernaut, my world will be pretty rocky for a while. But it won't be the world I knew before Isle Royale. Never again.

Jim comes in on a Sunday to tell me that my dad is on his way.

"Really?" I ask, blank-faced.

"Well, he was here before. Apparently, he stayed with you while you were unconscious in the ICU. He had to go to Offutt Air Force Base in Nebraska to make arrangements for a transfer to the U.S. Looks like you two may be moving to Omaha. He said he'd be back tomorrow."

"Tell him not to bother. He hasn't been my guardian for years."

"But—"

"He didn't even call me. I've been awake for three days."

"Hector—"

"I don't want to talk to him."

He gives me a knowing look. It's a friendly look, but still. "The doctors say you may be able to leave the hospital in a few days. Can't stay here forever. You have to go with your dad. He's not your uncle, right?"

"I don't want to. Look, most of the time, I took care of myself anyway. I wrote the checks for the bills. I bought the groceries. I held down a job and kept up a B-plus average in high school. Can't I just...live by myself?"

I wait for the no. I don't even know why I asked, since there's no way, but Jim started jotting down a few things.

"You have no support system. No other family around. I can't promise anything, but let me look into it." When I give him a surprised look, he continues. "There may a slim chance you could become an emancipated minor. But don't get your hopes up."

An emancipated minor? How could I have not known about this? Oh, of course. I was too busy focusing on actual physical escape to even consider talking to a lawyer. And my social worker never mentioned it existed.

After a lot of calls, my mother is willing to wire some money to get me started. It turns out, my mother has been trying for years to get my contact information, but my father kept blocking her. The fucker. Soon after, she invites me to come and visit Seoul for a while, but I say no. I can't move to another country when I can't even handle living in the one I'm already in. But we speak on the phone once. I cry the whole time, like a kid, because she's so happy to finally speak to me. It's amazing how much Korean I still remember.

Na-neun neo-reul sa-rang-hae. Na-neun ne-ga geu-rip-go bo-go-sip-gu-na. Na-ui sa-rang-seu-reo-un a-deu-ra.

I love you. I miss you and wish to see you. My beloved son.

Jim starts the paperwork for emancipation and says a judge will have to get involved. It's all starting to happen, even before my dad arrives in two days.

"You'll have to tell him," Jim warns me.

"I'll send him a letter."

It's going to be an epic letter, let me tell you.

...

Anda haunts my now non-medicated dreams every night. I see her standing in her fluttering white nightgown, up to her calves in lake water. She's beautiful, and terrible, staring out at the surface of the lake and beyond. She never says a word to me. I think it's because she's waiting for me to say something first. After all, she had dealt the last hand.

I'm still alive. So is my uncle.

Nothing changed.

Everything changed.

The first ferry back to Isle Royale is on May 3, 7:30 a.m. Right now, it's almost December. If everything goes okay, I might be taking extra classes to make up for my lost months of school so I can actually graduate on time. One of my doctors asked me what I want to be when I graduate. Of course, the only thing that occupies my mind, 24-7, is the island. How the island, in its own way, needed taking care of. I like that, being needed by something so powerful as nature. I also liked being away from buildings and crowds of people and knowing that I could take care of myself without so many human trappings. So when the doctor asks me again, the freakiest answer comes out of this city boy's mouth.

"A park ranger."

The doctor chuckled at me. "Oh, I get it. You're joking, right?"

"Right," I say, but I'm not.

I spend too much time thinking. I've seen things in this last month that were never meant to be seen. Some days, I'm not even sure that I didn't just imagine everything. Like, maybe I accidentally ate some weird mushroom my first week there and tripped the whole time.

Anda is something that wasn't meant to live in my world. I know exactly what she's capable of and it's no fairy tale, despite my wishing. I don't know if I can reconcile the Anda that spent the night with me in the lighthouse, the Anda that saved my life, and the Anda that could decimate a ship full of lives. Like that.

I promised Mr. Selkirk that I would explain things to her. The whys. Though I'm not sure what there is to explain.

I don't know what I'm going to do on May 3.

Five months is a long time to decide.

Chapter Sixty-Six

ANDA

The lighthouse and I have an understanding.

We don't agree on everything, but we at least know each other. One by one, I go to make peace with the others. The Rock of Ages lighthouse, Rock Harbor Lighthouse, and even Passage Island lighthouse. Their very foundations shudder when we meet, but it doesn't last for long. They sense the change in me. I make my apologies, and they do, as well.

Someday I will visit them again. The proper way, in a boat. I will have to learn how to use one. Transportation is a clunky, hefty word that fits into a human world. One I'm learning to live in, without constantly snagging myself on sharp corners of common sense. It's not easy. I've been bruised pretty badly, but I like the marks they've left on me. Like Hector. He's a bruise that reminds me of violets in the shade.

Hector.

I'm not ready to think of him yet. Wait, just wait, I tell myself.

I listen for advice from Mother, but my choices are making it harder to hear her.

I listen for Father, but the vacant silence only upsets me. I've added a lot of salt water to the lake this month. For so long, we've lived in each other's periphery, even when we're only feet apart. But that distance mattered little when he was *there*. Now that he's gone, the emptiness that's filled his place is yawning and enormous. I bounce around it, not knowing which way is north. Not knowing where the center of the earth is anymore.

But there are some things I know. There's a darkness inside me that won't ever go away, but I cannot be a slave to it anymore. It hurts to rearrange myself, the devotion to this other side of me, the light. Reaching into the growth of the island and finding that it can nourish me if I let it, if I accept the struggle. It's strange, not running away from the wealth of strength there. I had annulled the choices before in accepting November as the only time when I could truly renew myself, through the carnage of sinkings.

The lighthouse was right.

November is not the only answer.

It will always be a struggle. But I won't partition myself off anymore, and there is no more Father to beg it of me. After all, the extremes pushed to their furthest limits away from each other have wreaked havoc. There is light and darkness in life, and in death. Neither is purely good. Neither is purely bad. But it's taken me this long to understand, and it is still a fight, every minute. But that is what I get for nurturing this humanity inside me. The constant testing of oneself; the constant effort of being better than I was only minutes ago.

At the end of December when the last of the police and park rangers left the Isle, I left my hiding place on

Menagerie Island. Once again, it was just me and our little house near Windigo. Once again, Isle Royale sat there like the queen it is, the eye of the wolf. She lay half immersed in water and continued to sleep the winter away.

I was alone. I was safe. But not from everything.

The house was full of ghosts. I'd see Father folding clothes into the drawers, putting a pound of butter into the small refrigerator, warning me not to break the weather radio. I'd see Hector scraping fish scales on the back porch, and Mother's voice enticing me to join her in the lake's oblivion.

I'd sometimes spend an entire week, just studying the stones on the shore by our house. Sometimes, I cook food and expect Father to come indoors, sniff the air with surprise, and thank me for a plateful. But the door never opens. He never comes.

Oh God, he never comes.

I ask why, and I get no answers.

Sometimes, I weep for days on end.

But I also know where he is. I've dreamed about it. I see Mother embracing his inert form, cradling him and bringing him to the shore, spent and sagging. She pushes away at the earth and places him in there, replacing stone and soil as if each were a gift, weighing his corpse down with adoration. She lets the lake water rain over the spot, and kisses it with her winter's wind.

In the spring, crocuses will crack through the top layer of cold earth. It won't be Father, back in anyone's arms, will it? But when I let my soul quiet down and stop my own whimpers of loneliness, I can feel his warm smile on my cheek.

What I can't sense anymore is Mother. She's noted the change in me. She's aware of the battle. Several large storms come to the island, coaxing me back to the water, but I don't go. My thirst for death is slowly slackening, but it's there. I understand it is necessary, and it will never truly go away. But I also understand that I can parcel it out in a way that makes more sense. Not having to save it until November means I can be gentler with what I take and when I take it.

When I grow too weary of my dreams, I go back to the water. I need it less than before, but I still need it. I allow the winter lake, drowsy at dusk, to swallow me whole. My arms reach west, toward the coordinates that play a crooked tune in my head.

N 47°53'1.06", W 89°28'1.79"

Down in the depths, the newly broken ship lays, grimacing and uncomfortable on her new bed. I touch the still-strong, smooth metal hull with my hand and enter the cabin, where the steering equipment is still perfectly intact. Trout and muskellunge swim through the broken glass and visit the glints of metal that have yet to be covered by summer algae. I sit down in the corner and hug my knees to my chest, staring across the cabin to the company I keep here.

The captain greets me with a fixed, morbid smile. His unmoving body lies crumpled at the bottom. His polyester clothes are still almost new-looking, but his body is succumbing to the elements, even with this heavy pressure and damning cold. I wait a long time. I am very patient. Eventually, he begins the conversation.

You're sad.

"I am."

You miss the boy?

"I do."

Well. It's not up to you, anymore, is it?

"But I'm not happy."

You weren't happy or sad before you met him. It's a curse, isn't it? To be even partly alive for once?

"Yes. It is."

Are you ready? Do you really want that sort of tedium?

I nod, unsmiling.

There are hearts beating in boats on the water, but my hunger for them has lessened so much now. With the captain, I feel a roiling pain inside myself, too. Empathy is a new emotion I've only just met.

The captain recedes back into silence. I kiss the tattered flesh of his cheek and say my good-byes. He sighs and comforts his ship. She still mourns her own death, more than her own captain does. His soul will stay there until she's sung her final song and is, at last, ready to fade.

He is a good captain.

D ecember. January. February.

I begin preparing. I read all the books on Father's shelves to squeeze in lessons on how to be. I practice phrases like, "Nice to meet you" and "As you know, dolphins are highly intelligent mammals." I use the boat to steal supplies from the storerooms in Rock Harbor, because I've been living with a selfish companion who's finally come to stay these days—hunger.

March. April.

The Isle has been awakening. The trees have long since sprouted their proud green leaves. The red-breasted mergansers and grebes have returned, as well as the humans who are working hard to get the park ready for new visitors. I study the Grand Portage ferry schedule for hours at a time.

May 3 arrives. A Wednesday.

I practice my story and walk into Windigo when the first ferry appears in the distance. One of the park workers is at the dock, and she looks at me with shock when I walk onto the pier in my boots, Father's canvas jacket, and messy hair. No nightgown. I look like them. Sensible and work-worn, like I've been preparing for visitors. Like I belong here. When the woman won't stop staring at me, I take a breath, forcing words out of my mouth.

"Hello. I'm Anda Selkirk."

"You're…are you related to Jakob?"

"Yes. I'm his niece. He told me to look after his cottage if anything ever happened. I arrived a few days ago with some of the park employees."

The lines come out only a little bumpy. To my own ears, I sound like a foreigner. What shocks me more is not that I'm speaking them—it's that the middle-aged woman with wiry auburn hair in two braids over her shoulders can see me without effort. I feel naked.

"I'm so sorry, Anda. We liked Jakob a lot. Welcome to Isle Royale."

I nod and wipe away tears. Discreetly, I taste them on the back of my hand. It never fails to surprise that I weep seawater even though the lake runs in my veins.

It's nine thirty in the morning. I'd rather hide behind the same tree as when I first saw Hector on the island, but the good sense that's shakily taken root inside me says don't. The ferry grows in size in the distance, and my skin flushes with nervousness when it finally touches the dock. Eager campers disembark with their stuffed, oversize backpacks, happy to be the first on the isle for the season. My eyes hungrily read each face, searching, searching. I look for tall bodies, for handsome brown skin, for forgiveness.

Finally, the captain exits, and the ship tells me what I already know.

Hector is not on board.

On Saturday, I do the same thing at nine thirty. And then on the next Wednesday again.

I've become obsessed with the ferry schedule. I want to discuss it endlessly with the house, with Mother. But no one answers my questions. Even down in the deep—if I could visit him—I know the dead captain would refrain from telling me anything at all. Even he would know how hopeless I've become.

The lady I met at the dock visits me once a week. Her name is Cecile. She thinks I'm lonely (she's right) and brings me things to eat because she thinks I'm too thin (she's right) and brings me tiny animals she's knit of nubbly gray wool. I don't know what they're for. She asks if I would like to learn to knit. The idea of creating something not made of soil and air and chitin and microbes fascinates me. I grow calluses from the pressure of knitting needles and crochet hooks. I make an afghan in the shape of a walleye, and Cecile says it's quite unique.

I believe she is called…a friend.

The island is bustling with the pitter-patter of hiking-booted feet. It's strange to no longer need to hide as I walk around the island and take short hikes. Spending money (Father had something called "an account" at the Windigo store) for food, because I need to consume nourishment like a baby, every few hours. I am thankful that no one comments on the half dozen Hershey bars I occasionally take home with me from the camp store.

I blend in with visitors on the island. It used to be that they couldn't see me, because I wouldn't let them. Now they can't see me because I share their common tale of existence.

I'm glad their glances pass me over. It would hurt too much to have any set of dark eyes on me that aren't the ones I'm seeking.

June comes.

Then July. With its arrival comes air that is warm and marmalade sticky. The mosquitoes and black flies have woken up. The first Wednesday ferry has just left for McCargoe Cove on its trip around the island, but this time I did not go. I take a long hike to Feldtmann Lake instead. It never stops, that knifelike sensation that comes when the last person leaves the boat and he's not there, so I experiment to see if the sensation happens even when I don't watch—and the pain arrives anyway. The void inside my rib cage grows with time, marking its permanent residence within that tells me the truth.

Hector is not coming back. He's forgotten me.

Mother has not, but the changes within me have made her quieter. We will never be the same. The threads binding her to me have frayed; we sense each other still, but at a distance, as if through memory. I am still there to keep the soil acidity just so, to bring about the death of a goshawk chick that isn't ever meant to fly. Both make me cry; both make me smile. And she nods when I do these things, before going back to gathering what solar warmth she can into her breast before winter.

I walk home through the woods. As changed as I am, I

can't completely escape the creature I was. The birds and insects still flee from my footsteps. The bloodthirsty insects look elsewhere for salty red comfort. But I'd welcome a bite. It would be a distraction, having myself consumed by something else for a change.

The house is quiet and still, and the breeze plays dully against the eaves. I listen quietly and hear nothing. It's been like this for months now. No whispers on the wind anymore. I reach for the cottage door when I trip over something on the slate step.

It's half a dead lake trout, scaled and cleaned.

I throw open the door and race from room to room in my fish-bloodied boots, but no one is here. I run outside, frantically looking left and right, listening.

All I hear are the waves of the lake, lapping on the rocks by the shore. So I tear through the back path that leads to the lake, under the canopy of verdant leaves. I crunch mercilessly on the millipedes whose scurrying legs aren't quick enough. I dodge the thimbleberry bushes and push away the foliage, running as quickly as I can.

The dappled sunlight on the lake water blinds me at first. A shadow, ten feet out, soothes my eyes.

Someone stands in the lapping waves, wearing a sagging gray hoodie. His bare feet are immersed, pant legs rolled up to muscular calves. Hands in pockets, he hears the sounds of the brush being stepped upon behind him.

Hector turns and sees me.

And the world around us disappears.

Acknowledgments

Any story has roots in imagination, but it takes real friends, family, and keen eyes to help transform it into a book. I am deeply grateful to my husband, Bernie, and my children for being so supportive of my endless hours of laptop shenanigans. I'm so proud of each of you, and you make me beyond happy. Every day.

My deepest thanks to my mom and especially my father, for his patient answers about all things Korean. As always, you're a tome of wisdom! Kate Brauning, my editor, saw something special in this manuscript, and I will be forever grateful for her guidance. She pushed me, pushed Anda, and pushed Hector to be our perfectly imperfect selves. I am indebted to my entire team at Entangled—I couldn't be more thrilled to bring this story to fruition with the support of so much human awesomeness!

I pestered John Heneghan and Gwenn Aspen with Isle Royale questions, and finally went to visit IR in person in August 2016. It was so beautiful, I cried. A huge thanks to the rangers and the National Park Service for taking such good care of Anda's island.

Justina Ireland and Lamar Giles, an enormous thank-you for the reads and early, honest feedback. Leo Monardo and Ben Su, I appreciate the beta reads. You promise to be my beta readers forever, right? Thanks to Ohsang Kwon, Alice Kang, Maurene Goo, Christina Ahn, and Haerin Jung for the hangul help! The very sweet Karin Akins answered all my foster care questions, and thanks to Sydnee Schmidt and Emalee Napier for keeping life chaos at bay and for never freaking out when I'd randomly talk about gross stuff like corpses. And an enormous thanks to Mindy McGinnis, Elle Cosimano, Maurene Goo, and Marie Lu for your support. You guys rock.

To the Kang/Kwon family—squishy hugs from your Eemo/aunt Lydia/sister, and thank you for never questioning my weirdness. Thanks to Tonya Kuper for indulging the post-event-burger runs and being there whenever I need her and for helping me find a home for this book. For Lenore, Dushana, Val, Gale, Ilene, Cindy, Anna, Angie, Alice, and so many other friends, near and far—I owe you all a lot of lattes. To Angie Ralph, thank you for being a champion of authors and young adult lit. To my colleagues and patients who kindly ask, "Hey, Dr. Kang—are you still writing?" The answer is, always! Thanks so much for caring and asking! And for Isabelle Pagani, who is probably too young to read this but hopefully will someday—you probably already know this, but your dad loves you. A lot. I hope you love the book!

GRAB THE ENTANGLED TEEN RELEASES READERS ARE TALKING ABOUT!

LOST GIRLS
BY MERRIE DESTEFANO

Yesterday, Rachel went to sleep curled up in her grammy's quilt, worrying about geometry. Today, she woke up in a ditch, bloodied, bruised, and missing a year of her life. She's not the only girl to go missing within the last year...but she's the only girl to come back. And as much as her dark, dangerous new life scares her, it calls to her. Seductively. But wherever she's been—whomever she's been with—isn't done with her yet...

VIOLET GRENADE
BY VICTORIA SCOTT

DOMINO (def.): A girl with blue hair and a demon in her mind.
CAIN (def.): A stone giant on the brink of exploding.
MADAM KARINA (def.): A woman who demands obedience.
WILSON (def.): The one who will destroy them all.

When Madam Karina discovers Domino in an alleyway, she offers her a position inside her home for entertainers in secluded West Texas. Left with few alternatives and an agenda of her own, Domino accepts. It isn't long before she is fighting her way up the ranks to gain the madam's approval. But after suffering weeks of bullying and unearthing the madam's secrets, Domino decides to leave. It'll be harder than she thinks, though, because the madam doesn't like to lose inventory. But then, Madam Karina doesn't know about the person living inside Domino's mind. Madam Karina doesn't know about Wilson.

27 Hours
by Tristina Wright

ZERO HOUR MEANS WAR

Rumor Mora fears two things: hellhounds too strong for him to kill, and failure. Jude Welton has two dreams: for humans to stop killing monsters, and for his strange abilities to vanish.

But in no reality should a boy raised to love monsters fall for a boy raised to kill them.

Nyx Llorca keeps two secrets: the moon speaks to her, and she's in love with Dahlia, her best friend. Braeden Tennant wants two things: to get out from his mother's shadow, and to unlearn Epsilon's darkest secret.

They'll both have to commit treason to find the truth.

During one twenty-seven-hour night, if they can't stop the war between the colonies and the monsters from becoming a war of extinction, the things they wish for will never come true, and the things they fear will be all that's left.